Praise For
The Witch Haven

"Smith opens a trick door between bruising history and glittering fantasy, to a place that will leave you drunk on secrets and dreaming of magic (and murder). *The Witch Haven* is spectacular, singular, and spellbinding."
—Casey McQuiston, *New York Times* bestselling author of *Red, White & Royal Blue*

"A beautiful story filled with sisterhood, mystery, and interesting magic. This book will keep you turning the page with immersive prose and clever, memorable characters. I will be dreaming about this story for a long time."
—Adrienne Young, *New York Times* bestselling author of *Sky in the Deep*

"As dark and lush as it is utterly enrapturing, *The Witch Haven* is sure to enchant."
—Alexis Henderson, author of *The Year of the Witching*

"A positively spellbinding debut. Smith has crafted a delectably immersive mystery packed with magic, enchantment, and an absolute powerhouse cast of women."
—Adalyn Grace, *New York Times* bestselling author of *All the Stars and Teeth*

"*The Witch Haven* is a dazzling debut—a wonderfully thrilling, sinister take on a secret school for witches. Sasha Peyton Smith deftly balances a nuanced exploration of loss with a page-turning magical romp through 1911 NYC. I grieved, raged, and swooned right alongside Frances."
—Jessica Spotswood, author of *Born Wicked*

"*The Witch Haven* is a mesmerizing atmospheric historical fantasy fraught with spellbinding magic, mystery and nail-biting twists and turns." —*B&N Reads*

"*The Witch Haven* by Sasha Peyton Smith is a dazzling historical fantasy novel about a school for witches in 1911 New York City." —*PopSugar*

"Devotees of Libba Bray's *The Diviners* will enjoy debut author Smith's affectionate group of witches breaking through straitlaced expectations in a historical New York." —*Publishers Weekly*

"This intensely dramatic story presents Gaelic-influenced magic as a means to empowerment and shows the strength in sisterhood." —*Kirkus*

"Mystery and adventure abound in Smith's spellbinding debut." —*Booklist*

Also by
Sasha Peyton Smith

The Witch Haven

SASHA PEYTON SMITH

SIMON & SCHUSTER BFYR

NEW YORK LONDON TORONTO SYDNEY NEW DELHI

An imprint of Simon & Schuster Children's Publishing Division
1230 Avenue of the Americas, New York, New York 10020

Also available in a SIMON & SCHUSTER BFYR hardcover edition
Interior design by Tom Daly
The text for this book was set in Adobe Garamond Pro.
Manufactured in the United States of America
First SIMON & SCHUSTER BFYR paperback edition August 2023
2 4 6 8 10 9 7 5 3 1
Library of Congress Cataloging-in-Publication Data
Names: Smith, Sasha Peyton, author.
Title: The witch hunt / Sasha Peyton Smith.
Description: First edition. | New York : Simon & Schuster, [2023]
Sequel to: Smith, Sasha Peyton. Witch haven. | Audience: Ages 14 up. | Audience: Grades 10-12.
Summary: Seventeen-year-old Frances and her fellow witches travel to Paris, where family secrets, lost loves, and dangerous powers await.
Identifiers: LCCN 2023013254 (print) | LCCN 2023013255 (ebook)
ISBN 9781534454422 (paperback) | ISBN 9781534454415 (hardcover) | ISBN 9781534454439 (ebook)
Subjects: CYAC: Witchcraft—Fiction. | Witches—Fiction. | Wizards—Fiction. | Paris (France)—History—1870-1940—Fiction. | LCGFT: Witch fiction. | Novels.
Classification: LCC PZ7.1.S6555 Wj 2023 (print) | LCC PZ7.1.S6555 (ebook) | DDC [Fic]—dc23
LC record available at https://lccn.loc.gov/2023013254
LC ebook record available at https://lccn.loc.gov/2023013255

For Charles. I'm so lucky to love you.

If you have ever gone to the woods with me,

I must love you very much.

—Mary Oliver

THE
WITCH
HUNT

PARIS, 1913

The Seine was full of life. The teenagers who danced along her banks basked in the twilight of their own wild youths, the purple of the sun dancing along their unbruised skin.

White-teeth smiles and a bottle passed between them felt like promises to never grow up. High up on the hill, the Sacre Cœur loomed over the city, benevolent as a proud mother.

But beneath the cobblestones that had long ago been washed of blood sat a man.

He was sitting, as he had most of the nights of his life, in front of a doorway. This guarding was a formality. He and his brothers knew the stories well; the door had not budged in nearly one hundred years.

Somewhere, across a great dark ocean, a girl slept, dreamless and unaware of all she had awakened.

Deep underground in a passage made of bones, something that was once dead began to stir, and a lock on a door, once sealed shut, clicked open.

CHAPTER ONE

New York, June 1913

Nineteen sets of eyes are looking at me.

I should be used to it by now, the strange reverence in their gazes, but I don't think it's something that will ever feel normal.

I turn to face the blackboard instead. The piece of chalk in my hand snaps as I go to write the spell. I've pressed too hard again.

In and out, Frances, just breathe.

It's funny to think now, just how deeply I hated the Emotional Control classes I was forced to take my first year at Haxahaven Academy, how I resented Mrs. Li. She's become a trusted colleague, the deep breathing exercises have become a habit, and I have grown steadier right along with them. There's a joke in there, probably. Something about growing up.

I do feel it sometimes, growing up as the days pass, like a flower tilting almost imperceptibly toward the warmth of the sun. At least I do in the moments where it doesn't feel like I'm pretending.

It feels like pretending now, standing in front of a class, *my* class. Nineteen baby witches, all looking to me to learn the basics of elemental and magical manipulation. The magic isn't complicated—simple spells to unlock doors or float something across the room. But my broad-shouldered stance and unwavering voice are all playacting.

"Is everything all right, Miss Hallowell?"

Of course, it's Bernice who asks, the little teacher's pet. She's sitting in the front row, her hands folded politely in her lap, her freckled face looking up at me. She's the kind of perfect student I never could manage to be.

"Everything is fine, just lost in thought. And it's Frances, Bernice. Please." I'm barely their teacher. Just last year I was sitting in the same seat she was. It's only out of necessity that I'm standing in front of the blackboard now.

Headmistress Florence called me into her office last fall to ask for "a favor." I think she thought it would be good for me to take on some responsibility. I overheard her wife, Ann, tell her it might help me to stop moping around the library so much.

I took umbrage with that. Sure, I sometimes sulk. I rarely mope.

Bernice nods with the wide-eyed enthusiasm of a golden retriever. You'd never know her power was awakened just three months ago after her mother passed.

"Have you all been practicing?"

Their nineteen little heads nod at me.

"Very good then, please turn to page thirty-eight in your fall semester packets."

Copying spells down from the *The Elemental*, the book Lena, Maxine, and I found in the woods, what feels like a lifetime ago, was no easy task. In the end, it was Oliver who did it. In his neat, university student penmanship, he created a curriculum from the disorganized spell book. For all the trouble it once caused, the magic inside of its pages proved worth knowing. At least some of the spells.

On page thirty-eight my students find, in bullet points and careful diagrams, instructions for how to spark a small blue flame between their thumb and forefinger.

We've been working on object manipulation for the past few weeks, and moving on to elemental magic has become one of my favorite things about being a teacher.

I talk them through the spell, then release them to try it themselves.

Bernice furrows her brow as she snaps her fingers over and over again.

"Snapping isn't part of the spell, Bernice," Bess whispers next to her. In the next moment, a light pops into being between Bess's fingers. She shouts and stands so quickly she topples over her chair, right into Georgia, who falls directly into Charlotte's lap. The movement bumps Yael's arm, sending her flame colliding with Berta, whose cape immediately catches fire.

Yael shrieks, then uses the small cup of water I've placed on everyone's desk for this exact reason.

No one is any worse for wear except for the hem of poor Berta's cape, which drips sadly onto the floor.

Once the chaos has calmed down and all the chairs have been righted, the ruckus starts right up again as Theo in the back row creates a spark of light and holds it too close to their desk, burning a hole right into the wood.

I can't help but smile at the scene.

The first semester I taught this lesson, no fewer than three students burst into tears. Another went back up to her room, determined to practice, and burnt her curtains to a crisp.

I might feel like barely a teacher, but there is nothing more rewarding as an instructor than communicating to my students, *Yes, that giant, awful, incredible, endless power you feel within yourself is real. You did not imagine it. You truly do contain that much.*

It's teaching them what to do with it that remains the hard part.

It's hard keeping my secret too. The students don't know yet.

At least I don't think they've figured it out.

If they have noticed that I stopped demonstrating months ago, they haven't said anything. I read from the textbook and ask students to come up and practice, but it's been ages since I performed an actual spell myself.

It's made even worse by me not knowing how to explain it. It's not that my magic is *gone*; it's just . . . wrong.

It's unpredictable, it zaps and stings like a live wire. Every day, it feels further out of reach; like a lighter without fuel, it sparks but it doesn't catch flame. I can feel it, but I can't make it bend to my will like it used to.

It started slowly. My demonstrations in class didn't work right, or when I tried to close a door while lying in my bed it would slam instead of gently latch. Ann noticed too. We were rolling out pie crusts in the kitchen together. I tried to float a stick of butter from the butcher block to the ice chest, but halfway across the room, it splattered all over the floor. Maxine magicked a ball of embroidery thread across the sunroom for my latest cross-stitch, but I was unable to stop it and it smacked me directly in the forehead.

At first it was embarrassing. Now I'm starting to panic.

The first few weeks, Florence thought it was nerves. "You've been through so much," she said kindly as I clutched a steaming tea mug in my hands and cried in her office.

But it hasn't gotten any better.

In fact, it's getting worse.

Florence promises me we'll find an answer, and I'm trying not to worry, but the truth is I am. I thought Finn stealing my magic was the worst thing that could happen to me, but this almost hurts more. The part of me I love the most is just out of reach.

It nags in the back of my mind now, a shadow to the joy I'm witnessing on my students' faces.

Florence can't come up with an explanation for what's happening to my power. Neither can Maxine or any of the library books or terrifying Therese Theresi or the other hedge witches at the Bizarre Bazaar.

I haven't told the students. There's no reason they need to fuss over me too.

What is the saying, again? *Those who can't do, teach?*

For ninety minutes nineteen sets of hands loop and twist, their mouths trying to make sense of old Gaelic. Once they've mastered the simpler spells, they can move on to working on creating bigger fire with more creative, less precise magic.

But when it comes to fire, I've learned to start with the basics.

At the end of the ninety minutes eight girls have created flame from nothing, which I count as a success.

Despite the pride I feel as a teacher, I find it a relief to retreat upstairs. There's something profoundly exhausting about being looked at like I have the answers when I don't even know what is happening within myself. Teaching is more difficult than I anticipated but more rewarding, too. It's nice to have something to pour my focus into. I don't know what I'd do otherwise.

Usually this time of day I'd head to the kitchens, make myself a cup of coffee, and settle in the library for a few hours of independent research before lunch. I'm making my way through a stack of books on the magical history of the Scottish Isles looking for anything useful, anything that might help me understand what is happening to me. Nothing has been helpful so far. It's like searching for a needle in a haystack without knowing if a needle is in there at all.

Or I'd find my mother in the solarium, where she's taken to tending a particularly finnicky group of orchid plants after her morning lessons.

It was Florence who suggested moving her in after her release from the asylum. After all, she's hardly the first Haxahaven pupil over forty, and her magical education wasn't finished when she ran away with my father at eighteen.

She's still fragile, still . . . my mother in all the good and bad ways, but like her orchids, she's begun to bloom.

She's in class now, or I'd say goodbye in person. Instead, I slide a note under the door to her room saying I'll miss her and be back before she knows it. I hugged her goodbye at breakfast too, and she hugged me back tight around my middle and told me to have a marvelous time.

I hear Maxine before I find her, the swearing coming from behind the door to her room on the second floor.

I don't bother knocking. The door is unlocked.

I should have known better than to let Maxine wait until the last minute to pack.

"Lena is going to kill you," I say from the doorway.

Maxine glares up at me from the nest she's made of discarded clothing on the floor. "She wouldn't dare. She'll be too happy to see me."

I sink onto her bed, becoming one with the chaos, and throw a brimless hat at her, aiming for her head. She ducks at the last minute, and it lands in yet another pile of clothes next to her vanity. "She won't see you at all if we miss the ship."

"We're not going to miss the ship. Stop being dramatic."

Maxine tosses a tangle of stockings into her suitcase, all knotted together like some kind of sea creature.

I click my tongue at her. "We're going to be late."

Maxine throws me a murderous glance. "We're not going to be late."

The door swings open. Mabel leans up against the jamb, riding goggles up on her forehead, pushing back her curly hair.

"You're going to be late," she says, eyeing the mess.

"Jesus Christ, not you, too," Maxine replies.

"Don't act like my awareness of the concept of time is a personal affront, I beg you," Mabel laughs.

My darling roommate has agreed to be our chauffeur to the docks in Hell's Kitchen, where a very large ship is waiting to ferry us across a very large sea.

Maxine shoves the ball of fabric into a final waiting trunk and snaps the latch with a flourish. "There now, quiet, the both of you."

Together, we drag her trunks and hatboxes down to the awaiting ambulance, where my singular case rests in the back, taken down hours ago, well before breakfast.

It's so bright, I'm soon sweating under my cape. Though no longer technically a student, I couldn't find it in myself to let go of Haxahaven black. I've thrown the cape on over a simple traveling dress. Maxine and I wear near-identical hats, with small brims and black ribbons trailing off the back.

It's strange to be going anywhere that isn't here. The most traveling I've done in months requires only walking from the courtyard garden to the kitchen. We're growing carrots now. I've grown roots too, gotten good at staying put.

And while I'm excited to see Oliver, I'm nervous, too. Haxahaven once felt like a prison, but of late, it's become a sanctuary. I remember what happened the last time I longed for adventure. The last year has been spent wrapping myself in a cocoon, building a quiet life where I cause no more destruction. Am I ready to leave?

Maxine slumps into the front seat, and I situate myself amongst the luggage in the back, a solid, sharp-cornered reminder that this is real. We're truly going.

Mabel is, blessedly, a much better driver than Maxine, and hurls us through the wide boulevards of Queens and across the bridge into Manhattan.

All the while, I try to quiet the riotous butterflies in my stomach. There's the buzz of excitement, but there's something else, too. Dread, probably. Fear, perhaps. I don't want to admit that I'm still scared of Finn, but I am.

I knew what I was agreeing to when we planned this trip. I also knew it was my fault Maxine didn't understand my reluctance at first.

"Oliver is studying at the Sorbonne. My family home is right across the river, and Maman has been begging me for a visit to Paris. Frankly, it doesn't make sense for us not to go," she insisted one night after dinner a few months ago, while we were playing cards in the drawing room. I was losing like usual, both at cards and the conversation.

"I don't have the money," I muttered half-heartedly, looking at the two of hearts in my hand rather than meeting her eye.

"You know that's not an issue," Maxine replied, laying down the hand-winning card.

"My classes . . ."

"Ann has said she'll cover them. The tickets have been purchased. I'll drag you there in my trunk if I have to."

I knew she wasn't bluffing. It wasn't Maxine's way, in cards or in life. And so the plans were made. My cases were packed.

I never told my friends or Oliver of Finn's letter, the one that arrived one year ago, currently lying hidden under piles of documents in my desk drawer. *Soon, Frances, we will be together again,* he promised. *Together in Europe.*

In the moment, I was ashamed of how frightened I was. Then, it was easier to pretend he didn't exist at all. We never spoke of him, as if by rule.

But there's a knot in my chest. It's been there since the letter arrived, and today it's squeezing tighter.

There have been no more letters. Maybe I've gotten lucky and he's forgotten about me. Perhaps he's found some other girl to dream about.

Am I a fool for bringing myself across the ocean to him, or is it brave to not let fear control me?

Regardless, I truly was excited to see Oliver, so I was perhaps too easily convinced.

His letters are as poetic and sweet as his soul, but a very poor substitution for a hand held in comfortable silence.

It's been only three months since he's been gone, but it feels longer. Maxine would laugh at me if I said it aloud, but it feels true.

We make it to the city in record time. I drum my fingers against the fabric of my skirt the whole way. Just six days now until I see him. Just a single ocean to cross.

It sets a jittery feeling under my skin whenever I think about it. It's silly to be nervous to see someone I've known nearly all my life, but what will he see in me? Will he think I'm changed? What if he thinks I'm the same and he's the one who is changed? That would be even worse.

I haven't mentioned the strangeness of my magic in our letters. It would only worry him, and I've never known how to explain the ins and outs of my power to him. He's spent a fair few weekends at Haxahaven, surrounded by floating food and showers of sparks coming off fingers and flowers that bloom out of nowhere. He takes it all in good humor, but there is so much he doesn't understand.

The docks are bustling with people, the weather-beaten wood nearly blinding in the midmorning sun. I squint as I hop out the back of the ambulance and immediately have to duck as two porters haul a trunk right over my head. I can smell the sea and the strange scent of rot that never quite leaves the river.

Next to me, a woman weeps in the arms of a man who looks mostly bored by her show of emotion, and a mother tugs two boys wearing matching sailor suits by the hand to the awaiting ship.

I miss Manhattan less and less as time goes on. I've made a home in the peace of Forest Hills, but there is something about this bubble of noise, this gentle hum of chaos, that comforts me.

The skyline has already changed in my short absence, but I force my eyes away from the skeletons of buildings reaching up into the sky to instead look at the ship, my home for the next week.

The ship. I've never seen something so big in my life.

It's a behemoth, like someone has taken one of the skyscrapers from the financial district and tipped it on its side.

I can't imagine ever learning anything that would make sense of its ability to float.

"If this thing sinks, I'm going to haunt you for all eternity," I hiss to Maxine.

It's been a little over a year since the sinking of the *Titanic*, and every single newspaper article I read from last April flashes in my mind. All those bodies, frozen in the middle of the night in the

North Atlantic. Some of the more macabre girls at school are still talking about it over breakfast.

Maxine laughs. "You truly think we couldn't scam our way onto the lifeboats."

The fizzy excitement of seeing Oliver dissipates as the nerves bubble back up. "I wouldn't bet my life on it."

I'm mostly joking, but the prospect of spending six days floating out at sea has my stomach turning.

I still can't stand the sight of water. This is the first time I've been this near the river since Helen, Finn, and I dumped a man's body into its depths nearly two years ago.

How time flies when you're repressing the memories of the murders you once committed.

Mabel rises up on her tiptoes to give us both a kiss on the cheek.

I'll miss her, but I think she's probably secretly glad to have our room to herself for the next month. I haven't been sleeping much lately, and though she's too kind to tell me, I'm sure my tossing and turning is keeping her up.

From out of the open driver's-side window, I take her hand in mine. "I'll miss you terribly. I promise to send so many postcards you'll drown in them."

She preens. "I can't wait."

"Don't let the little girls sleep in my bed while I'm gone!" I shout over the roar of the engine kicking to life.

"You know I'm a pushover!" she yells as she pulls away, disappearing into a cloud of dust and down the street.

Maxine and I bend to haul our trunks to the awaiting ramp.

Then, from out of the crowd, as bright as the rising sun comes a face I've missed deep in my bones. One I haven't seen since she left Haxahaven on a cold Tuesday two Decembers ago.

There are some things that don't change.

Lena's smile and the relief it brings me is one of them.

I run through the crowd, not caring how it looks to others, and fling myself into her arms.

She hugs me tight and together we sway, basking in the relief of being together once more.

"You are never allowed to leave again," I say.

"You hate being alone with Maxine that much?"

Maxine collides with us, throwing her arms around both our shoulders. She laughs, but I know she feels it too, the completeness of being a trio once more.

This is how it's supposed to be, a homecoming. There are elbows and laughter and someone might be crying a little, but none of us will admit to it.

"Never leave me alone with Frances again. She's so bad at cards, Lena, it's not even fun beating her anymore," Maxine says, face burrowed in the crook of Lena's neck.

Lena pulls back and takes us both in. I wonder what she sees in our faces, nearly two years older than the last time she saw us.

She looks the same, beautiful with her big brown eyes and hair so black it seems to glow in the sun, but she's more settled, somehow, like she's made a home of her body.

Maxine reaches up and runs a finger over the brim of Lena's hat, a beautiful baby blue dotted with silk flowers.

"Take a look at the fancy painter."

Lena rolls her eyes. "Don't jinx it. We don't even know if they'll exhibit my work."

"They'll love it, how could they not?" I say.

"You haven't even seen it. How could you possibly know?"

"Because I know you."

It's not entirely true that I haven't seen her work. Lena, always an expert in beading, embroidery, and with an eye for beautiful things, has taken up painting in her time at home. She sends Maxine and me weekly postcards, decorated with hasty watercolors, so vivid they take my breath away no matter how many she sends. Maxine's deceased father was an art dealer, and her mother is now a donor in the art world. She's arranged for Lena to study in a few salons while we're abroad. Women artists are rare, but if we're lucky, someone with modern sensibilities will purchase her work.

Lena rolls her eyes but she smiles, and it's so achingly familiar I can't believe how long I've lived without her by my side. I could spend the rest of the morning gazing at her face, but the smokestacks on top of the ship bellow, pouring steam into the bright blue sky.

"Girls, they're playing our song," Maxine says.

She flags down a strong-looking group of young men, and with a well-deployed smile she has them hauling our trunks across the pier and right up to the loading dock.

Waiting at the base of the ramp is a mustached man in a navy-blue uniform. He tips the brim of his hat as we approach. "Ladies, good morning, tickets if you will."

Maxine reaches into her handbag and produces three tickets, printed on thick paper edged with gold leaf. They arrived in the mail weeks ago. I haven't yet had the stomach to ask what they cost.

The man in the uniform grins. "An honor to welcome first-class passengers aboard. Your porter will show you to your suite."

Maxine smiles the smile of a person used to being treated well, and together we step onto the chrome ramp.

Lena's hand grips mine as we climb up and up, our heels clicking on metal, over the churning dark water where the river meets the Atlantic. I don't look down. I try my best to feel brave.

If the ship looked big from the ground, it is even more overwhelming to be aboard. The length of at least a city block, the upper deck gleams with neat rows of polished oak and the blinding white of fresh paint on metal hulls. Smokestacks sit like four identical, enormous cigarettes, painted tan at the bottom and capped with charcoal gray.

Staff in the same navy-blue uniform as the ticket taker rush by, luggage and papers in their hands. Families in neat traveling clothes mill about the deck, their eyes as wide as mine.

Maxine and Lena race to the railing and tilt their faces up to the midmorning sun, letting it wash over them. From just over their shoulders peeks the impassive face of the Statue of Liberty, far off in the bay.

And deep in my pocket rests a piece of paper with an address. Just a single scrap, but it feels so heavy.

The paper is a formality at this point, really. I've stared at it so often; I have its contents memorized.

36 Rue de Vis, Paris, France.

They don't need to know, I reassure myself, staring at my friends who stand across the deck, pressed against the railing, letting the ocean air tangle in their hair. They're laughing at a joke I didn't hear, and I'd never shatter this moment for them, rob them of the peace they've earned. They didn't need to know about Finn's letter then, and they don't need to know about the address now.

I'm sparing them the confusion, the heartache.

What's one more thing to bury in the graveyard of my chest?

What is a secret, if not an act of love?

CHAPTER TWO

Our cabin is larger than any bedroom at Haxahaven, even Florence and Ann's apartment on the top floor. Lena and I both gasp as the porter swings open the door. Maxine barrels through, treading dirt from the dock into the thick beige carpet and throwing a hatbox onto the settee in the parlor room. We have a *settee* in a *parlor room.* I don't know what we could possibly need a full set of bone china for during six days at sea, but we have an entire cabinet of it, next to the dining room table, polished so bright I can see my own reflection in it. I count the teacups instead of staring out the round window that looks out onto nothing but the endless, dark-blue expanse of the Atlantic Ocean. Twelve teacups. Twelve teacups and thousands of miles of water to cross.

The porter at the door clears his throat. "Welcome to your suite. I trust you'll find it to your liking, decorated in the style of King

Louis the Fifteenth. I assure you no detail has been spared. Please ring any of the bells placed about the living quarters for an attendant and one will be with you shortly."

The moment the door closes behind him Lena dissolves into a fit of giggles. "Why on earth would King Louis the what-have-you style be what we want?" She gestures to the general absurdity of the suite. There's even a golden statue of a cherub blowing a trumpet in the corner.

"Wasn't he the little creep who was obsessed with clocks? Or was that his son? Which one was beheaded?" Maxine drums her fingers along the polished dining table, leaving a trail of smeared fingerprints in her wake. "You know, they call this the Versailles of the Atlantic. Let's hope it ends better for us than it did for them."

I wish I had it in me to laugh, but I'm still feeling green in the gills. Is it possible to be preemptively seasick?

Lena appears at my side and crouches down to lay her head on my shoulder, gazing out the window alongside me. "I hate it too," she says. "Something terrifying about coming face-to-face with endless nothingness."

I take a jab at her ribs. "Have you always been this profound? My, you are an artist."

She jabs me back and rolls her eyes. "Maybe I got smarter away from you and Maxine."

From the settee, Maxine yells, "You know I can hear you, right?"

I wish I had the distraction of unpacking, but they've managed to do that for us too. In the smaller room with the two brass beds off the main living quarters, Lena and I find our clothing already hung up. We don't have much between us. I'm sure we'll end up stealing whatever Maxine has brought as we usually do.

We find Maxine in the master bedroom sprawled out on a four-poster bed. "You look like King Louis himself," I say.

"I'd look better in the crown."

"You'd make a prettier head in a basket, too," Lena agrees.

We kick off our boots and throw ourselves onto the bed with Maxine, and staring up at the heavy velvet canopy, their warm bodies next to mine, it is easy to imagine we are back at Haxahaven once more.

I've never left New York before, never had a reason to until now, but I still feel at home, here, with them. The kind of warmth that buzzes just above my rib cage, the kind I feared I'd never feel again after my brother's death. It's the comfort I craved so badly I nearly ruined my own life. The comfort of knowing the people who love me won't always leave me.

Just then, the ship groans and jolts. The china from the other room shakes like insect wings. And then, with a mighty lurch, we are off, pushing out into the great wide world.

Oliver, my heart hums. I'll be in his arms soon, in another kind of home.

There is another feeling that nags, but I swallow it down. I'm getting good at it, ignoring the guilt that pools in my stomach, and why shouldn't I be? I've got eighteen months of practice.

As predicted, Maxine dresses Lena and me both for dinner. She explains on these kinds of ships most first-class passengers bring their own staff, but we have to make do with her.

I steal a pale pink gown of heavy satin, tied around the waist with a white lace sash that trails along one side of the skirt. Lena looks radiant in a gown of deep red, set with dangling jet beads along the neckline.

"How many dresses did you bring?" I ask from over the dressing screen.

Maxine magicks a hairpin over the top of it, and sends it flying at my face. "Ha! And you tried to convince me not to overpack. Eat your words, Frances Hallowell."

I roll my eyes and send the hairpin flying back at her. The magic, blessedly, obeys me. "I'll do no such thing. I never told you not to overpack, I simply told you to pack faster. There's a difference."

Maxine steps from around the silk screen wearing a gown of brilliant cobalt blue. "Ta-da!" She twirls, giving us a full view of the bouffant Lena pinned pearls into.

I spend most of my days in black wool covered in chalk. Maxine has taken to wearing trousers most of the time. This morning was the first time I'd seen her in a skirt in months.

Wearing Maxine's borrowed gowns used to feel like playacting at being an adult. Tonight, they feel like camouflage. What would the passengers of the SS *France* truly think of the three young witches in their midst? They'd probably use Louis the XV's fine wooden tables as tinder to burn us on the starboard deck.

The three of us stand in front of the gilt-edged vanity and take ourselves in. It's like a trick mirror to another world, another life in which we are ladies instead of whatever it is we turned out to be instead. Maxine cracks a smile. "Good enough to fool them, I think."

We walk to dinner, as we do most things, hand in hand. Down a staircase carpeted in lush green with swirling patterns of tan, through ornate oak-paneled halls, I'm reminded briefly of the Commodore Club where the Sons of Saint Druon used to meet. They still do meet there, probably. I know only the barest details of their activities now. It is Florence who keeps tabs on them. Maxine and I are under strict instruction to focus only on our studies and our students. "Romps into the city, I encourage," Florence told us. "Late-night break-ins and blood on your hands, I do not." We could have ignored her warnings, she knew that as well as we did, but it was a relief to allow myself to rest.

Florence and Ann took their evidence of the Sons of Saint Druon's life-costing factory negligence to the city. The witches and the Sons buried their dead, and the centuries-long stalemate between the witches of Haxahaven and the Sons of Saint Druon resumed.

I've heard nothing of the Sons in nearly two years, save for a single piece of information. Finn D'Arcy, my brother's killer, my friend, my . . . something more, perhaps, was run out of New York City as punishment for his failed coup attempt. Turns out the leaders of industry and magical magnates of New York didn't take too kindly to an eighteen-year-old murdering their friends and colleagues in a power grab. He was lucky to make it out with his life, we heard. He hasn't been seen since.

I don't know where they buried Boss Olan, but we buried Mrs. Vykotsky on the edge of the back lawn, under a gnarled old oak tree. She wouldn't have wanted to rest anywhere other than the school, I'm sure of it. I go to the grave when I can't sleep and want to apologize again. I visit her often.

"All right, I'm starting to understand the 'Versailles of the Atlantic' thing," Lena says as we step into the formal dining room.

Our three heads tilt in unison to look up at the domed ceiling, easily two stories up, set in a Tiffany-glass mosaic.

"If this thing sinks, that'll be the first to go," Maxine quips from beside me.

"I hate you," I reply.

We give our names to the tuxedoed host who shows us to our table. As three single young ladies, we're seated with two old widows, one young Englishwoman, and her husband, who might be the oldest person I've ever seen in my life. He's hunched in his chair wearing a tuxedo that probably once fit and a gold watch so large it must be difficult for him to lift his thin wrist.

She introduces herself as the Countess of Essex, and with a gesture of the diamond-covered wrist says, "And the Count of Essex." I'm not sure if her husband hears her. He's too busy muttering something to himself about mutton.

"You're American," I say more to myself out of surprise than to her.

"From Louisville," she confirms. "The count and I met while I was abroad. It was love at first sight."

Next to me, Lena chokes on her water. I pound her back a few times as she swallows down a cough.

The widows prove to be a lot more fun. Rose Salisbury and Hedda Heely from Philadelphia, on their way to Paris because, "Why the hell not?" Hedda laughs.

If anyone has anything to say about the color of Lena's skin, they aren't brave enough to say it in front of us. I'd like to see them try. There are so many sharp knives in this room, it would be so easy to make something look like an accident.

Waiters in identical white tuxedos serve course after course. Escargot, then French onion soup, then beef bourguignon.

Hedda and Rose crack each other up at one end of the table; the Count and Countess of Essex sit in mostly icy silence. The count makes exactly one comment as the snails appear on his gold-edged plate. "The French, absolutely mad," he mutters, and his wife laughs like it's the funniest thing she's ever heard.

I don't understand his comment. They taste mostly like butter to me.

Lena and Maxine and I do a halfway convincing job of acting like respectable young ladies. We claim to be students studying at Barnard College.

Maxine spins an elaborate story of our history of art studies. We're going to Paris to study medieval portraits of the Virgin Mary, she explains.

"How lovely," Hedda says.

"Always found her more interesting than the rest of the family," Maxine says with a raise of her glass.

I swallow a laugh at their horrified expressions.

Even with our false identities, dinner is a bore. I'm surprised by how quickly I've come to miss the barely controlled chaos of meal-times at Haxahaven.

One of the little girls climbing into my lap to finish her dessert, or Maxine keeping me updated with who was caught with whom in the second-floor broom closet this week.

I sometimes fear my life at Haxahaven is boring. Most days are the same, rising early to eat breakfast with the same people I always see. In the afternoons I teach groups of wide-eyed young girls how to use the magic that lives within them, and in the evenings I read or walk or let Maxine beat me at cards until I'm tired enough to fall into sleep. It's a quiet life, but one that feels true.

This, the social farce and pretense and having to ever pretend a man is funny, I don't think I could stand. The Countess of Essex is a stronger girl than me.

It's right before the dessert course when it happens: a butter dish scoots across the table as if gliding across ice. It's the small kind of magic we do all the time at school. I haven't seen anyone open a door with their hands in ages.

Next to me, Maxine sports a wicked grin, and the game begins.

Lena responds in kind, lifting Maxine's dessert fork up a fraction of an inch, then dropping it back down onto the white tablecloth with a small *ting*.

I go next. Feeling bold and bored, I direct my magic at Maxine's knife and spin it in a full circle. The magic responds, and I sigh in relief. It's so like Maxine to not treat me with kid gloves despite her knowing the strangeness of my magic lately, and I love her for it.

Lena swallows down a laugh.

I've wondered before if Maxine ever regretted giving up her high society life for Haxahaven. I know now she's telling the truth when she says she doesn't miss events like this, people like this, having to sit straight-backed and polite like this.

Lena sends a ripple through Maxine's water, and Maxine floats Lena's napkin up off her lap and onto the floor.

I'm next. The tendrils of my magic reach out and take hold of Maxine's dessert spoon, lying gracefully above her plate.

I mean to nudge it, so it's lying vertically instead of perpendicular.

But the second I try, a shock goes through me like zapping my finger on a doorknob after shuffling through carpet but ten times worse.

The dessert spoon launches itself across the table, shooting across the crisp white linen tablecloth and directly into Lena's crystal water glass, which shatters.

The countess gasps, clutching her literal pearls.

Hedda rubs a hand across her eyes and blinks slowly a few times.

Maxine, Lena, and I hold our breaths.

A waiter appears immediately, sweeping away the broken glass and dabbing at the soaked tablecloth with a clean towel.

Maxine widens her eyes at me, and I shrug my shoulders. Lena places her hand on my knee under the table, and I turn to give her a small nod.

I need to reassure them that I'm all right, but am I? *What is happening to me?* The question makes me want to throw up.

"What on earth happened, darling? Are you all right?" Hedda asks Lena.

Lena smiles thinly and says, "The ship . . . moved."

Hedda looks to Rose, but no more is said.

Another waiter arrives carrying a tray of Baked Alaska, already ablaze.

He sets down my slice and the flames lick at my face. They burn through the alcohol soon enough, but I still can't bring myself to move.

The Baked Alaska is fine, but I can only manage a few bites, my appetite having vanished.

The waiters come around asking if anyone wants sherry. Hedda declines. "The wine has already gone to my head," she laughs. "I could have sworn I saw a spoon and a butter dish move themselves by the end of the meal."

I lower my face and pray she doesn't see how my cheeks flush red.

Hedda and Rose leave us with, "Good night, dears, don't study too hard!"

"We never do!" Maxine chirps back.

We leave soon after, abandoning the Count and Countess of Essex to their sherries alone.

The minute the door closes to our suite, I'm confronted by Maxine.

"That was reckless."

I sigh and sink down on the hard velvet settee. "First, you started it. Second, I didn't mean to do it."

Lena's brows furrow in confusion as she sits down next to me.

I'm mostly just embarrassed. I don't want to be someone they have to take care of.

"Shh, breathe." Lena rubs my back in slow circles. "It was just a stupid game, don't be too hard on her, Maxine."

"I'm sorry." It comes out a little broken, too pathetic for such a minor incident.

Maxine walks to the bedroom, stripping off her gown as she goes. "No apologies needed. I just thought you were going to give that poor woman a heart attack."

We follow her to her room, and together we help one another out of dresses and corsets and hairpins.

We collapse into Maxine's bed, and if it weren't for the rocking of the boat or the strange incident at dinner, this might be a perfect moment.

We fall asleep like that, tangled in one another, Lena's breath on my neck and Maxine's arm thrown across my belly.

Lena and I have our own beds, and I'm sure we'll sleep in them tomorrow night, but for now we allow one another this. The tactile reminder we're together once more.

The darkness shimmers, ripples, *moves.*

"Hello?" I whisper to the emptiness.

There is no answer, just the rhythmic rushing of waves.

Shhh, they whisper, *shhh.*

"Hello?" I call once more. It's dark here. Dark like Forest Park on a cold November night. Dark like the part of myself where I bury the things I don't want to face.

It's navy blue in every direction, like I'm in the middle of the sea or a starless sky.

It bends, the world bends, ripples once more.

And then—a figure appears.

It's small at first, out of focus as it crests the horizon of the dream space.

Then, illuminated in silver moonlight, comes a person, walking, water up to their knees. It sloshes as they make their way toward me, agonizingly slow.

"Hello?" I call to them. In this moment, I want so desperately not to be alone.

They say nothing, but move, steady through the water, through whatever strange space this is.

I try to move my feet but find I am rooted to where I stand. Cold water soaks me, up to the knees of my tea gown, making the white translucent.

The light shifts as the figure moves closer. A moonbeam lands on a hazel eye, on a grin, on a head of curls.

Finn.

The name alone sends me reeling.

My brother's murderer.

The boy I once thought I might've loved. *Did I love him? Does it matter?*

I want to call out to him, but his name sticks in my throat until I'm choking on it.

Finn.

I gasp awake, sweaty and panting, still in Maxine's bed, sandwiched between her and Lena.

The ship rocks, an ever-present reminder of where I am, somewhere in the middle of the freezing Atlantic.

Lena is awake too. She nudges my knee with her foot. "Are you all right?"

I roll my ankles under the heavy covers, feeling little snaps as they shake off the stiffness of sleep.

My heart pounds in my chest. Despite the feather duvet, I'm struck with cold terror.

"Yes," I whisper, staring at the dark ceiling. I don't have it in me to tell her I've just had my first dream in nearly two years.

CHAPTER THREE

The next morning, Lena, Maxine, and I make our way for the women's lounge on the direction of our porter. After a breakfast of hard-boiled eggs and pastries that pale in comparison to Haxahaven's, we walk together to the glass atrium on the starboard deck.

There's an itchy feeling under my skin I can't shake. Does it mean something that I've dreamed for the first time while on my way to Europe? It has to.

I paste a smile on my face, not wishing to worry my friends, and enter the women's lounge.

It's beautiful, paneled in glass with endless views of the Atlantic Ocean and warm wood furniture on which to lounge.

We meet Opal Bright, a woman who looks at us with such disgust I think for a moment I must have personally done something to someone she loves.

The countess is there too, bored, staring off to sea with fresh pansies in her hair.

There's a pair of sisters named Sylvie and Simone who smile brightly and ask us in accented English if we'd like to play shuffleboard.

I've got terrible aim, but the sisters smile encouragingly at me. On the court next to us, Lena and Maxine won't stop bickering about who's winning.

"The movement of the ship knocked my puck sideways," Maxine insists.

"It absolutely did not." Lena tries to wrestle the golf pencil out of Maxine's hand to correct her score.

While they argue, I feign seasickness and return to our cabin. The silence is comforting after the overstimulation of the ship.

I sit at the polished dining room table and focus on the shelf of bone-white teacups. One by one I levitate them off their saucers. It feels normal, blessedly easy, but then—

That awful shock comes again, starting in my fingertips and traveling up to the hollow of my throat. The last teacup on the row shatters.

I curse. And then I cry.

The only comfort is the address in the pocket of the overcoat in the closet and the promise of the answers I might find there.

Dinner is much of the same as the night before. Again, we steal Maxine's gowns and walk arm in arm to the dining room.

They're serving shrimp tonight.

The countess makes a face at her plate.

"More for us!" the widows laugh. I wonder where they've spent their day. It wasn't in the oppressive quiet of the women's lounge on the starboard deck.

Tonight, the game starts after the soup course, with Maxine levitating Lena's roll.

I go next, refusing to be left out. The incident with the teacup only makes me more eager, like picking at a scab to see if it still hurts. I stir Maxine's soup spoon with a flash of small magic. It works for a moment. Then stutters like a heartbeat and falls to the edge of the porcelain bowl with a *ting*.

Maxine shoots me a look of concern. Lena looks more pitying than anything, her diamond necklace reflecting rainbows in her dark eyes.

The dining room is a cacophony. No one notices a spoon falling against a soup bowl among the clanging of china and raucous voices. But we still feel the echo in our tiny universe of three.

We return to our room that night. Lena and Maxine laugh beside me, recalling something the count did at dinner, but my stomach is in knots. I don't want them asking what happened with the stupid magic game.

In the end it's Lena who asks; of course it is. "It's still happening, then? It's not getting better?"

Dread pools in my stomach. "I'm sorry."

Maxine looks confused, ripping pins from her hair. Behind her, Lena undoes her silk-covered buttons, then tugs at the laces of Maxine's corset.

"I wasn't looking for an apology. You certainly don't owe us one," Lena says kindly.

"I—" I start. I don't know what I mean. I don't know what happened. Do I tell them just how frightened I am? How the magic not coming when I call reminds me so intensely of the day Finn stole my power from right out of my chest?

I don't want to cry in front of them.

Maxine laughs, attempting to lighten the mood. "I'm going to tell Florence you need to be enrolled in Basic Manipulation class the moment we return to school. Put you with the baby witches."

The joke doesn't quite land. Lena lays a reassuring hand on my shoulder as I hold back a wince.

Maxine magicks a set of neatly folded men's pajamas from a drawer, levitating them through the air and right into her own hands.

She helps me out of my dress next, her fingers kind and careful. There are no errant pinches, none of the small swats I've come to expect from Maxine. She must sense how on edge I am.

That night, Lena and I sleep on our own beds, side by side in the dark.

"I'm here," she says. "If there's anything you need to speak about."

"Same to you," I reply.

The ship rocks me, but my eyes stay wide open, staring at the ceiling, afraid of dreams and who might wait for me in them.

Lena, Maxine, and I fill the next two days on the pool deck, sunning ourselves, despite the cold Atlantic breeze, or in our quarters, reading novels, catching up with Lena. Letters are well and good, but did nothing to stop us from missing her fiercely.

Over breakfast the third morning she shocks us both.

"There's a boy back home," she says as nonchalantly as if she was telling us the weather.

My fork clatters to the marble table. Maxine nearly chokes on a bite of French omelet.

"A boy?" I ask.

"Tell us everything," Maxine demands.

Lena takes a sip of her coffee and grimaces. Maxine reaches over and plops two more sugar cubes into her cup.

"Fine, fine," Lena says reluctantly, as if she weren't the person who brought the topic up in the first place. If she were Maxine, I'd kick her under the table, but she's not Maxine.

"His name is Mark. He's kind, works in lumber, his grandmother is my grandmother's best friend. I came home from Haxahaven and the fix was in. They'd spent months conspiring to fix us up."

"What happened next?" I prod.

"We went on a walk. He was . . . sweet. He's continued to be sweet." Lena looks at the ground and smiles softly. My chest warms at seeing my friend so happy.

"Why didn't you tell us?" Maxine asks.

Lena shrugs. "I'm not sure. It felt too big to tell you in a letter and I wasn't quite sure how to. We can't all be Frances, who meets the love of her life at eight years old."

I blush, thinking of Oliver bounding up our steps, a raggedy baseball in his hand. The way I'd watch him from the window, fascinated by him even then.

It's a nice thought, that we've been fated to be together all along, but it's not that simple. Our growing together has been a gradual thing, something that feels fragile even now. It's not that I don't trust Oliver, it's just that we haven't had enough time together as the people we are becoming.

It's hard with me living all the way up in Forest Hills and him being uptown at Columbia, immersed in the life of a university student. The time we have together is composed of stolen moments, stitched together with weeks of absences in between.

When he does come up to Haxahaven, it's nearly impossible to be alone together with all the little girls scrambling all over him, showing him their new magical tricks. Even Maxine steals him away. She says he's a more worthy gin rummy opponent than I am.

When I make it into the city, it's often for dinner at his parents' house or with his dining club at school. He's taken me to a few theatrical shows. He always holds my hand carefully in the dark.

But I pray for a time when we don't have to be so careful around each other. I'm still waiting to be someone who is good enough for him. Maybe once I learn to control my powers or feel as if I've properly atoned for all I've done, I'll be able to relax around him. I'm happy to be with him, truly I am, but I'm always just a little on edge, terrified to say or do the wrong thing. Oliver deserves a perfect girl, one who didn't earn him a bullet to the stomach.

"We're not engaged or anything," Lena continues. "I just . . . care for him."

"You deserve that," I say emphatically.

Maxine nods in agreement and takes a sip of her own coffee, barely recognizable as coffee for all the cream. "I'm sure he's a much better fit for you than me."

Maxine does get kicked under the table, but it isn't by me. "What was that for!" she yelps.

Lena gives her a withering glare.

"Oh, like Frances doesn't know we'd meet up to talk behind her back. If we kissed a little, we kissed a little! That was years ago, and Frances really did deserve it. You were so whiny back then, we like you much better now," Maxine says.

"You!" I whip my head, looking between them. Lena is blushing terribly; Maxine is as casual as you please. "You two—" I can't complete the sentence.

"Once!" Lena insists.

Maxine takes a bite of omelet and shakes her head. "Three times."

"I can't believe no one told me!" The other passengers are looking at us now, so I duck my head, lower my voice. "I can't believe you were talking behind my back!"

At that, Lena laughs. "Oh, that I'll defend, you were briefly insufferable. We love you, but you have to admit it was a lot there for a minute, Frances."

"She thought I was a murderer." Maxine nods her head in agreement.

Lena points to Maxine with her coffee spoon. "You thought Maxine was a murderer."

I roll my eyes, but know deep down she has a point.

"I'm going to tell Maria," I laugh.

Lena's eyes go wide. "Maria? You two finally worked it all out, then?"

Maxine shrugs, a lock of hair falling in front of her sharp eyes, stormy like today's pale gray morning. "No, that's over now."

I'm surprised by the news and hurt she hasn't told me sooner. "Since when?"

"A month? Maybe two. It was hard with her in the city, and you know how things could be with her. It's for the best, I'm fine. Truly, I am."

"What happened to May?" Lena prods.

Maxine takes a sip. "Moved back to Connecticut. Married a nice boy with lots of money."

"Oh, Maxine, I'm sorry," Lena replies.

Maxine shushes her. "Stop, stop. I'm fine! Look at me!"

"You deserve it too. Happiness, I mean," Lena says.

Maxine laughs but it's hollow. "Happiness, what a boring goal."

After breakfast, Maxine goes for a swim in the onboard indoor pool, but I never learned how to swim, and putting on a bathing costume and learning now doesn't seem worth the trouble.

Lena and I end up, as we have most days, in the women's lounge reading novels and listening in on conversation.

"I'm sorry about the game at dinner," she says between sips of too-sweet tea. "I'll tell Maxine to stop."

I shake my head. "I don't want you to worry about me."

Lena does the awful thing she does where she looks at me up through her lashes, quirks an eyebrow, and makes me feel like she sees right through me. She always has. "I'm your friend. It's my job. Maxine's, too. This will get better, I believe that."

I think of the address. I believe it too. I have to believe there are answers waiting for me in France.

"I don't want to be someone you have to worry about. This is a holiday. We're supposed to be having fun."

Lena bends down the case that contains her watercolors and pulls out a few tins of paint and a square of paper. "Who said I'm not having fun?"

The ship creaks the worst at night. Back and forth, vibrating and swaying and making awful noises.

Maxine sleeps right through it, snoring from the other room. Lena sighs and rolls over.

I stare at the ceiling in the dark and pray I don't fall asleep. If I don't fall asleep, I won't see him. I won't have to face what it means.

By day five on the ship, we have finally found our sea legs. We greet the porters by name, make jokes with the widows at dinner; even the countess begins to open up a little. She calls the count "that man" when he's not around, and I have to stifle my laughter every time. She has plans to replace the brocade drapes at her estate with something more modern, and can't wait to give her old housekeeper a heart attack.

Only two more sleeps until I see him. Or at the very least, two nights of avoiding sleep, so I don't see something I don't want to.

When I finally lose the fight, I dream of slipping under the churning dark ocean. Salt water fills my lungs. But at least I am alone.

We dock in Le Havre, France, on a bright-blue morning six days after leaving New York. I hear it before I feel it, the groaning of the great boat, the Versailles of the Atlantic finally coming home to the shores of France.

I peek out our porthole and see it, precious land. It isn't until I lay eyes on the small seaport that it settles in just how far from home I am.

I still don't feel quite ready for any of it, for Oliver, for seeing somewhere that isn't New York, for the address in my pocket, but I'm learning to let go of the need to feel ready for things. I don't think I'll ever find it, the sense of finality I'm craving.

Maxine and Lena pack up our suite in a hurry, flinging clothes, shoes, and hats across the room, both by hand and with magic. A sapphire hatpin comes zooming by my head like a sparkly insect. "Watch it," I snap. "Death by hatpin isn't how I dreamed of going."

"But what a story!" Maxine responds. The pin lands gently in her hand. She throws it in her trunk with the rest of the detritus.

If they notice me packing my things by hand, they don't mention it.

I step off the ship, and don't miss it at all.

CHAPTER FOUR

The docks at Le Havre are significantly less crowded than the docks back home. Nearly all the passengers shuffle the same way we do toward the singular train platform nestled among fish sellers and terra-cotta-hued plaster buildings.

The train doesn't feel all that different from the boat. There's the same rocking, the same people. The count and countess are in the compartment next to us, but I wish it were the widows. They'd be more fun to eavesdrop on.

On plush red velvet seats, we settle in for the hour-long journey into Paris.

Maxine buys us lemonades and roasted nuts from the snack trolley, and I sit in silence, my face pressed against the cool glass, and watch the world go by.

The trees are different here, spindly and twisting up to the sky, nothing like the squat, sweeping oaks from back home.

"If that was the Versailles of the Atlantic, is this the Versailles of the Rails?" Lena asks from across the private train car, looking in amusement at the fine carved mahogany paneling.

"Ha ha," Maxine deadpans, flipping a page of her *Vogue*. She flashes us the page, a dapper-looking man wearing a waistcoat and a top hat. "Do you think this would suit me?"

"The hat?" I clarify at the same time Lena says, "No."

Maxine rips the page out, crumples it into a ball, and throws it at her. Lena tilts her head back and closes her eyes, drifting off to sleep. I allow the rocking of the train to bang my head steadily against the glass.

It's a relief when the train finally pulls into the Paris station, but my sense of balance is still off from the incessant rocking of the ship, and the ground still seems to tilt and sway beneath me.

Maxine guides us through the bustling train station to a sweeping archway where a man is waiting in a fine suit.

"Miss DuPre, a pleasure to have you home," he greets her in accented English.

"Bonjour, Pierre." She passes him the hatbox in her hand and gestures to us. "*Mes amies, Lena et Frances.*"

The man, Pierre, tips his hat to us and flashes a smile. His blue eyes are weatherworn and kind.

"Pierre has worked for my family since I was small," she explains to us as we're led out of the station and to a waiting shiny-black Model T.

I nearly gasp at the sight of it, Paris in all its glory. It's like something out of a fairy tale, wide city blocks lined with buildings of white limestone, carved with angels on the eaves, wooden shutters flung open to let the early summer in.

The buildings aren't tall like in New York, and it makes the sky look bigger, stretching over the city.

"You coming?" Maxine calls over her shoulder.

"Yes!" I sputter, tripping over my own traveling shoes to hop after them into the automobile.

I've spent so much time dwelling on the journey, it's overwhelming to be here.

Maxine's family lives in a flat in the 8th Arrondissement on the Left Bank of the Seine. It doesn't take us long to drive there. I keep my face pressed to the window, drinking in the views like I've been starving for it.

The river Seine reflects the late afternoon light, shimmering as if from a dream. Along its banks groups of young people gather, chatting and passing bottles of wine between them. I wonder what their lives must be like, living in a place like this.

Even ordinary shops look like something from a fantasy, with shiny copper gutters and multicolored doors.

New York is all practicality, harsh angles, and dull gray. In Paris, it seems to be a rule that things must be beautiful as well as functional.

Maxine nudges my shoulder. "Pretty, isn't it?"

The "yes" I whisper in response seems inadequate, but I don't have words for my awe. If I'm going to find answers, surely it must be in this place. It's already so full of magic. It's somewhere worth running away to.

Once at the flat, Pierre takes us up the elevator while more household staff pour out of the magnificent building to fetch our trunks.

The elevator lets out into a marble foyer so similar to Haxahaven's that for a moment I have to stifle a laugh.

"Darling!" A woman who must be Maxine's mother comes exploding out of the doors that must lead to the living quarters. "You're here!" She takes her daughter in her arms and gives her two kisses, one on each cheek, before pulling back to look at her.

She wrinkles her nose in disgust. "Oh, *mon Dieu*, Maxine, what are you wearing?"

Maxine rolls her eyes. "Lovely to see you, too, Maman. These are my schoolmates, Lena and Frances."

Maxine's mother is one of the few Haxahaven parents who know the truth of their daughter's life. One of the few lucky enough to know their daughter isn't wasting away in a sanitarium, but a scholar at a school of magic.

It isn't expressly against the rules to tell one's parents, but most girls choose the path of least resistance. Who would believe the truth anyway?

As Haxahaven's resident Finder, Maxine is more bound to the school than other students. After one too many missed Christmases, she wrote home and told her family the truth. They seem to have taken the news well.

We mutter our hellos, and Maxine's mother waves us into the receiving parlor.

"Your father is working," her mother explains with a hint of a French accent.

"That man is not my father," Maxine replies with no real malice, lowering herself onto a pale pink armchair.

Before her mother has a chance to reply, the door swings open, and in a flash, a girl is colliding with Maxine. "You're home, you're home!" she yells.

This must be Nina, then.

She's the only person I've ever heard Maxine speak about with softness. Her baby sister, nine years her junior. Born to her mother and stepfather after Maxine's father passed away when she was young. Nina is Maxine's opposite in every way, short where Maxine is tall, hair so dark it is almost black, bouncy and loud where Maxine is, well . . . Maxine.

But the eyes are the same. I can see the ice gray of Nina's even from here.

They sway back and forth, then break out an elaborate handshake, and my heart swells, witnessing this show of sibling affection.

There was a stupid hand game William and I used to play every chance we got. We'd play at church and the schoolyard and evening in front of the fire until our mother begged us to stop. It involved doing a series of hand motions again and again until someone made an error. Our record was fourteen. Looking at Maxine and Nina I realize I'll never play the game again. Fourteen will stay our record forever.

That's one of the things I've learned about grief: you can't expect it, you can't control it, and sometimes the white-hot knife of hurt twists in your gut in the middle of your friend's Parisian flat and there's nothing you can do about it.

Lena and I let Maxine reunite with her mother and sister in privacy and follow another member of the household staff through the sprawling residence to our rooms. She gives us a tour on the way, pointing out the staff's staircase, the family wing, Maxine's stepfather's study, the parlor, the library, the butler's pantry.

Despite the palatial residence, Lena's and my rooms are right across the hall from each other, one bedecked in pink brocade, Lena's, and the other in blue and white chinoiserie, mine.

Out of habit, I check the window first. It latches and unlatches easily, opening to the fire escape with rickety steps that lead all the way down into the courtyard. I smile to myself, easy enough to sneak out of. *I'll need to, when the time comes,* I think.

It's strange, later that night, to not have Lena and Maxine fussing over me as we dress for dinner. I've grown so accustomed to Lena swearing as she tries to pin up my hair, it's a little disappointing to have one of the DuPre household lady's maids conduct the task in such silence. She's better at it than Lena, pulling my hair back into a stylish twist at the back of my neck, draping a string of pearls over the crown of my head, then securing it with a satin pink ribbon at the base of my skull.

Lena and I laugh as we exit our opposite bedrooms at the same time, bedecked in finery. Lena has a whole ostrich feather stuck in her dark hair. "Oh my," I say.

"All this for a simple family dinner?" Lena says. "They'd keel over dead if they saw what we wear at home."

"Tell me, what does your beloved Mark wear to dinner?" I joke.

Lena magicks the hem of my dress under my feet so I trip on it. "Ostrich feathers, a thousand of them. It's a sight to behold," she replies.

Lena and I are instructed to sit on one side of the table, facing Maxine and Nina, and a wall made entirely of ornate mirrors.

By the time the soup course comes I realize why people don't usually have mirrors in the dining rooms. Watching myself eat is strangely embarrassing, so I make faces at Maxine instead.

Maxine's stepfather sits at the head of the table in a white tuxedo with tails, but says barely a word to any of us, flipping instead through an English-language newspaper.

Maxine's mother is quiet and birdlike, sharp like her daughter, but hollow somehow, more fragile.

In a lilting voice she asks Maxine about school. "All is well," Maxine answers.

"But when will you marry?" her mother prods. "You must leave eventually."

Maxine makes a face at Lena and me from across the table before turning sweetly to her mother and saying, "When someone I can stand comes along."

"More like someone who can stand you," her stepfather mutters from behind his paper.

Later that night, Maxine takes us up to the roof. Up and up a spiral staircase, through a skylight, before we pop out into the night sky.

The buildings are so low here, for a moment all I see is stars scattered across the navy-blue dark.

The air is warm and heavy, the promise of summer no longer a promise, but something that's here. The promise of this trip is no longer a promise either, but something I'm living.

I've lived this trip in my mind so many times that it's disorienting to be doing it in reality. It feels sharper, more vivid, a little disappointing somehow too, but I think that's how imagination always goes. Minds are good at skipping over the boring bits.

But tomorrow I'll see Oliver, and tonight I am in the stars with my best friends and that is enough.

The limestone white buildings of Paris stretch beneath us like a parade of ghosts, and cigarette smoke wafts up from the street-side café below.

"I can't believe you're here," Maxine marvels.

"Me neither."

Lena picks an ostrich feather from her hair and drops it off the edge of the building.

Together, we watch it float gently to the ground.

It falls slowly, like it has nothing but time.

I wish I felt the same way.

I have plans to meet Oliver for lunch the next day. He's studying French literature at the Sorbonne for the spring and summer semesters, having abandoned his prelaw studies after being disillusioned with his father's career. He has no interest in becoming the great state of New York's next Judge Callahan. I find it preferable to hear him speak about George Sand than property taxation, so I've enjoyed the change. His absence I've enjoyed rather less well.

The sun is high in the sky this afternoon, a perfect golden circle reflecting off the rippling waters of the Seine.

My feet don't know these cobblestones, don't know these corners or alleyways, but it is nice to be in a place without memories.

I could pretend to be someone different here, if I didn't have a perfect boy waiting for me and an address sitting heavy as a secret in my pocket. There is no outrunning myself, it seems.

I arrive at the café early, and choose a small table in the corner under a red awning, close enough to see the river.

I fiddle with the pearl buttons on the white cuffs of my dress and try not to look at the clock. Oliver wouldn't be late. It isn't his way.

I'm wearing one of my own dresses today, an old tea gown he's seen one hundred times, but I wanted to look like myself. The wide brim of my hat shields my face from the afternoon sun.

Ninety-two days, I counted each one, crossed them off on a little calendar in my bedside table.

And now I'm here, sitting in a wicker chair on an unfamiliar sidewalk under an unfamiliar sky waiting for the most familiar boy.

With Oliver, there are always nerves. Ever since I was young and saw his dimpled smile and something inside my heart went *oh*.

We still don't quite know what we are. We've been learning each other in fits and starts, not quite yet able to reach a comfortable stride.

There's the ever-present anticipation, the warmth in knowing we will one day *be* something. But we're still becoming. Neither of us is very good at the in-between.

I see him before he sees me. He turns the corner, head ducked low, muttering something to himself.

He's arrived five minutes early, blue hydrangeas clutched in his hand.

Then his eyes lift from his shoes and find mine. I'm standing before I realize what my body is doing, colliding into him, closing the distance between us.

It isn't until I hug him that I realize just how homesick I've been.

Oliver is the apartment on Hester Street, the soda shop on

Delancey Street, the rumble of the subway, Central Park on a quiet Sunday morning. He's a lifetime of quiet glances across a small kitchen.

I wrap my arms against the expanse of his rib cage, bury my face in the familiar warmth of his chest, and even in this strange city, I'm home in all the ways that matter.

"Frances." He breathes my name into my hair like a sigh of relief.

I peel my cheek from off his chest to look up at him. Same familiar green eyes, but his hair is a little longer than when I last saw him, dark and waving around his ears, pushed up off his forehead. There's a shadow of stubble around his jaw, and most horrifyingly, an attempt at a mustache growing above his lip.

"Oliver Callahan." I slap his arm. "You can't greet me after three months with a *mustache*."

He laughs and clutches his chest, performatively aghast. "I thought you'd like it."

"I hate it."

He sinks down into the seat across from me and I follow suit. "You hate me?"

"I hate *it*. . . . You I like very much."

He smiles, dimples in his cheeks, so fond it makes my chest hurt. "The feeling is very mutual. God, it is good to see you again."

Other than the horrible little mustache, he does look well. Sun-kissed and more relaxed than I've ever seen him, and the tight coil of his shoulders has unwound a little in the months we were apart.

I want to hold his hands across the table, to feel him as a real solid thing, rather than the idea of a boy in my head, but I resist the urge. It wouldn't be appropriate, not here in public.

As if reading my mind, he extends his hand across the table.

The tips of our fingers brush, just barely, and this is it.

"How was the journey?" he asks.

"Dreadfully long. I hate the ocean, I think. Too large. That's my official review."

"I agree," he says. "Was the food good?"

"I ate snails."

His eyes go wide. I could stare at him forever. He's always made it easy to forget everything else. My world is narrowed to a single point, to a single color, the spring-grass green of his irises.

"Metropolitan! What'd you think?"

"I was underwhelmed." I wave my hands in dismissal. "Enough about me, enough about snails, tell me everything! I want to know everything about Paris."

He grins. "You sure you're not sick of it after all my letters?"

"Not at all. I want to hear it directly from you. Spare no details, tell me everything."

And he does.

I don't remember what we eat. I barely notice the food on my plate or the drink in my glass.

I stare at the pink of Oliver's mouth as he speaks and his long fingers drumming on the table as he gets lost in his own stories.

"The classes are incredible," he says, eyes bright. "Just two days ago I spent the whole day with my professors at the Louvre. Took a lecture right under *Winged Victory*."

I nod like I have any idea what he's talking about. There are so many ways in which Oliver and I speak the same language, but academics isn't one of them. It's embarrassing to remind him I left school right after learning complex multiplication. I never learned much about art or language or any of the other fancy things he knows. And it's fine, really. He doesn't understand the magic I teach or the classes I attend either.

"And the people, Frances, you're going to love the people. There's a show tonight, a brass band. You're coming, bring Lena and Maxine, too, I beg you."

It isn't hard to convince me to spend time with him. "Of course."

After our meal, we take a walk along the river in slow meandering steps, my hand in the crook of his elbow.

We don't quite fit, but we're learning.

It's quiet, peaceful moments like this that are the hardest. That's when the voices in my head are the loudest, when the memories roar back to life.

My boot slips on an unfamiliar cobblestone. Oliver steadies me.

The streets of Paris fan out in front of me, the buildings and hanging baskets of flowers like something from a dream.

But my vision tunnels until I'm somewhere else. There's the snap of a neck, the way her body crumpled to the floor, another body in a hotel room, one in a shop, my scissors in his neck. The bullet burying itself in Oliver's stomach, the bloom of blood spreading over his shirt as his eyes went glassy. It all happened so long ago, I don't have to remember it here. I could let it go, if only I could figure out how. The feeling has grown, like tree roots, snaking through my being, wrapping around my bones. We're now an inextricable being, this slick, sluicing guilt and me.

Oliver must see it on my face because he stops, reaches up, and presses a thumb right in the middle of my eyes, where my brow has furrowed. "You have that far-off look again."

I shake my head. "I'm here, I'm here," I reassure him.

I let the afternoon slip away as light bleeds out of the sky.

Oliver walks me right up to the door to Maxine's apartment and hovers for a moment. Neither of us quite knows what to say.

"I'll see you tonight," I say at the same time he says, "I missed you."

I look up at him, his skin golden in fading daylight. I pause, taking him in. He's looking at me too, not like he sees right through me, but just because he wants to look at me.

"I missed you too, you know I missed you," I say a little too quietly.

He smiles sadly. "Pfft, what am I, compared to magic?"

Everything, I want to say. *You're everything.*

"What am I compared to French girls?"

This isn't a dance either of us were ever good at, and distance has only caused us to forget the steps more. We're stumbling over our own feet, but we're trying. He makes me want to try.

He shakes his head. "You're Frances."

"And you're Oliver." His name feels like magic, but I don't tell him so.

He leans in, his eyebrows knit together, but pulls back at the last second, as if thinking better of it.

He places an awkward hand on my shoulder but only briefly. "Tonight." He pulls a pen and paper out of his pocket and scribbles down a time and address.

"Tonight," I agree. I take the address. I don't tell him about the other address in my pocket. He's good like Lena and Maxine. He wouldn't understand either.

CHAPTER FIVE

I blink hard a few times, attempting to focus on my own face in the mirror as Maxine's lady's maid pins my hair for the evening. Lena and Maxine are already dressed, Lena in a pale purple gown with a modern sort of bustle and Maxine in an emerald-green dress with a lapel collar like a man's suit.

They've put me in a dress of gray-blue, with delicate pearl beading along the trim. "You'll take Oliver's breath away," Maxine said when she handed it to me.

It's profoundly silly, the warring anxieties in my brain.

Is my magic gone forever? Have I done something that's destroyed my very soul? chimes right alongside *Will Oliver think I look nice? Will he try to kiss me tonight?*

Maxine's family driver takes us across the river, the three of us piled in the back, crammed in with our skirts around us, giggling every time the automobile takes a turn too sharply. Lena's sharp elbows dig into my ribs. I savor the reminder that she's right here beside me.

I take a deep breath and push magic and death and the address from my mind.

The driver turns onto Boulevard de Clichy, and I am immediately transported to another world.

The twirling, blinking lights remind me for a moment of Coney Island, and of the boy who once held my hand as music swirled around us.

I don't want him here with me, so I shoo him away, like a pest to deal with later. *Not now, please, don't make me think of him now.*

The club Oliver has asked us to meet him at is easy enough to find. It's lit up like the Fourth of July, with a door shaped like a mouth with literal teeth carved into the stone.

The name of the club is carved into stone too: Le Ciel et l'Enfer. Maxine snickers. "*Heaven and Hell,*" she translates. "My, what has our nice boy Oliver gotten himself into?"

"He said we were meeting friends of his tonight."

"Well, I'd hazard a guess they're interesting."

"Hmm" is all I manage to reply. One of my favorite things about Oliver is feeling as if I know everything about him. Has he become someone new in the months we've been apart?

Music spills out onto the street, raucous horns and the happy lilting tune of flutes. There's singing, too, a woman's voice in French singing a melody that has me tapping my feet before the driver has slowed to a complete halt.

The party has spilled out onto the sidewalk. Men in undone

tuxedos and half-buttoned shirts mill about smoking cigarettes, dates on their arms in fine silks, jewels dripping from their ears like icicles.

There's a man in a red silk suit, illuminated by the dim gas lanterns of the building's facade, waving a white-tipped cane. "*Entrez et soyez damné!*" he shouts over and over to passersby who giggle and look scandalized.

I look to Maxine for a translation. She arches a brow. "Enter and be damned."

"Good Lord, they really are leaning into it," Lena says.

The lights shift, illuminating a single point. Oliver is standing on the sidewalk in a fine suit with a shy smile on his face. He's standing perfectly still amongst the chaos, like he doesn't mind waiting at all. Even in the dark of the night, he still looks golden, and my heart does a little flip.

His smile grows as we approach him. "Frances, you came!"

"Of course I came." I laugh because he's shaved the mustache between lunch and now. "The mustache is gone."

"Never say I can't take constructive criticism."

He pulls Maxine and Lena into quick hugs, careful not to crease their dresses. "Oh, I missed you," he says to both of them and they hug him back, speaking about how dearly he's been missed as well. Oliver was Haxahaven's boy. The one boy we were allowed. He fit himself into our routines on weekends away from school. Haxahaven felt most like a real home when he was there. I miss watching him play cards with Maxine as the sun would set or pouring orange juice at breakfast for the little girls. His absence has loomed large these past few months.

It's a deeply heartwarming reunion until Maxine swats him square on the chest. "Oliver Reginald Callahan, I can't believe you tried to grow a mustache." She chastises him even though he's clean-shaven now. She howled when I told her of it earlier this evening while we were dressing.

"That's not my middle name, Maxine."

"You're missing the point entirely."

"I thought I'd look handsome with it. Dignified!"

A shorter boy I hadn't noticed before pops out from behind Oliver. "Do you not think this man is dignified?" he asks in a thick French accent. The boy is shaped like a barrel, squat and broad chested. His brown hair is parted down the middle, revealing a face with ruddy cheeks and a kind smile.

"Ladies," Oliver says.

"Not a lady!" Maxine interjects.

"Ladies, Maxine," Oliver continues, "meet Pascal!" He gestures to the boy. "Pascal is my friend from school and my generous, unofficial Parisian guide." Pascal grins at the praise. "And Pascal, these are my friends Maxine, Lena, and . . . Frances."

He hesitates on my name like he wishes to say something more.

Pascal nods politely at each of us, extending his hand for a handshake. "A pleasure to meet you. Oliver speaks highly of you."

"Pascal, if you're the one encouraging our dear Oliver's sartorial choices, I'm afraid I can't say I'm pleased to meet you," Maxine replies.

Pascal clutches his chest with mock horror. "I'm wounded, *ma cherie!*"

"No scaring him off yet, Maxine. The night is young."

Oliver pulls a wad of francs from an engraved silver money clip in his breast pocket and pays the price of admission for all five of us, 1.25 francs a person. He hands it over like it's nothing.

A man in a top hat and ridiculous devil's mask waves us in, chuckling at our stunned expressions.

Inside the club is chaos wrapped in velvet and doused in candle smoke.

There's a brass band playing somewhere. The bass thrums in my veins right through to the tips of my fingers.

All around us people are dancing, limbs and noise everywhere. Lena, Maxine, and I take identical pauses, our eyes wide at the sight of it all.

Oliver just smiles like he's been here one hundred times before. He probably has been.

Pascal, like Oliver, seems totally unfazed, shouting over the din, "I'll find champagne!"

The candlelit sconces on the wall have set our faces in shadows, warping our expressions into something just this side of grotesque.

Oliver maneuvers us into a round booth. We slide in, one after the other, the fine silks of our dresses slipping over the blood-red leather.

Pascal arrives a moment later, balancing five champagne flutes in his large hands. They slosh and spill as he collapses into the booth next to Oliver.

"*Mes amis!*" he yells. I wonder if he's drunk or if he's always like this, so full of unbridled glee at the company of strangers.

This isn't the kind of place I usually feel comfortable, but I'm not in New York anymore, so maybe I don't have to be the person I've always been.

I tilt my head back and let the music take up the space in my brain where the horrible thoughts usually live, until I feel as light as the bubbles on the champagne flute.

Under the table, Oliver's pinkie brushes against mine.

It's a simple gesture that sends heat radiating up through the small bones of my wrist. There's comfort in the *I'm here* of it all.

I glance up at him, squished so close next to me in the packed booth. His eyes are questioning, his face soft.

"Not my usual scene," he says so low only I can hear.

"You could have fooled me," I say, smiling. Oliver is one of those rare people who has the ability to blend in anywhere. I envy him for it. I feel like I'm always sticking out.

"We can leave," he says.

But from over his shoulder, I see Lena and Maxine laughing uproariously at some kind of close-up magic trick Pascal is doing with a napkin. Flickering candles reflect in their bright eyes and I don't want to leave. Not at all.

"No, no, it's all right. It's just . . . new. But I'm having fun, truly."

"'New' is a word for it."

Cautiously, like he's afraid I might startle and snatch my hand away, he threads his fingers through mine, our palms brush, and it feels holy even in his decidedly unholy space. I take comfort in that no matter how time and distance and my own cursed nerves may make what exists between us feel fuzzy and unformed, we still have this, how perfectly our hands fit together.

"So this is what you've spent your months in France doing?" I tease. "I pictured you wasting away in a classroom."

"I promise I've been a devoted student. Besides, Pascal is a horrible dance partner, he never follows my lead."

His eyes crinkle at the corners and we share a laugh, alone in this bubble of two we've created among the music.

"I'm on Pascal's side, I'm afraid. I've never been good at following a lead either."

Oliver takes a drink, untangling my hand from his, then sets down his glass and lays his hand palm up on the table. "Dance with me?"

My heart swells. "What if I step on your toes?"

Oliver smiles. "I'll survive. I'm very strong."

"What if I'm bad?"

He shakes his head. "Impossible." He's trying to be sweet, but he ruins it almost immediately by frowning and saying, "Wait—weren't you and Will banned from Prussia by Mr. Nowack because you were so bad at dancing?"

"I mean . . . I don't think it's diplomatically enforceable but—" He laughs and I can't help but join him.

I haven't danced much. Only during a few school socials, and once at a neighborhood New Year's Eve dance the winter I turned thirteen. It was thrown in the basement of a church two blocks from our old apartment. I remember they tacked a few sparkly streamers to the ceiling, and when one fell to the floor, my brother picked it up off the ground and tied it into a bow around my head. Oliver wasn't there that night, he was at a fancy party with his parents, but William dragged me around the dance floor, and together, the Hallowell siblings performed perhaps the worst mazurka the Lower East Side had ever seen. Katya Nowak's dad was on tuba, and he laughed so hard he cried and then begged us to get off the dance floor.

"Up, c'mon," Oliver insists. "If we cause a diplomatic crisis with our terrible waltzing, so be it."

I place my hand back in the warmth of his, and he pulls me to my feet. Pascal, Lena, and Maxine cheer behind us as he guides me to the dance floor.

The band slows, the horns drop a few octaves, and the strings kick up into a waltz.

He doesn't drag me to the center. He stays right on the periphery where the carpet meets the parquet.

Oliver straightens his already perfect posture and raises my hand in his to shoulder height.

"Other hand on my back. Right between my shoulder blades," he instructs.

I comply and hope I don't blush at the warmth of his body under my palm.

The song the band plays starts slow. The percussionist hits a chime, and then the song swells in earnest, and Oliver and I are spinning across the dance floor, joining the flurry of other couples.

Oliver is a strong lead. He takes sure, quick steps and points the way with his shoulders before we change direction fully.

I've only ever waltzed once, in physical education class in the gym of PS 042 with Mary Dombrowski as my partner. We stepped on each other's toes until we dissolved into a fit of giggles and were threatened with a switch.

I don't feel like laughing now. My heart is in my throat. Oliver tugs me closer. "That's it," he encourages softly. "It's easy. *One, two, three, one, two, three.*"

"How are you so good at this?" I resist the urge to look down at my feet. His green eyes catch mine and he smiles.

"Too many cotillion classes. They sure are paying off now. I owe my mother an apology."

"Send my thanks as well."

He closes his eyes for a heartbeat and breathes out softly. "God, I love this song."

"What is it?"

"Tchaikovsky. The opening waltz from *Sleeping Beauty*. In the ballet she meets the prince in the woods, and they dance to this."

That sounds right. This song sounds like it's from a dream. Well, not one of my dreams, but someone else's. "Then what happens?" I whisper.

"The usual. A monster. A curse. A kiss."

We turn again. We've made a whole circle around the dance floor. "Hmm," I say. "Sounds boring."

By the second circle of the dance floor, I'm no longer tripping over my own feet. I only step on Oliver's toes once.

I've never been one for dancing, but I'd dance with him again and again if he asked, because it makes me feel like I'm *here*, in my body, instead of watching the scene play out from afar.

We return to the table flushed and out of breath.

"You looked great out there," Lena says.

"We'll look better!" Pascal exclaims, and hauls Lena to her feet as a new song kicks up. He takes Maxine for a turn next, and Maxine laughs hysterically as she and Pascal both fight to lead.

Not long after, Maxine takes Lena onto the floor as someone onstage pulls out an accordion and a polka springs to life.

They collapse back into the booth when the song concludes, already fighting over who polkaed the best.

We sit at the table for the better part of an hour, finishing a bottle between the five of us easily. It hums in my veins, warm and only half-familiar.

I lean my head against the back of the booth and let the sounds of my friends' laughter and the music wash over me.

Oliver squeezes my hand, bringing me back to reality. It's comforting to watch the people I love most feel such joy. I brush away my racing thoughts, my sharp guilt, my fear, and I let the joy take me, too.

It's when Maxine stands from the table and declares it's her turn to get onstage with the band and show off her elementary-school flute lessons that we decide our time in Heaven and Hell should come to a close.

"You're just afraid to let me because you know I'm a better flutist than all of you, all of you combined! You're intimidated by my musical talent!"

"We have zero doubts that's true, darling," Lena consoles her, her arm draped around Maxine's shoulders. "But we fear the people of Paris don't deserve the show you'd give them. Best leave it to the imagination."

Maxine gives in easily, collapsing against Lena, burying her head in the crook between Lena's neck and shoulder.

"One day you'll all be sorry," she says, but she's laughing as she says it.

We stumble out of the club and down the cobblestone streets of Montmartre, arm in arm, stretched five people across, even Pascal, who is laughing hysterically on the end.

We're not the only people out tonight. The city is awash with starlight and bustling with youths, free from the social constraints of daylight to laugh as loudly as they please.

The air tonight is thick and heady with unfulfilled promises, and though I have no idea where we are, I don't feel lost.

It's easy to brush aside the magic and the address, to pretend I'm a different person, one who hasn't ruined so many things. If I pretend to be the kind of girl who is fun, perhaps I will become her.

Pascal drags us through winding streets, up and up so long my legs begin to burn. From this high, we can see the entirety of Paris sprawled out under us, sparkling little dots following the winding river, like something from a painting. Warm yellow electric lights on the top of the Eiffel Tower blink lazily, like lightning bugs in the darkness.

Finally, he stops at the top of the hill, at the white steps of a cathedral, glowing nearly blue in the moonlight.

It's a specter on top of the city, looming above everything. There must be at least one hundred steps up to the entrance, which is bigger than any church I've ever seen in New York. It makes Saint Patrick's look like a corner store.

The points of the onion-shaped domes reach up into the dark, disappearing into the small puffs of clouds floating gently above the city.

"What a night!" Pascal declares, collapsing onto the steps. The four of us join him, in varying states of wobbliness. Lena is a little unsteady on her feet. Oliver catches her by the arm and lowers her gently down.

Pascal grins and pulls an entire bottle of wine from inside his coat. I don't think he's far gone, none of us are, but by the look on his face, I'd guess he wants us to be.

"Did you swipe that?"

He shrugs. "It was on the bar, they weren't using it. It was begging to be drunk! It would be an insult to let French grapes go to waste."

"Open it then, if you insist," Maxine says, head lolling back on the stairs, one leg propped behind her, the other stretched out front. She's hiked her skirts as high as she can around her shins, and her hair is coming loose from her lady's maid's careful pinning.

Pascal fiddles with the wax wrapped around the cork, peeling it off bit by bit with his thumbnail. When the cork is finally revealed, he looks at it through narrowed eyes, as if he's only just realized we don't have a corkscrew.

He tucks the wine bottle in his coat again and turns away from us. Lena's eyes are closed, Maxine's face is tilting up toward the stars, and Oliver is looking at me. But I am looking at Pascal, and what I've just seen doesn't make any sense.

He pulls the bottle of wine from his lapel with a "ta-da!" It's been uncorked. He tips the bottle to his lips, taking a swig.

I blink a few times, but I know what I saw. I didn't drink more than a glass of champagne at the club.

Pascal didn't have a corkscrew, so he couldn't have just popped the cork out of the wine bottle like it was nothing. I'm not an expert on wine bottles, but I am an expert on magic.

Before I can say anything, Maxine sits bolt upright, her eyes flying open.

"You!" she exclaims, her arm outstretched and pointing at where Pascal is sitting dumbfounded, his mouth stained red.

"Me?"

"You . . ." As soon as the word comes out of her mouth she thinks better of it. Her eyes narrow, calculating, she glances around and sees we're alone on the cathedral steps.

She finishes her thought. "What did you just do?"

Pascal hesitates. "I opened the bottle of wine?"

"How," she demands, stony-faced. I don't envy anyone on the other end of Maxine when she has that expression on her face.

"I—" Pascal trips over his own words. "I do not know the words in English."

"*Dis-moi en français, alors,*" Maxine replies in fluent French.

Silence stretches between them as the three of us watch. Then, slowly, a smirk spreads across Maxine's face. She's caught him like a fox catches a mouse.

"You're one of us."

CHAPTER SIX

Pascal sputters. "I don't know what you mean."

"Does Oliver know?" Maxine presses.

"Does Oliver know what?" Oliver asks. His brows knit together, and I repress the urge to press my fingers between them and soothe the lines that appear there.

"Yes, Maxine," I say. "What does Oliver need to know?"

"That Pascal has magic," Maxine quips. Her gaze flits between the two boys. She's still leaning as casual as you please on the cathedral steps, but her face has changed. Her sharp eyes glint as she grins like a cat with a canary in its teeth.

"How do you know that?" Oliver asks. There's an edge to his voice, like he's just found out we're all in on a joke at his expense. But I'm as shocked as he is.

"I felt it," Maxine says matter-of-factly. "I felt it when he opened that bottle. I am rather good at that, sensing power. That's the whole thing about me."

Pascal presses his lips together in a tight line. "Magic? *Qu-est-ce que la* magic?"

Maxine tsks. "I know you understand us. You've been speaking fluent English all night."

"Maxine, be nice," Oliver says. "You've had some champagne. Pascal goes to the Sorbonne with me. He's in all my art history classes. Sometimes people are just people."

Oliver's panic at the idea of Pascal keeping a secret from him sends a fissure through my heart. I'm keeping secrets from him too. He deserves better, but I can't help it.

"Oh yeah?" I don't like the look on Maxine's face. It's the same look she gets when we play cards or fight over whether to stay in Forest Park for the weekend or take the ambulance into Manhattan. It's the look she gets when she knows she's just been faced with a challenge she can win.

She stands up, brushes herself off, and pulls a pin from her hair. It's got a blue-and-green enamel butterfly on one end, and a sharp silver point on the other.

I should stop it, tell her it's time to go home and to be nice to poor Pascal. But I'm too curious to see what she'll do next.

This late, mist pours in from the river, leaving the city below us looking as if it's suspended in a bank of clouds.

We all watch in silence as she lays it carefully in the palm of her hand, narrows her eyes, and then with a flash of magic, the pin flies, pointy end first, directly at Pascal's face.

He gasps in shock, and then, as if it was swatted down from the air, the pin falls to the stone steps with a harmless little *ting*.

For a second, we all sit there breathing, trying to process what we just witnessed. Maxine begins to laugh, and sits right back down on the steps next to Pascal, who looks too stunned to speak.

Maxine turns to Oliver. "Told you so." After nearly a decade of honing her power, Maxine is never wrong.

And instead of shock or surprise, the first emotion I feel is the sickening roil of *jealousy*. Because here's another person who has magic that works when mine doesn't.

I couldn't have protected myself from Maxine's hairpin. It makes me feel exposed all over as the realization dawns I can't protect myself from *anything*.

Am I still a witch if my magic doesn't work like it should? Am I still me at all?

Pascal smiles brightly, before fracturing into a full-body laugh. He slaps his knee with glee, collapsing nearly in half. "You!" he exclaims, pointing at Maxine. "You are gifted as well? Oh, how marvelous! Oh, how exciting! You'll forgive me my reluctance in admitting it. We are not supposed to tell!"

Pascal may be laughing, but Oliver looks panicked. I can't imagine how it must feel to hear that his closest friend in Paris has been keeping such a big secret from him. At best, it's an innocent lie by omission. At worst? It's too terrible to consider. We know all too well the cost of trusting the wrong boy with an easy smile.

Pascal gestures between Lena and me. "You are like me as well?"

Lena gives a cautious closed-mouth smile and levitates the wine bottle off the steps as her wordless answer. I just nod, feeling useless. I'm glad he doesn't ask me to demonstrate.

Pascal claps Oliver on the shoulder with a big hand. "Oh, my friend did not know! But now he does!" He bends over in a fit of giggles once more.

I feel equal parts fear and fascination. I've never met a magical person outside of New York. Nearly everyone else I know is a Haxahaven witch. I knew the Sons of Saint Druon, too, once upon a time, but I don't want to think about them, here, on such a lovely night. I know a few hedge witches from the magical market in the city, but even then, most of them were educated at Haxahaven at some point, so it doesn't feel like it counts.

"I attended Saint Bosco's School, right here in Paris!" Pascal exclaims. "I've heard of a magical school in New York. Haven something?" He drops his *H*s so it sounds more like *'aven*.

"Haxa," Lena says, looking a little taken aback at Pascal's reaction to being found out. "Haxahaven."

"Saint Bosco's?" Maxine asks, cradling her head in her hands, her elbows resting on her knees.

"It's Paris's own school of magic! The finest in the world!"

Maxine scoffs, "In your opinion."

"Of course, of course!" Pascal brushes her off, as animated as ever.

Lena shoots me a sidelong glance and I know what she's thinking. *The last time we met a boy with magic, it didn't end well.*

"You'll forgive us if we're cautious," I say. The truth is I want to ask him one million questions. I want to sit in on Saint Bosco's classes, to meet with their instructors and see if any of them have answers for what is happening to my magic. But I can't get ahead of myself.

Pascal nods. "Of course, but please, my friends, do not be."

I turn to Oliver, and scoot until our sides are pressed together. "Has he asked you for anything? Said anything?" I ask him under my breath.

Oliver worries his bottom lip, thinking. "No . . . He's just been my friend."

"Did you tell him anything about me? About us?" I can't think of anything Pascal could want from us, there's so little I could offer, but this coincidence makes me nervous.

Oliver looks down at me through his lashes. "I've told him loads about you, Frances. But I've omitted the magic, I assure you."

What have you said about me when I'm not around? I want to ask. But now is hardly the time.

"Come see, I insist!" Pascal says. "Come for lunch on Monday, let me be your host."

"All right," Maxine agrees immediately.

"Could be fun," Lena acquiesces.

I'm cautious of Pascal, but I don't want what happened with Finn to have destroyed my ability to trust people. I tamp down the discomfort that rises in my throat. "We'll be there," I confirm.

And here it is, the sense of adventure, the sense of hope I've been desperately searching for. Perhaps France will have the answers I seek. Under the sparkling Parisian stars, I promise myself I'll be brave enough to keep looking for them.

But something in my gut nags. What if everyone at the school looks at me and can sense that something about me is broken?

Pascal bids us good night at the bottom of the cathedral steps with a dramatic bow and a "*Bonsoir!*"

Oliver insists on seeing us home. He hails a pedicab for us outside the Moulin Rouge, which is still bursting with activity despite it being well into the night. Down the street, the party at Heaven and Hell has also shown no signs of slowing down. The music is as loud as ever, no longer sweeping waltzes, but echoing horns.

I admire Paris's commitment to after-hours entertainment, but I cannot wait to be back in bed. All the drive home, my eyes hang heavy, and I have to resist the urge to drop my head onto Oliver's shoulder.

He steps out of the automobile first and opens the door for us with a polite bow of his head. I almost make fun of his manners and his cotillion classes, but I stop short. Oliver isn't doing this for show. He's doing this because he's a kind person.

Maxine and Lena step away from us, pretending to fiddle with the key to the gate of the building, but I know what they're truly doing is giving Oliver and me a stolen moment alone.

He pushes the brown waves off his forehead and glances to his shoes.

I can feel my heart beat in the tips of my fingers, and the buzz under my skin has nothing to do with the champagne.

For such a kind boy, Oliver has a sullen mouth. It's turned down now, slick with alcohol, and I want to kiss it, to catch his bottom lip between my teeth, to feel the expanse of his back under my hands.

His eyes flick to my lips. I want this with him, I always have.

The gates to the building groan open with a push from Maxine, and the spell of the night is broken.

"Good night, Frances."

"Get home safe, Oliver."

* * *

Sneaking out the next morning isn't difficult. Upon our return from the Sacre Cœur, Maxine's mother and stepfather, having just gotten home from their evening engagement, invited us into the parlor for a late-night game of charades. Maxine and her mother kept bursting out into laughter at inside jokes in French, and her stepfather insisted we "make the game more interesting" by laying down stacks of francs on the table. Lena made a killing, but I suspect her clairvoyancy skills had more to do with that than her skill at charades.

I joined in for one round, but quit after not being able to guess the clue "the particular emotion of making a sandwich."

Sleep was blessedly dreamless, though it did take me a long time to feel calm enough to drift off. Waltzing with Oliver and the incident with Pascal left me feeling as seasick as if I were still on the ship.

The house is quiet this morning. The only sound is the shuffling of the housekeeper across the flat in the kitchen.

The family will take breakfast in bed this morning as I'm sure their post-champagne headaches demand.

I dress myself quietly as the first golden rays of dawn creep over the city. Then, on socked feet, I creep through the halls like a thief . . . well, not *like* a thief, I suppose. I *am* a thief.

I don't have to steal a map. I could ask to borrow one from the housekeeper or buy one from any number of stalls on the street. But I mostly want to see if I still can. It's like scratching an itch. This need to do *something* still nags for reasons I can't explain.

I stop at the door the housekeeper pointed out as Maxine's stepfather's study the first day.

I tug the handle. Locked, as I suspected it would be.

"*Briseadh,*" I mutter under my breath, waving my hand over the brass knob. I mutter a prayer to the magic: "Please work."

Again, there is that strange feeling of being shocked. Despite how many times it's happened, I can't get used to the sickening sensation, the way the pain travels down my limbs and up through my throat, leaving me choking for air.

I jerk my arm back and massage my fingers with my other hand. I blink back the tears of frustration. This won't last much longer, I promise myself, because today I am going to the address in my pocket, and soon I will have answers.

I push on, mostly because I've never found a bruise I won't poke at. "*Briseadh.*"

This time, the door unlocks. I sigh in relief.

Maxine's stepfather's study is deeply ordinary. A green leather armchair behind a glossy wood desk, bookshelves lining the walls, a globe in the corner. Stripes of early-morning light paint the floor as the sun peeks through the slats of the blinds.

I find what I need easily enough, a map of the city in a neat stack of paperwork on a squat table near the entrance.

I snag it and tuck it into the thick ribbon tied around my waist.

The maids didn't dress me this morning, so my hair is in a simple braid, and it's nice to cling to this small piece of normalcy on a day that fills me with such fear.

Maxine and Lena have plans to go shopping with Nina this morning. There's a new department store Maxine wants to terrorize.

If I'm lucky they won't notice I'm gone. If they do, I've left a note on my bed that simply says, *Couldn't sleep. Off to sightsee. Will be home in time for lunch.*

The street outside is quiet this early. Across the street, a baker in a tall white hat lugs bags of flour into his shop. One of the bags has broken, and flour floats through the air, blanketing everything in a hazy coat of white, like the beginnings of a snowstorm.

I pull the map out of my pocket, scanning each of the tiny streets for the name I need.

It takes only a moment before I find it. *Rue de Vis.*

It isn't terribly far, probably just over a mile and a half.

I set out walking, swallowing my own nerves, and wrapping myself in the surety that I have no other choice but to do this.

A young dark-haired man passes me on a bicycle and in his face, I see my brother.

What would William think of me now? Would he make this same choice if I were the one who was dead and he were the one who was alive?

I think he would. But he'd walk with balled-up fists ready for a fight.

I wish I felt angrier. Right now, I just feel scared.

I have a mile and a half to arrange my face into something impassive. I can't afford to show up looking emotional. I refuse to give him the satisfaction.

I turn onto Rue de Vis, my heart hammering in my chest.

The cobblestone street is dreamlike, bathed in the gray light of early morning.

On one side of the street are rows of the elegant homes I've come to expect from Paris. On the other is a large redbrick building, covered almost entirely in dark ivy. Flat-roofed and elegant, it takes up almost the entire length of the block, surrounded by a tall wrought-iron fence.

I don't know what I expected, perhaps an apartment building or a row home. Certainly not whatever this estate seems to be.

I approach the gate and swallow hard. I've crossed an ocean for this; there is no turning back now.

I tilt my face up to the sky and say a simple prayer to something I don't believe in.

Don't let me cry in front of him.

The gate is closed, but unlocked. It whines as I press it open.

The front lawn of the building is empty, neatly manicured in rows in shrubbery.

I climb the steps and approach the double doors, tall and set with glass. Through them I see a white-checkered tile vestibule leading into a long hallway.

Next to the doors, there is a plaque.

SAINT BOSCO'S SCHOOL. EST. 1489.

Saint Bosco's. It's the same school Pascal attends. Is it a coincidence? Do I even believe in those anymore?

The main hall is empty, but from upstairs comes the rustle of voices and the muffled steps of feet. Classes must start soon. I don't have much time.

I make my way down the hall, scanning the row of offices for a familiar name. He has to be here. She said he'd be here.

Ah.

My heart lurches.

It's right there, his name on a gold plate, drilled into the second to last door.

I don't bother knocking. It's a courtesy he doesn't deserve.

Three, two, one. I take one breath to close my eyes and steady myself.

The brass knob is freezing under my palm. The door opens easily, but still, it is one of the hardest things I've ever done.

In the end it's so simple, this moment I've spent a lifetime imagining.

It's smaller, harsher in the light of reality. There are no tears, no screams. It's just a moment, one like a million others.

It's just a man sitting at a desk.

He's here.

I thought I'd prepared myself, but there was no preparing for the brute force of having to look him in the eyes.

He's sitting at the desk, a startled look on his face.

For someone who has loomed so large in my brain, he looks so small here in front of me, his mouth in an O, a cup of tea held halfway up to his lips.

"Hi, Dad."

CHAPTER SEVEN

He springs up from his desk, then sits back down. I stand awkwardly behind the empty chair across from him and wait to be invited to sit.

He opens his mouth, then closes it again.

It's like all the blood has gone to my head. It pounds in my ears so terribly, rushing in and out, in and out with the beat of my heart. I take a seat without being asked because being rude is less embarrassing than fainting.

The office is barely larger than a closet. It's difficult to find a pathway to the chair that isn't blocked with teetering stacks of books and loose paper.

The room smells like chalk dust and stale coffee. What little light comes through the small window high above the bookshelf is made even dimmer by the sheer amount of dust caked over the glass.

"I—" He looks like he means to protest, to tell me that I'm mistaken. But he takes a moment to stare at my face and thinks better of it. He must see it too, our identical noses. His hair is graying at the temples, but the rest of it is the exact shade of brown as mine, as William's, too, once upon a time. His eyes are blue like my brother's were. If I squint, I can imagine him as the young man he once was. The man who wrote my mother love notes in secret and convinced her to run away from Haxahaven with him.

"Are you truly—" he asks.

Truly what? I want to say. *The daughter you abandoned?*

"Here?" is what he settles on. "Are you truly here?"

He looks so stupid, sitting at his overcrowded desk in a moth-eaten sweater, confused at the sight of his own child. If I didn't need answers from him so desperately, I would pick up the ceramic mug of old coffee and smash it. Then I'd use both my arms to sweep the books and papers off his desk and onto the ground. I'd scream until my voice was hoarse and he was forced to explain why he left us.

But the world doesn't respond to rage. The world wants sweet girls and fathers want sweet daughters, even if they did everything in their power to make them bitter and broken.

So I swallow my rage until I am choking on it. I unfurrow the tension between my eyebrows. And I pretend.

"Yes. Got in from New York a few days ago."

"Wow." He shakes his head in disbelief. "It's been so long since I've been to New York. What a fantastic city."

I'm not sure what I expected, but it wasn't this. I clench my jaw. "I'm aware."

"Frances! My darling girl!" He's so excited, like this is a heart-warming family reunion instead of a confrontation. "You must be what, fourteen now?"

He has to be joking, so I laugh. He doesn't laugh along with me.

"I turned nineteen in February." I eye the mug again and picture shattering it. Would the shards go everywhere or would it be a neat break?

"That can't be right." He looks genuinely baffled, staring at me with a slightly bewildered smile.

"I'm fairly certain I'm right."

"Well, I guess you would know."

"My own age? I— yes, I would."

He settles back in his chair and takes a sip of tea from another mug. There are so many stupid, discarded mugs in this room. He can't remember to put away his dishes the same way he can't remember to take care of the children he fathered. "So, what brings you here, across the world to see me?"

He's speaking to me like we're old friends, like I've known where he was all the time. "You don't seem surprised."

He shakes his head. "No, no. I've learned not to be surprised. I've always hoped you would come visit." There's something sad in the way he says it.

The tenuous control I have over my facial expressions breaks. "You never told us where you were," I say sharply.

He scrunches his face up. "Surely, I did. I meant to. Your mother, she knew. That's for certain." He may be telling the truth. But I have no interest in talking about my mother.

"So, this is what you've been doing all this time? This is why you—" I want to say *abandoned us, left me behind.* But I didn't come here to fight with him. I'll never get what I want from him if I let my rage win. "This is why you left New York?"

"Oh, not the entire time. I've been doing a little of this, a little of that. You know how it goes."

"No, actually. I don't."

"I'm an academic. A magical researcher. I'm sure your mother told you." He waves his hand like he's annoyed he's being forced to tell me something I should already know.

"She didn't. I'd like to hear it from you, the whole story, if you'd be so kind."

For months I've been searching for answers as to why my magic is behaving strangely. None of my classmates have been affected by this strange shift. Lena and Maxine are as powerful as ever, as are Sara, Cora, Alicia, and the rest.

My mother, even now that she lives at Haxahaven, still all but refuses to do magic. Her power comes in the form of small object manipulation, never anything more than scooting a butter dish across a dining room table.

We're different in so many ways, my mother and me. Magic is the love of my life. In her mind, magic ruined hers.

I had only two people left whose power was connected to mine who I could seek for answers.

And hunting down my absentee father was still a more appealing option than the alternative.

I knew my father belonged to the Sons. Mrs. Vykotsky told me my parents had magic, and my mother confirmed it a few months ago. It was an offhand comment about William walking in his father's footsteps by working at the Commodore Club. It was easy to put two and two together.

Magic runs in families, though not always. Lena's grandmother is a witch, but Maxine's family seems perfectly powerless.

Finding my father was a long shot, but it was better than nothing, and I refused to sit around doing nothing.

But I never dreamed I'd get this lucky. He's a magical researcher. He might be able to actually help me. I'll play his game of father-daughter catch-up if it's what I need to do to get answers from him, but I came for information and information only.

He nods. "Of course, of course. I grew up in Philadelphia. Came to New York when I was eighteen. I'd heard there were others like me there."

"Like you?" I prod.

"Possessors of magic," he explains. "Like your mother, too. I'm sure she's told you all about it."

It takes effort to continue to look impassive.

"I came to the city, joined the Sons of Saint Druon. Fine fellows. I'm sure you know them, too."

I nearly choke. "Vaguely acquainted."

"Good, good." He continues, "Worked with the Sons for a bit, came to Europe on business. Fell in with a literary sort of crowd, you know how it goes. Hopped aboard a few archeological projects. Traveled to Egypt, Greece, China. Uncovered all sorts of interesting things. When my knees started aching, I settled into teaching. I've been a professor of magical history here at Saint Bosco's for . . . oh, it can't be a decade, surely? Perhaps eight years? Time is lost so easily, I fear."

Not once in his accounting of his life does he mention his wife or the two children he fathered or why he left us. I was prepared to deal with someone cold and unfeeling. I wasn't prepared for this, the ramblings of a man who seems more criminally careless than evil.

Is it worse that he simply didn't care that he left us? That he never spared a passing thought to us, cold in our two-room apartment while he was gallivanting in Greece? It must have been nice. I bet it was warm.

He's no villain. He's just a man.

It's so pathetic I almost feel sorry for him.

When I was little, I pictured him as this larger-than-life figure. I believed he must have been living an incredible life if it was worth leaving my brother and me behind for. I asked my mother for years when my father was coming back. I wanted to show him how good I'd gotten at hopscotch and sounding out my letters. "Soon," my mother would promise me. I think she believed it too; that's the worst part.

I waited for him the morning of my fourth birthday as my mother tied lilac ribbons in my hair.

I waited for him to appear in the audience of the Christmas pageant where I had a solo in "O Little Town of Bethlehem."

I waited for him after my hands slipped off the metal bars at Tompkins Square Park and my ankle snapped. William carried me home and held a washcloth to my forehead as I became feverish. The bone healed and the fever receded, but still my father didn't come.

There was no moment in my life too important to miss.

I grew up and I realized that "soon" meant "never," and he morphed into something else in my head. A villain from a play with a cape and an evil plot. It was easier to believe that than to believe I might be someone worth leaving behind.

Christmases and birthdays and funerals ticked by and he never darkened our door. He might as well have been dead, because he was dead to me. It was a slow death. One he earned with each act of neglect.

Then I stopped thinking about him at all. It wasn't until my magic started acting up that I considered finding him.

And now he's sitting in front of me, in another sort of resurrection.

"So!" he exclaims. "I've ought to be off to class soon, but I would love to catch up. We have"—he glances at a clock on his wall—"six minutes."

Six minutes. How do I distill a life down into six minutes? He hasn't seen me since I was a baby, and he gives me six whole minutes to catch him up.

"I'm at Haxahaven now. I came to Paris with a few friends for a holiday." It seems like the wrong place to start, but I don't know where else to begin. I can't very well begin by asking him for information about my power.

"You teach at a school of magic?" I prod. I know what Saint Bosco's is because of Pascal, but I'd like to hear more about my father's role here.

"Ah, not quite like Haxahaven. Older and larger, more prestigious to be sure. I've always thought of Haxahaven as more of a country institution. It's quaint."

"I'm an instructor at that *quaint* institution." I've tried so hard to remain polite, but the facade slips for a moment.

He slaps his desk with both hands, a wide grin spreading across his face. "Oh, thank goodness! We've been trying to get in touch with you witches for months, but Ana Vykotsky hasn't been answering our letters or telegrams. It really is quite urgent."

"You've been trying to reach Mrs. Vykotsky?" I blink a few times, giving my brain the space it needs to catch up to the conversation. I despise the way it breaks my heart as the knowledge settles that he was looking for someone. He sent telegrams and letters for months to Haxahaven. I just wasn't the witch he was looking for.

"Well, it makes sense she wouldn't be writing you back," I deadpan. "She's dead." I don't tell him I was the one who killed her. I blink away the horrible image of her neck snapping in that final, awful, unnatural way.

I pinch the bridge of my nose and close my eyes for a moment, finding my way back into my body.

"Dead?" He shakes his head in disbelief. "Oh, that really is a shame. Not because I was particularly fond of her, no, that is no great loss."

"Depends on who you ask, I suppose."

He shrugs. "Who is in charge now?"

"Florence Poole."

My father shrugs disappointment. "No, no. I do not know her. That would explain all of the unanswered telegrams. It is convenient you're here. Have you been having the same issues in New York that we're having here?"

I'm confused. "Issues?"

He nods excitedly, takes a sip of coffee, and then nearly chokes on it continuing his story. "The Sons are in a tizzy, the New York chapter and the European chapters," he explains. "Someone's mucked up the veil between the living and the dead. The magic has gone all funny. It's clouding the clairvoyants' visions. And then there are the lunatics, the fundamentalists who believe they can use the damage to—" He stops himself. "We don't have time to get into all that. But have you witches noticed?"

The veil between the living and the dead. My blood runs cold. Suddenly I picture myself back in a basement, talking to my brother through a mirror.

I'm terrified to tell him *yes, I've noticed the magic going wrong.*

"Get into what?" I clutch my hands in my lap to stop them from shaking. I can't quite follow what he's talking about but those words he's using, "the veil," the talk of magic going wrong, it's ringing true in a way I don't want it to. This is the answer I've been searching so desperately for.

"The Sons of Saint Druon believe the veil between the living and the dead has been damaged by some idiots performing death magic they had no business doing. There's a reason things are forbidden, but rules never do account for sheer stupidity. Nothing like this has happened in about one hundred years."

"What happened one hundred years ago?"

"Well." He takes a sip of his coffee. "That is why I was trying so desperately to get in touch with Ana Vykotsky. She was the only one who knew the whole story. Well, her and Boss Olan, but he is dead too, I hear."

I nod, my heart in my throat. I barely know what my father is talking about, but I am well aware of the deaths of Ana Vykotsky and George Olan. I wear them like wounds, like scabs I can't stop picking at.

It takes me a moment to find my voice. "What's the story?"

"Ahh, we don't have time. I really shouldn't even be telling you this. The only reason I am is so you can tell your current headmistress to write me."

"Surely you can provide me with more details for her. The more I know the better," I press. I need to know more.

He tsks. "I'm afraid not."

He springs up from his desk, dropping his mug with a clumsy clatter. Muddy coffee splashes over my shoes.

Distantly a bell rings.

"Well, that's time for me! I do hope you'll come see me again while you're here in town. I have office hours most days from two to four p.m."

It's beyond insulting being invited to my own father's office hours, but right now, I'll take what I can get. He doesn't seem to be interested in a father-daughter relationship. It's all the same to me. I'll take these unsettling business meetings if it will get me the answers I need.

He walks me to the door, but pauses as I adjust my hat.

"And my son," he asks. "How is William?"

I've thought about this part, how it would hurt to deliver the news. I suspected he'd ask and I would be the one to have to tell him, but I couldn't have imagined a sting quite this horrible.

I take a breath. "He's dead. About two years ago now."

He blinks slowly, the spark of light in his eyes snuffing out like a candle at the end of the night. It's the first show of genuine emotion I've seen from him since my arrival.

". . . Dead? No, that can't be right. He's so young."

"He was nineteen," I say. "When he was murdered."

He leans heavy against the doorjamb, something within him deflating. "Murdered." He says the word like a marvel, like it can't be true. "How? Who . . . who killed him?"

There are a thousand reasons I can't tell him the whole story, so I settle on a half-truth. "It was a misunderstanding with someone he thought was a friend. He drowned in the East River."

My father shakes his head. "I'll be . . . that is . . ." He struggles to find the words. I find some satisfaction in witnessing his discomfort. I hope it hurts, I hope it hurts worse than anything he's ever felt.

Because at least I got seventeen years with William before he was gone.

My fool of a father will never get to know him. He can't begin to imagine what a profound loss that is.

"Bad" is the adjective my father settles on. "That is very bad."

I will not comfort him. "I thought so as well."

He still looks dazed as he walks through the door, eyes no longer focusing on me, but somewhere far off. I imagine he's picturing William as he last saw him, a baby just learning to walk on chubby legs.

He doesn't walk me to the door, but bids me goodbye with a half-hearted wave.

"I do hope you'll come again."

"I will." It's a promise, but not one for his benefit.

I walk out of my father's office in a daze. The hallway, so empty when I walked in, is now crowded with students bustling to class. In shiny black shoes, they clack over the checkerboard marble floor, chatting and clutching books and shoving one another laughing.

The ruckus makes me miss Haxahaven. I don't even know what time it is there. Are my students sitting in class or are they warm in their beds?

From over the din of voices I hear someone shout, "*Frances!*"

I turn, out of instinct. I doubt whoever is calling my name is calling me.

But I'm surprised to see I am the Frances being called. On the grand staircase behind me stands Pascal, a bright smile on his face. I should be less surprised to see him. He did say he was a student here.

I tamp down the nausea and anger from the meeting with my father and give him the warmest smile I can muster.

"Hello, Pascal."

With a concerned look on his face, he fiddles with the tie of his uniform. "Please forgive me, I thought our meeting wasn't until Monday."

"Oh!" I exclaim. "I'm sorry to have worried you. I was here on other matters."

"What matters?" he asks. He's blunt, like Maxine. It makes me like him more.

"A research project." It isn't quite a lie.

"Did you find your visit useful? There is a library on the fourth floor, I could show you."

I stop him as an idea comes to me. "Are there any faculty I could speak to? I didn't find the professor I came to see particularly . . . helpful."

Pascal nods. A knowing smile spreads across his face. "Ahh, I'm afraid you won't find the instructors at Saint Bosco's very . . . forth-coming."

The crowd of students in the halls is thinning. A second bell chimes—we don't have long before Pascal will be drawn back to class.

"What do you mean?"

"The curriculum is strict. The professors don't encourage free thinking. It's why I so enjoy my extracurricular lessons with Oliver. They are a welcome change of pace."

I deflate. "So the library is my best resource for more information?" The idea of combing through more historical texts searching for anything remotely relevant feels like returning to square one. I can't bear it.

Pascal narrows his eyes. "Perhaps not. There is a community of people just outside the city, a group of young magicians who live together in harmony, who dream of a better world. They share magical knowledge freely. I lived there all of last summer before returning to the city for university. I go back as often as I can. It's only a short train ride away."

"Can you take me?" The question bursts out of my mouth, the desperation clear, spilled all over the floor of Saint Bosco's.

Pascal quirks his head, curious, but not unkind. "Of course."

"How soon?"

"Monday, with your friends? We can meet here and travel together."

It's perfect. We already had plans to tour Saint Bosco's together anyways.

A third bell chimes. Pascal glances up the stairs. "I'm sorry, *ma cherie*, but I must go now. I will see you soon! Give Maxine and Lena my fondest regards!"

Sometimes I picture my magic as a living creature, small and curled up and golden in the space right behind my heart. It's weak now, but it's still breathing, and I'm not giving up on it. I'm not giving up. I've fought too hard for it.

"Thank you!" I call after him as he bounds up the stairs.

I step out onto the quiet cobblestone street, and pick up the pace of my steps. I can't get away from the school quickly enough. I'm walking like I can outrun myself, when the skinny heel of my boot catches on the edge of a cobblestone, sending me careening to the ground. Panting, I push myself up off the ground and assess the damage. I'm all right; I've escaped the fall with two scraped palms and a bruised knee. The blood from my hands runs down the tips of my fingers. I wipe it on a handkerchief in my bag and set off once more, with a pounding heart and a single question plaguing me. *What have I done? What have Finn and I done?*

CHAPTER EIGHT

"Are you all right?" Lena asks me later that night at the DuPre family flat.

"That's a silly question," I say through a forced smile. "I'm in Paris with my dearest friends. Who wouldn't be thrilled?" They don't need to know of the panic I'm feeling. I barely understand what my father was talking about. There's no need to draw them into it yet.

"How'd you hurt your hands?" She nods to where they're scraped and scabbing over.

"I tripped on a walk this morning." It's the truth.

But she must sense I'm distracted, because she narrows her eyes like she doesn't believe me.

I've done my best of putting on a brave face all day, smiling as we strode through the Jardin de Luxembourg after lunch, or picked up baguettes from the bakery across the street.

Everything about Paris feels dreamlike. Like the whole city was painted in watercolors of pale blue and baby pink. They bleed together into rain-soaked lavender. But it's all left me feeling unmoored, as if I could float right out of my body and up, up, *up* into the candy floss sky.

After the conversation with my father this morning, I think perhaps I want to. I want to be anyone who isn't me. Any one of the other millions of people on earth who didn't accidentally rip the fabric of magic itself.

I tell them I ran into Pascal on my walk this morning. It's a difficult coincidence to believe in a city of so many, but if Lena and Maxine don't believe me, they don't question it to my face. "He's said he wants us to meet his friends outside the city after a tour of the school. They have some kind of magical community."

Maxine and Lena shrug together. "That's fine. Just let me know what shoes to wear," Maxine says.

The following days pass with strange lurches. Lena spends most of the day in painting lessons, and returns at night with colors caked under her fingernails and light in her eyes. It's a joy to see her so happy even if I feel on the edge of panic. Maxine and I are left mostly to our own devices and fill our time with shopping and museums and lunches in cute cafés. I end up with a trunk full of new kid gloves and a stack of silk bust-bodices. We take Nina with us sometimes, but seeing the sisters together, bickering and splitting plates of mussels, makes me miss my brother more fiercely than I have in months.

The nights drag on and on. I'm still not sleeping. God, I wish I could sleep.

I haven't had another dream since the boat, but I can feel one coming, like the drop in barometric pressure right before a storm blows in off the ocean.

Sometimes I wander the house like a ghost, peeking in drawers of fine silverware, admiring Maxine's mother's art collection. Other times, I gaze up at the silk of the canopy and try to think of anything other than what my father said. But there was truth in his words; I know it as well as I know my own soul. Because something has changed within me, within the magic that resides next to my own heartbeat. Like the days, it too lurches.

Sometimes it works completely fine as I magick my toothbrush under the water of a running sink, or close a drawer from across the room. Then comes the blessed sense of relief. In those moments it's easy to convince myself that I am overreacting, imagining it, even.

But then, sometimes there is the terrible zapping sensation instead. It shocks all the way up my arm from my ring finger, to my elbow, to my collarbones, to my spine, leaving me sputtering for air, and I know that I have to fix this as soon as I possibly can.

The day before we're meant to meet up with Pascal, I lie awake in a cold sweat as a terrible realization dawns on me. If we allow Pascal to go ahead with the Saint Bosco's tour like he's promised, there's a good chance we'll run into my father, and that would require more explanation than I am currently capable of.

So in the morning, I wake up with a lie on my tongue. Not a complete lie; something harmless.

Lena appears at my bedside and pokes my pillow. "You're running late," she scolds. "We're meeting Pascal in less than an hour."

I peer up at her from my pillow, giving my saddest eyes.

"I don't think I want to go."

She sinks to the edge of the bed and places a hand on my shoulder. "But you were so excited."

I scoot up a little. The feather pillows crinkle under my head. "I only meant to the school. Seeing students learn magic while mine . . ." I trail off. Lena understands like I knew she would. "It just sounds too painful to bear. Can I skip the school tour and meet you at the train station?"

Pascal sent instructions two days ago, and Maxine's family valet purchased the tickets on our behalf. His friends live a short ways outside the city. The plan is to spend nearly all of today on a day trip away from Paris with his community of magicians.

Lena sighs. "Of course."

"You'll tell Maxine?"

Lena pauses in the doorway and rolls her eyes. "You're lucky I'm less scared of her than you."

"Thank you, I love you."

"I love you too. Rest up. See you at the train station."

The housekeeper dotes on me all morning, bringing me eggs and hot tea to eat in bed while the others are off. The maid buttons me into one of my old dresses, a white tea gown with fraying lace around the high neckline. I think she feels bad for the shabby state of my clothing because she attempts to fancy up the outfit with a thick ribbon of baby-blue silk tied around the chignon at the base of my skull.

The DuPre family driver kindly drops me at the train station right as the clock chimes ten. Maxine, Pascal, Lena, and Oliver are waiting for me.

Oliver raises his hand to shield his eyes from the midmorning sun. "Aren't you a sight for sore eyes," he shouts as I cross through the crowd.

He smiles as I reach them. "How was the tour?" I ask. "I'm sorry to have missed it."

Pascal shakes his head. "No apologies needed. Your friends told me of your predicament. Fret not, friend. If anyone can solve your problem, it is the leader."

My predicament. I'm annoyed. I'm sure it was Maxine who told him of my magic not working. It's so like her to reveal my secrets like they are hers to tell. I try to catch her eye, but she pointedly avoids me. I'm uncomfortable that they've been speaking about me, pitying me behind my back. Oliver's eyes are full of concern and I hate it.

"The leader?" I prod, hiding my annoyance. Creating a scene won't get me what I want, which is as many answers as possible.

Pascal nods enthusiastically. "Yes, the leader of this group. A brilliant man, the most intelligent magician I've ever met. An excellent teacher. I am lucky to know him. And now you will know him too."

Small butterfly wings of hope flutter in my chest. Coming to Paris was the right choice, I know that now. We'll find answers here, I'm sure of it.

Pascal claps his hands together. "You'll love it! It's utopia!"

Oliver raises his brows. "'Utopia' is a strong word."

Pascal elbows him in the ribs and throws a fond arm around his shoulder. "You shall see, my friend! You shall see!"

The Gare de l'Est train station on the east side of the city is bursting with people on a Monday morning. Maxine is nearly bowled over by a woman pushing a pram. She mutters something I assume is a curse in French. "We should have made the driver take us."

"It's over an hour away, and besides, there would have been no room for the boys," Lena says.

"We tie Oliver to the roof. Pascal attaches a rope to the back and holds on as he rides a bicycle."

I snort. "We'll keep it in mind for next time."

The train itself is only slightly less crowded than the station. The four of us cram into a carriage, leaving Pascal on his own in another car. I'd feel a little bad, but he's so good-natured about everything he waves us off with a "Goodbye, new friends! Have a pleasant journey!"

"Is he always like that?" Maxine asks Oliver.

"Like what?"

"So . . ." She struggles for the word.

"Cheery?" Lena supplies.

"Yes, that's it. So sickeningly cheery."

Oliver laughs. "We can't all have your depth, Maxine. Pascal is nice, he's just nice. Is that so hard to believe?"

Maxine shrugs. "I don't trust any man who has that much to smile about. Plus, there's the lying about magic."

"Oh, hush," Lena says. "I think he's fine."

"You're so judgmental! Can't people just be friendly and welcoming?" Oliver says, but there's no malice in it.

Maxine rolls her eyes.

"Tell me about this morning. What did I miss?" I ask.

"It was good. A school. They had a library and a dining room and uniforms that were less dramatic than the Haxahaven capes. We met a few students. They all fell in love with Maxine at first sight."

Maxine nods enthusiastically. "It's true."

"Sounds like I didn't miss much?"

Oliver turns to face me. "No. We just missed you."

It's a warm feeling, to be missed, and my earlier annoyance dissipates. "I missed you too."

I tilt my head against the window of the train and let the trees blur into one another, a sea of green and blue and brown. My head knocks against the window as we zip by, a steady thrum that almost hurts as the train jostles on its tracks. *Cheer up, Frances,* William would say if he were here. He'd love Pascal. But he's not here. He never got to go to Europe.

The train takes only an hour, but the countryside feels so different from Paris.

Our stop is a local platform, quaint in its smallness. A train station guard doffs his neat little navy cap to us as we step off the train.

He asks a question and Maxine responds in French.

We look at her for a translation. "He asked if we had any luggage. I told him it was only a day trip."

I tilt my head up to the blue sky and breathe. The air smells like wildflowers here, verdant, like something growing. It reminds me of being back home in the garden of Haxahaven.

Pascal takes off down the dirt road that leads into the trees, nearly skipping with excitement.

"Only a short walk, friends!" he says.

We follow him in a neat line to avoid the carriage tracks dug into the road after years and years of use.

We walk the opposite direction from town.

There are no houses around. Just meadows and spindly trees stretching into the distance like something from a van Gogh painting.

Everything in France feels a little unreal, like someone took globs of paint to a canvas and it dried only moments before we arrived.

I'm not nervous. I even like Pascal. His energy is more amusing than suspicious, but it's been a long time since I've walked into a thicket of strange trees. It didn't end well for me before.

On we stroll, Pascal singing songs in French that Maxine occasionally joins in on.

Pascal is right about the walk. After about thirty minutes, the tree-lined path curves, then opens at a lake.

I blink at the scene. It's like something from a storybook. Sunlight skips off the glassy surface of the water, throwing beams of gold across the camp set up upon its shores.

Perhaps a dozen white tents have been pitched in the ground, staked with pale wood posts, with arching roofs like mini cathedrals. Each has a small pendant flag, each of a different color, waving cheerily at the top. There are chairs scattered about the camp, some armchairs as if from a fine estate, embroidered with silk, fading and fraying at the edges. Others are wooden dining chairs, set around a still-smoking firepit dug into the ground.

There's a long dining room table set up right on the pebbles of the shore, covered in mostly melted, tall, white taper candles, placed on an ornate rug that's sun-bleached and covered in dust.

There's a surreal quality to the place, like something from a dream.

"*Mes amies*! Welcome to the home of Les Selectionnes!"

"What's a Le Selectionnes?" Lena asks. She's kind enough to keep the sarcasm out of her voice, but it's there, glinting like steel in her eyes.

At Pascal's noisy arrival, a few others have come spilling out of the tents. People all about our age, girls in white tea gowns, stained brown at the hems, their hair unbound around their shoulders; there are more of them than the boys, but there are boys with white shirts unbuttoned around their throats, wearing suspenders and trousers.

"*Bonjour*!" a few of them call over.

One of them, I'm not sure which, magicks over a tray of lemonade in crystal goblet glasses.

I grab one hesitantly, as do the others. The ice clinks. There's a sprig of French lavender floating in the center.

"Thank you," Oliver calls tentatively to the awaiting group, ever polite, the gentleman his mother raised him to be.

"What is this place?" Maxine asks.

Pascal turns toward the glinting water. "It is a home for those who could not find one elsewhere."

"They live here?" I ask. The tents are beautiful, but I can't imagine that they offer much protection from the elements.

"Some, yes, but not all. We are wanderers. We go where we feel called. We practice magic together in peace. We care for each other like a family," Pascal explains.

Pascal waves his hand cheerfully and summons the group to stand in a semicircle around us. He says something in French, and the group nods and smiles at us. "Hello!" they shout in accented English. "Welcome!" They greet us with just as much enthusiasm as Pascal.

Voices bright, eyes sparkling with sun just like the lakeside they've made a home, they wave us farther into the camp.

I don't speak French, but follow Maxine to where she's been

directed to sit at the head of the candle-covered table.

I sit down next to her, and shoot her a look. "They've made lunch," she explains, but her face is as skeptical as Lena's on the other side of her.

"Are you all right?" I whisper to Lena.

She nods, tight-lipped. "I just find them all a little . . . odd."

She's hardly wrong. Pascal's friends have the same baffling joie de vivre he does. But I don't want to be someone who can't trust other people, so I brush away my uneasiness and smile. "'So are we."

Lena nods, but she doesn't touch her food.

Pascal looks thrilled. Oliver looks on edge. The last time he was in a group of magical men he brought home a black eye and a ruined suit. I apologize for what happened in the basement of the Commodore Club the night of the *Cath Draíochta* at least once every two months, even though Oliver still insists none of it was my fault.

I nudge him. "Can you ask him which one of them is the leader?" I don't want to be impolite and turn my nose up at their hospitality, but I took the train today with one goal in mind. I'm here for answers, not a party.

Oliver whispers to Pascal. Pascal nods, then leans around Oliver to answer me directly. "The leader is not here at this table. We will go to him once we are finished."

"Can we go now?" I prod.

Pascal pulls a melting petit four from a robin's egg–blue plate and eats it in one bite. "Why would we want to do that? The party is just beginning."

A girl with blond hair in tangled waves nearly to her waist

appears beside me with a platter of cucumber sandwiches cut into neat little circles, like from a tea party.

Another girl with black hair cut a little unevenly at the back floats over to Oliver a whole baguette and a crock of sunny yellow butter.

The seats of the table are soon filled, the surface bursting with food.

Those who didn't manage to snag a seat at the table are scattered around the camp in those odd chairs or sitting right on blankets spread on the ground.

One of the girls stands and announces something in French, and then a cheer goes up and plates are passed and the clinking of silverware begins. Near the firepit, a boy sitting on the ground pulls out a fiddle, filling the lakeshore with cheerful music.

"What'd she say?" I ask Maxine of the girl's announcement.

"She welcomed Pascal and his guests. They're happy we're here. She toasted the founder of this place too. They all did."

Someone at the table snaps and the taper candles spring to life, dripping more wax on the tablecloth.

A bowl of green beans is levitated into my hands, and I spoon them onto my plate.

Despite not being able to understand a word my hosts say, despite the unease, I sympathize with these people.

Being a person at all is lonely. Being a person with something big to hide about yourself is even lonelier. To live among people like you, to not have to hide, is a priceless gift. It's what we're trying to achieve at Haxahaven. And although I don't see myself moving into a tent anytime soon, they seem to have achieved it here. However strange the world might think these people, they have one another, and isn't that worth something?

I don't know who suggests it first, Pascal or the boy with the fiddle, but soon half the camp is running full speed at the lake. There's a rushing sound as a dozen people break the glassy surface of the water, splashing as they go.

Some dive in headfirst, submerging their entire bodies. Others wade in only to their ankles.

Oliver appears at my side. "Are you going in?" He looks unbearably perfect like this, haloed in golden light, gazing down at me.

"I never learned to swim." I glance behind me back to the now quiet camp. "Should we go look for the founder instead?" I appreciate Pascal's welcome, but I'm finished playing around. Witnessing the casual joy with which Pascal and his friends use their power has only made my longing for magic worse and anxiety about the veil heighten. The itchy feeling of dread doesn't go away, even in a place as beautiful as this.

Oliver nods, concern across his face, but then Pascal calls his name. "Come on!" Pascal urges.

I can see Oliver is torn. He wants to support me, but we are here as Pascal's guests, and it would be rude to wander off.

"Let's wait just a little while longer?" he asks. "I'm sure Pascal has a plan."

The old me would have argued with him and run off alone, but I don't want to make Oliver's life difficult, so I nod and wade into the water by his side. My heart leaps to my throat. It's ice cold, glacier runoff, I suspect.

My dress is turned gauzy in the water, floating around my legs like a specter.

Pascal splashes Oliver on the side of the face, and water drips down his dark hair. He brushes it back, and it should be a perfect moment, but it's not because something inside me is broken.

I plaster a smile on my face and hope no one notices that I don't join their games or the way I keep looking back to camp.

We wade out of the lake and lie down on the soft grass, letting the sun warm us where the water chilled to the bone.

The same blond girl from earlier appears. She stands over where Maxine lies on the grass, casting a shadow over her. The girl is smiling brightly and says something to Maxine in French. I turn, waiting for her translation. "She says the founder is in. He's just returned from town."

"Finally," I breathe.

"He's ready to meet you now."

I spring from the ground and immediately regret following Oliver into the lake. My wet dress hangs cold and heavy around my ankles.

I thought perhaps I'd go alone, but Maxine, Lena, and Oliver push themselves up off the ground as well. Pascal is already standing. He claps his hands together. "Oh, I am thrilled! You will love him! He is the best man I've ever met! A genius! A visionary! A true friend to all of us here. What a gift it is, to have so many friends in one place."

I've been on edge all day, but now my nerves have kicked into high gear. A thousand what-if questions burn in my head. *What if this man can't help me, what if he thinks I'm lying, what if he doesn't care, what if Pascal has made it all up?*

He walks us to the largest tent on the far side of camp. It's set under a weeping willow tree, shrouded in sun-speckled shadows, as the light moves through the branches. Unlike the others, this tent is built on a wooden platform, giving it a small front porch, making it look more permanent than any of the other structures.

There's a hush on this side of the clearing, a quiet peace, removed from the raucous laughter near the lakeshore. It's colder here too, in the shadows.

"What is his name?" Oliver asks Pascal.

"He doesn't have one. He doesn't need one," Pascal answers.

"Who doesn't have a name?" Lena whispers, so low only I can hear. A chill goes through me and I'm not sure I can blame the lake. What have I gotten us into?

"Hello!" Pascal calls toward the tent in English. It's so still it's hard to believe anyone is inside. "I have brought my dear friends to meet you! It is an honor!"

For him or for us? I want to ask.

A cool breeze ripples through the trees, and I'm painfully aware of just how wet my dress is. I'm barefoot against the grass, my boots abandoned somewhere near the water.

I reach out my hand to take Oliver's, but he's just a breath too far away and he doesn't notice me reaching for him, so I tuck my hand back to my side, alone and untethered. I take a step forward.

Just then, the entrance to the tent moves. The white canvas is pulled back by a hand, sure and quick; it sweeps the fabric aside.

A person, a boy, strides out onto the small porch.

I blink against the sun, as the ground tilts underneath me.

Because it can't be. He's gone. He's a ghost.

But the boy in front of me is not a ghost.

He's older, his hair a little longer, with a shadow of stubble along his sharp jawline.

But I would know him anywhere, in any time. I would know him in hell. And I certainly know him here.

My old friend. My brother's killer. No longer haunting me in my head, but here, solid and real and awful.

Finn D'Arcy.

CHAPTER NINE

I stumble back and clap my hand over my mouth in shock. A sound like a swarm of bees roars in my head.

Finn's impassive face cracks for the briefest moment, revealing *something*, pain, maybe, except I don't believe Finn feels pain, not like normal people do.

In the space of a stuttering heartbeat, I take him in. This is a familiar daydream, Finn with his broad shoulders and awful hands. His fine face dappled with fluttering sunlight, surrounded by trees. His golden curls cascade across his forehead and he looks like an angel, even with the bruise-dark circles under his eyes.

But these are not our woods.

This is not my Finn.

My Finn. I scoff at the concept. My Finn was a construction in my own head, a character he played. My Finn never existed.

And this is not a dream. It's achingly real, and it hurts right down to the soles of my feet to see him standing in front of me.

It's as if time is frozen, like infinity exists in the single gasp we both take at the sight of each other.

"We're leaving," Maxine declares, clear and decisive. She turns and Lena follows, shock and anger falling over her beautiful face.

Every ounce of color drains from Oliver's cheeks, and for a second I'm afraid he might faint.

Finn says my name like it is an inevitable thing. "*Frances.*" Then he grins. "I see you got my letter."

It's enough to send me careening through time, back to every other time he said my name.

I used to like it best when he said it in the dark, like it was a secret just for him, but it sounds like poison now, a curse.

Fury rises like bile in my throat.

I hate him, I hate him, I hate him.

But—a voice in the back of my mind whispers.

But—

Maxine marches away. I admire the way she doesn't look back. She's always been stronger than me.

"Maxine, wait!" I call.

Oliver turns and looks at me like I've lost my mind. He stands so still in the grass, like he's forgotten he has a body at all.

Maxine turns to me too. "He tricked us, Frances!" I don't know if she's talking about Pascal or Finn. Pascal looks completely baffled by the scene currently playing out, so either he's an incredible actor or this is the worst coincidence in the history of coincidences.

"I—" I don't know what to say to Maxine, how to explain it. "Stay, please, just for a moment."

"Stay?" I didn't know it was possible to say a single word with so much ire. She's looking at me like she hates me too. I wouldn't blame her if she does.

I wish I knew how to explain. I never have the right words. She doesn't know how empty I feel without my power, she doesn't know how hollow and terrifying it is to possess something and then have it go away. Nor does she know what my father said about the veil between the living and the dead.

I'd do anything for more information, even this.

Finn has always known more about magic than the rest of us. I came to Paris for answers, and as much as I despise him, Finn may have them.

"He may still have answers." I feel guilty I led my friends into believing today was nothing more than an innocent day trip.

"What use would it be?" Lena says. "He could say anything and we'd still never believe him."

She's right. Of course she's right.

"But I have to try."

My friends look at me in identical stunned silence.

Finn smirks. I want to slap the expression off his face. "Come in, then, you're welcome." His Irish accent lilts like poetry.

"Frances . . ." Oliver sounds so hurt. I wish I could fix this, but I don't have time to explain. I don't know how to make him understand when I hardly understand myself.

"I won't be long."

"You aren't going in there alone," Lena says.

"He's not going to do anything." Finn is many things, a monster among them, but I don't believe he'd hurt me. "I'll be all right."

With a wave of his hand, he magicks open the entrance to his tent and waves me inside. I take a step forward.

I brush aside the sick feeling that rises in my throat at his simple use of magic because I know what it means.

"Frances, please don't do this," Oliver begs.

"I won't be long, I promise."

He shakes his head sadly and the gesture breaks my heart.

"*J'ne comprends pas.* I do not understand," Pascal says quietly, more to himself than to us.

"We knew Finn back in New York," Oliver says. It's such an oversimplification of our actual relationship to him, I nearly laugh.

"Finn?" Pascal asks.

I would laugh if I didn't feel so close to vomiting. It is so like Finn to not even tell them his name and somehow amass a new band of naive magicians. I'm sure he smiled as he lied to them too.

My footfalls feel like sins, one after another, committed so publicly, as I walk across the clearing to Finn's tent. The weight of my friends' gazes is heavy as their eyes follow me.

He waves me into his tent, and the flap to the entrance falls behind us in a hush.

The tent is surprisingly homey. There's a threadbare carpet on the wooden floor, a twin bed frame made of rough-hewn wood, neatly made with a white quilt. There are two chairs around a small breakfast table, and a few leather trunks stacked in the corner.

The sunny afternoon is made dimmer here.

He paces for a moment, awkward in this small space, then takes a seat at the table.

I stay standing in the entrance, but he waves me over and I relent.

Get in and get out. Just tell him what you need to tell him. It would be pointless to stand sniveling waiting for an apology I know won't fix anything.

I sit across from him at the small oak table and for a moment we just breathe. I don't know where to begin.

"Frances—" I wish he wouldn't say my name. I wish he'd stop smiling at me like he missed me.

I don't know what happened to Finn's magic after that awful night at Haxahaven November before last. The night he betrayed me, admitted to killing my brother, and nearly killed my friends. When I stabbed him in our shared dream, and left him for dead on the icy lawn, I thought I'd taken away his magic permanently, or perhaps it was just an easier fantasy to live in than letting myself be afraid of him forever.

But I know what I saw when he waved the tent flap open like it was nothing. Power exists in him still.

Finn's eyes are downcast, landing on my palms, on the bruises and scrapes still healing there from last week's fall outside of Saint Bosco's.

He goes very still, his breath catching in his throat.

His brows furrow, then slowly, so slowly, he extends a hand, his outstretched fingers nearly brushing mine before I pull back, as if snapped out of a trance.

"Your hands," he says quietly, still not meeting my eye. "Did someone hurt you?"

"I . . . ," I begin. "Why on earth would you care if they did?"

"Who hurt you?" he asks, deadly serious.

"Are we asking questions now? How'd you get your magic back?" I snap.

He sucks on his teeth and pulls his hand back from mine reluctantly. "Another thing I'm afraid we'd disagree on."

"Did you steal it, Finn? Did you trick some other poor, lovesick girl the same way you tricked me?"

He sighs. There's something exhausted in it. "Lovesick? I didn't trick you."

"You did trick me! Revising the past doesn't make it true!" I didn't want to resort to yelling. I swallow my anger, refusing to give him the satisfaction of a reaction out of me. He's already had so much of me. He doesn't get more.

He said in his letter so long ago that what he was building, he was building for us. Is this whole camp for me? This tent? The narrow bed in the corner, illuminated by a single lantern?

"Why are you here in the first place? I thought you were supposed to be the fancy leader of the Sons of Saint Druon. Wasn't that the point of your whole little plot? This seems like quite the downgrade."

A dark look crosses his face. "I don't associate with the Sons anymore."

"How lucky for them. Probably increased all their life spans by decades."

He's looking at me like he sees right through me. "I missed you, too." Then he smiles, smug and sure. "I knew you'd find me."

Anger rises in my throat, hot and fast. "I didn't *find* you. We were brought here by Pascal. Which I assume is your doing."

"It isn't," he says simply, undeterred by my anger. "Perhaps the universe just wanted us together."

I don't know much about the universe, but I hope it doesn't hate me enough to want this for me.

Get in and get out. I don't have time to waste by arguing with him. "I'm not here to flatter you. I'd prefer if we never spoke again. But I fear I have no choice. There is an urgent matter."

The worried look that crosses his face is genuine. "Are you all right?"

It is often the case that time softens memory. People become perfect with distance and the passage of time. It has certainly been true of my memories of my brother; every rough edge has been rounded with the glow of nostalgia and the haze of grief. With Finn, it is the opposite. In my memory he is a monster, but sitting in front of me is just a boy. A boy with a scar on the back of his hand I never noticed before, and the blush of a sunburn across his gently freckled cheeks.

"How I am is no business of yours," I reply. It comes out sounding petulant.

"Did you get my letter?" He leans slightly across the table, fingers reaching for me.

Some terrible part of me wants to touch him just to see what it would feel like.

"I did."

His eyes search my face. "Did you read it?"

"That's not why I'm here, Finn." It's been so long since I've said his name aloud. It sticks in my throat like stale candy floss.

He cocks his head. "Then why are you here, Frances?"

"I'm here to ask if it's happening to you, too."

His hazel eyes narrow in confusion.

The tent is stifling, but my wet skirt has me feeling waterlogged and shaky.

"Is *what* happening?" I've captured his full attention now. No longer is his mouth set in a teasing smile. The question has torn through his facade. It's all the confirmation I need. Finn's and my magic is so wound together. When we opened the veil to speak to my brother, we tied our fates together.

"The magic, is yours behaving strangely too? Does it not come when called? Does it stop and start? Does it hurt?"

His eyes widen just the tiniest bit, and in them, I see the smallest flash of fear.

It's happening to him, too; I know for certain now. The confirmation should feel like victory, but it makes me sick. This is confirmation that my fears were correct, that what my father said about the veil is correct. It's connected to Finn and me, to our very souls, and now we have to figure out a way to fix it.

"I think we've done something terrible, Finn." Outside, the wind blows, and the canvas walls rustle around us. Shadows from the weeping willow branches dance across Finn's frightened face.

"Something terrible?" he whispers.

I nod. "I spoke to . . ." I nearly say *my father* but Finn is the last person I want to admit my secrets to. "I spoke to an instructor at a magic academy here. He says the veil between the living and the dead has been opened by someone performing forbidden magic. They're trying to locate those responsible, to figure out how to close the veil. Only Mrs. Vykotsky and Boss Olan knew how. This is our fault. We have to fix this."

I wait for understanding to dawn on his face. It would feel comforting to have him look as afraid as I feel.

But he blinks and the mask falls over his face once more. His mouth is set in an impassive line, his eyes dark. "Interesting."

I nearly kick him. "'*Interesting?*' That's the best you can offer me?"

He presses his lips together. "You asked to speak to William. I gave you that. I don't know why you've shown up to blame me for things that aren't my fault."

I want to spring up from the table and shout, but I restrain myself. "So your powers are perfect? You haven't felt what I feel?"

I ask the question, but I already know the answer. He must feel the skeins of connection between us. Unspooling like the yarn that used to litter a desk marked with my name.

"Magic is . . . fluid. It feels different for me all the time."

"You're lying. You feel it. I know you do. If you don't help me figure out what is going on, your magic will be gone too." *Help.* The word is as sharp as a blade in my throat. I once asked for Finn's help and paid every price imaginable. But here I am, asking again. What is it they say about insanity?

"Do you believe yourself to be such an expert in my emotions, still?" His thick Irish accent usually sounds like music, but it only makes his words come out harsher.

"So you won't help me?"

Finn sighs. "With a fairy-tale task? With fixing the impossible? I don't know what there would be for me to help with."

I should have anticipated this, just how deeply he'd disappoint me. But I still feel the sting of betrayal.

"I'm a fool for thinking you'd understand."

He shakes his head sadly, his curls in a riot around his face. "I'm afraid the feeling is mutual." I stomp to the entrance of the tent and brush back the flap, blinking as the full light of day stings my eyes.

From behind me, Finn says, so low I wonder if he means for me to hear it, "I do hope you'll come back."

I whip my head around, hoping my words sting him back. I don't want to give him anything, but if he insists on pulling things out of me, tugging and tugging on the spool of thread, let him only yield disappointment. "I won't." I pause at the entrance to the tent. "If you find anything, write me."

He laughs humorlessly. "I won't."

He doesn't follow me out.

Oliver, Maxine, and Lena are standing in a row outside the tent, their faces in the same awful expression of disgust and confusion. Poor Pascal just looks confused. He's off a ways from them, shuffling in the thistle.

I wonder how much of our conversation they overheard.

My feet carry me forward, not pausing for my friends or for a final look at Finn's tent.

The grass behind me rustles as the others follow me. Together, we go in silence to the road, our footsteps crunching down the gravel in tandem.

The icy silence is heavy when compared to the joy that accompanied us as we walked into camp earlier today.

Oliver's silence is the loudest. I want him to hold my hand and tell me he isn't angry with me. But I won't ask for it.

His face isn't unkind. It's just confused, which feels worse.

Spindly trees sway slightly in the breeze, watching our sad parade.

It's as if I can hear my friends thinking. Lena is chewing on the inside of her cheek. Oliver's brows are knit together. Pascal looks so lost; I almost pity him. Maxine is walking faster than the rest of us, marching ahead like she can't wait for this day to be over.

But then she slows her steps until she's at pace with the rest of us and asks, "What did Finn mean by 'I see you got my letter'?"

Oliver and Lena turn to look at me. I look at the ground. Shame is a horrible feeling. I bite my bottom lip to stop the tears from coming. The feeling is made worse by knowing this is my own fault. I should have just told them.

"I received a letter from Finn last June. There was no return address. I burnt it like I could make it disappear." I take a shaky breath. "I thought if I didn't speak about it, perhaps I could pretend it never happened. I never intended to see him again. I wasn't trying to be sneaky. I was just scared. You have to believe me."

"What did the letter say?" Oliver asks, shoulders tense.

"He said he was in Europe, that he thought I'd be here with him soon. He said he was building something . . . building something for us."

"Do you know what?" Lena asks.

This is where the uncomfortable nag of uncertainty comes in. Was that little colony by the lake a gift for me? Or was it the remnants of what Finn was able to scrounge up of a life after all he's done? He looked so uncomfortable at the mention of the Sons of Saint Druon, I get the impression he fled New York in fear rather than leaving it on his own accord.

For all the space Finn has taken up in my brain this past year and a half, I've given little thought to what his day-to-day life must look like. I've been holed up in Haxahaven, slowly transitioning from student to teacher. It's a quiet life, one filled with novels and buttered toast and chalk under my fingernails. The days pass so similarly. It was easier to picture Finn D'Arcy as a vague threat, a shadow in the night, rather than a person who eats and drinks and thinks and feels. There's something embarrassing about the mundanity of his life on the shores of the lake after his turn, however brief, as the leader of New York's Sons of Saint Druon.

"No," I finally speak. "He didn't tell me what he was building. I wouldn't have believed him anyway."

"Is that why you needed to speak to him alone?" Maxine asks. There's a hint of sarcasm in her words, but I can tell she's genuinely curious.

The dirt path turns to stone as we approach the small country train station.

Only a few other day travelers mill about the platform. Some sit on simple wooden benches; others lean against the metal pillars. The open-air station is little more than a platform.

My mouth is open and I'm thinking of a way to answer Maxine's question, but Oliver stops me.

"Frances, may we have a moment?" The words are polite, but stretched thin, like he's a bowstring seconds away from snapping. The muscles in his neck and his jaw are tense with effort.

My voice is small as I reply, "Yes, of course."

Lena and Maxine throw me a questioning glance. "I'll just be a minute," I say. They nod, their faces sketched with half-hearted concern.

Oliver and I take a few steps away from the group toward the back wall of the train station, near the ticketing booth, tucking ourselves away from the other travelers.

"I can't believe you didn't tell me."

I brush off his concern with an unconvincing shrug. I've never been good at being casual. I'll never be breezy like Maxine or self-assured like Lena.

"I thought it was nothing," I lie.

"I thought we'd moved past the need for secrets like this, Frances. I didn't think we lied to each other anymore."

His words prickle like tiny shards of ice, because he's wrong. There are still so many things I'm hiding. I lie to him all the time. I'm lying right now.

I love Oliver too much to give him all of me. These broken parts, the parts I hate the most, I'll bury away, sweep under dirt, hide from him as long as I can. Maybe this will be my life's work: becoming someone who deserves him.

"It's over now." Another lie. "He couldn't give me the answers I needed. I can't imagine I'll ever have to see him again."

A muscle in his jaw twitches. "It's very clearly not over." I've never seen this look on his face before. His mouth is turned down into half a frown, his nostrils flaring.

"Is this a fight? Are you trying to have a fight with me right now?"

He throws his hands up in front of him. It's a desperate gesture for Oliver, who is usually so buttoned up. "I don't know how to get you to let me in! How do I convince you to share things with me? Do you not see how maddening this is? I cannot love you if you don't let me know you!"

Something inside me shrinks. I feel sticky and sick all over. I want to bite the inside of my cheek so hard it bleeds. I want to stop speaking forever until I can guarantee I'll only ever say perfect words.

I tilt my head to the ground so he doesn't see my tears fall.

I tense. "I'm sorry, I didn't realize this would be such an inconvenience."

"This is exactly what I'm speaking of! You don't have to martyr yourself! It doesn't make you easier to be around, it makes it more difficult."

It feels like a compromise to feed him this half-truth. I'll rip select pages out of this story for him to know. There's no reason he should be burdened with the whole thing.

I don't speak, so Oliver fills the silence. "Why didn't you say anything about the letter last year? We could have handled it together."

"Because it was nothing. There was nothing to say about it."

"You know that's bullshit!"

I've never heard him curse before. He used to scold William for it.

"I'm sorry," I mumble.

"You have to let me in." He leans forward and catches both my hands in his, clutching at them hard.

"I don't want to be difficult to love, Oliver. I'm not doing this on purpose."

"That's the exact opposite of what this conversation is. God, don't you see how impossible you make it to speak with you?"

I fold in on myself. Bite my tongue to keep from saying too much. "I didn't realize it was impossible to speak with me."

His frustration is evident. "You can't keep living like this!" he yells and it stings. He never yells.

"Like what?" It comes out broken, like a sob.

"Like you're haunting every room you enter." He's looking at me so open, wounded, green eyes glistening with tears he's too stubborn to let fall. "Be honest, Frances, if not with me, then with yourself. I don't know how to make you let me in."

"I don't know what you want from me, tell me what you want, I beg you!" My emotions boil over like a pot on the stove. There's no putting them away now.

He shakes his head, his too-long hair falling in waves across his forehead. "I don't want anything from you, Frances."

"Fine." My voice is thick. Tears rush down my cheeks. "Then you'll get nothing."

We look at each other, my face wet with hot tears. He doesn't cry, but his mouth is turned down into an awful scowl. I am laid bare under his gaze and I hate it.

I stomp over to Lena and Maxine right as the train pulls up. They say nothing about my tear-streaked face, but Lena rests a comforting hand on my shoulder.

Pascal goes to sit in another train car, this time without protest. He looks upset, but no one knows yet just how far we can trust him, so he slinks off, uncomforted and alone.

In the gentle rocking of the quiet train car, it's easy to pretend that what happened back at the lake was a dream. Or that I'm someone else. What a comfort it would be to be anyone else on this train but me.

My skirt is still wet. It sticks to the fabric of the seats. I've stopped crying but my eyes still sting and I have no doubt my face is puffy and red. Oliver doesn't look much better. I can't stand that I'm the one who's made him look that sad.

His words weigh heavy on my chest. *I cannot love you if you don't let me know you.*

"I want to explain," I confess, my head resting against the window. "I'm just not sure where to begin." I don't know how to make Lena and Maxine understand, but I'm less afraid of telling them than I am of Oliver. They have no Frances-shaped rose-colored glasses to be torn off. They see me for who I am, for better or for worse. I'm less afraid they'll cut themselves on the jagged parts of me.

"It's a long train ride. We have time," Maxine replies.

"Will you tell us the whole of it?" Lena asks.

"Please, Frances," Oliver echoes.

I don't want him to look at me at all in this moment. There are so many things I'm afraid he'll see in me if he stares too closely or for too long. It's only a matter of time before he realizes just how broken I am.

Now there is the question of where to begin. Perhaps the night Finn and I performed the resurrection spell that allowed me to speak to my brother from beyond the grave.

Perhaps I begin with explaining that I've tracked down my father.

Or perhaps I begin the story the night my brother went missing and something inside of me was permanently ruined, making me a person who does selfish, awful things.

Here's another secret. I never told Lena, Maxine, or Oliver that the resurrection spell, the spell I nearly ruined my own life over to gain the ability to speak to my brother once more, actually worked. They know Finn and I attempted the spell, they know Finn used my desperation to bind my magic to him, effectively robbing me of it. But when I told the story, they assumed Finn's theft meant the spell never worked, that it was all a ruse. I didn't know how to correct them, so I simply didn't. It seemed too awful and strange to speak about. How do I tell them I spoke to a ghost? How do I tell them it still didn't change anything?

Next to me, Oliver is silent, still looking straight through me. It's hard to tell if he's breathing or not.

God, I want nothing more than to reach out for him. The anchor of his hand might stop me from spiraling. But his hands are folded neatly in his lap, so untouchable, he might as well be across the ocean from me again.

So I lean my head on the back of the bench in our private train car and stare up at the red fabric ceiling. There's relief in truth telling. I should know that well enough by now, but it surprises me every time. I'd do anything to make the slippery, rotten feelings inside me go away, so I'll do the one thing I haven't done yet. I'll try being honest.

I thought if I could protect them from the mess of my life, from the ugliness of my guilt, I'd be being a good friend. But the truth has come knocking and I can't pretend anymore. I don't have the energy.

If a secret is an act of love, truth telling is an act of trust. Of handing the very worst parts of yourself to someone and asking if they'll hold them too.

"I found my dad," I say simply.

I keep my eyes trained on the ceiling. I'm not strong enough to look at them as I tell the story, but I can hear them gasp in harmony.

"Your dad?" Lena asks. "How?"

"It was stupidly simple, actually," I say. "You remember Alicia McClain?"

"She was in my clairvoyancy classes at Haxahaven. From Cobble Hill, right?" Lena replies.

"Yes." I breathe. "When my magic started going wrong, I cried in Florence's office and begged her to help me find a solution. She requested that all clairvoyancy students report any visions involving me directly to her. Honestly, it was really embarrassing. Not that many people had visions involving me, and those who did mostly saw me burning frittatas and cursing at the deer for eating my tomato bushes. I didn't think anything would come of it. In my spare time, I searched the Haxahaven library and the Bizarre Bazaar for any texts that might offer clues. In desperation, I even asked my mother about my father. She didn't have much to offer; she said last she heard he was in Morocco, then broke down crying. I felt so guilty I went downtown to search genealogical records for any clues, rather than pressing her for more. But then, a few months ago, Alicia came into my classroom as I was cleaning up. She passed me a small slip of paper. I could tell she'd agonized over it. Poor thing looked so wan. When I opened it, all that was written was an address. She told me she'd had a vision of me meeting with an older man. In her head, she could see the street name and house number. She said it didn't look like New York. I took enough elementary school French to know '*rue*' meant 'street,' so I combed through maps of Paris in the library until I found it. She described the man and I was hopeful he might be my father. It was more a hunch than anything, but I was correct."

"So, you found him? You spoke to him?" Maxine prods.

I've never spoken much about my family to either of them. They know William once existed and now he does not. They know about my mother, Lena through letters and Maxine because she lives at Haxahaven with us both. Maxine is gentle and kind with my mother, always bringing her cups of tea in the library and asking her quiet questions about her day at dinner. They also know I never knew my father. I've never felt the need to put any finer details on it.

It's Oliver who witnessed the true pain my father's absence caused. It was he who taught William to tie a bow tie, and his father who taught them both to shave. He was there when I broke my ankle too. He heard me cry for my mother and father, and he held all the doors open as William carried me into our apartment building and stayed until the doctor came.

"Your dad . . . ," he whispers. "Oh, Frances, I wish I'd known."

"He's a professor at Saint Bosco's, of all the things in the world."

Maxine's laugh is dark. "Like father like daughter."

"I had to tell him about William. He didn't know."

Oliver looses a breath. "I'm sorry."

Lena leans across the carriage and squeezes my arm softly. "Oh, Frances," she whispers.

"It's fine, it's fine, I'm fine." I take a breath but it sounds like a desperate gasp. I didn't realize quite how close I was to the edge of tears. "But things may not be . . . fine."

"What do you mean? I'm also still not sure what this has to do with Finn." Maxine's voice is grave.

So I close my eyes and I tell them. I tell them everything my father told me about the veil between the living and the dead.

Which requires telling them every terrible detail of what happened in the basement of the Sons of Saint Druon that November night. The night we spoke to William, and Finn kissed me and stole my magic. The night the two of us might have altered the fabric of the universe inexorably.

I leave one detail out. Lena and Maxine know the truth of what happened to Mrs. Vykotsky, but I don't have it in me to confess to Oliver, too. His eyes are always so soft when he looks at me. He treats me like someone who is worth loving. I'm not ready to let go of that just yet.

Golden sunlight dances in from the train window, painting the inside of my eyelids red.

I'm lucky. Maxine, Lena, and Oliver are good listeners.

They let me spill my guts like I'm vomiting. It burns just as badly on the way up.

It's easy enough to gauge their reaction by the speed of their breathing and the way it hitches in their throats.

I don't realize I'm crying until Oliver brushes a tear from my cheek.

"That's why I needed to speak with Finn. I know it's my magic that is bound to the veil, but then it has to be his, too. I can feel something going wrong and I can't stop it." The words are coming faster, in hiccupping sobs.

"I'm glad you told us," Maxine says. "We'll make a plan in the morning. We'll go see your trash can of a father. Or we'll find another professor. We'll figure this out together."

I'm relieved she's taking my confession so well, but it doesn't lessen the weight of my guilt.

"I don't want to draw you into the mess I've made." I scrub a hand across my wet face and will the embarrassing tears to stop falling.

"Well, we're in it," Lena says. "We've been in it since that night in the woods. There's no getting rid of us, even if you fling yourself into the great beyond."

"Wait, yes, can we please revisit a few particular details of your tale? Like when you so casually informed us of the dead living beyond death," Maxine says.

She's joking to relieve the tension, but next to me Oliver is standing stock-still and tense.

"You really spoke to him?" he breathes. "And your magic . . . I wish you'd told me."

I turn to face him for the first time since I began my story. He's pressed his lips together in a thin line; his face has gone pale. "I'm sorry I didn't tell you sooner." I mean it. I am.

The train pulls into the station with a lurch, and we step off. My skirt has dried.

The Parisian early evening glows gold, and all around us swish the fine silks of those on their way to dinners and entertainment. The music of an organ grinder floats by, nearly lost in the chorus of voices.

But Oliver doesn't seem to see any of it. He goes to speak to Pascal without us. They stand across the platform, too far away for us to hear them, looking small under the domed roof of the station. Oliver towers over Pascal, who looks up at him. I cannot hear his words, but he's talking with his hands, like he's pleading. I don't know about Lena and Maxine, but I do believe Pascal when he says he didn't know about Finn. Finn's words about the universe wanting us to be together rattle around uncomfortably in my head. Perhaps some things really are inevitable.

Oliver bids Pascal farewell with a brief handshake and crosses the platform back to us.

"He swears he didn't know."

"And?" Maxine prompts.

"And I believe him," Oliver says matter-of-factly. His confidence puts an end to the conversation.

Maxine harumphs, but there's no real malice in it. I think she and Lena know that it doesn't particularly matter what Pascal was or was not aware of. What is done is done. The reunion of our little study group from the woods of Forest Park has happened and there's nothing we can do to undo it.

CHAPTER TEN

Later that night, after the lady's maids have brushed out our hair and clicked off the lights, I'm startled by the sound of footsteps pacing outside of my bedroom. It's barely audible, the carpets here are inches thick, but it is unmistakably there. A soft *thump, thump, thump*. Pause. *Thump, thump, thump*.

"Hello?" I hiss into the darkness of the room.

Ordinarily, I'd use a simple light casting spell to dispel the long shadows stretching over the room, but I am terrified that the magic won't come, so I lean over to the bedside table and click the button on the wall to set the sconces alight.

There is no one in my room. The baby-blue damask wallpaper is no longer cast in threatening shadows. But the thumping footsteps have not stopped.

It could be any of the number of household staff. It could be a ghost, or my imagination.

Or, an awful part of me considers, *it could be Finn. He did so love to come to me in the night.*

"Hello?" I whisper once more.

The door swings open with a crash, sending me yelping and scrambling across my duvet. I throw a stupid little tasseled throw pillow at the door more out of pure shock than an attempt at a counterattack.

"Ow!" Lena yells as it hits her in the arm. She picks it up off the floor and hurls it back at me. It bounces directly off my head.

"I did not deserve that! I'm the one who is currently the victim of a home intrusion."

"This is my home," Maxine quips from where she stands behind Lena.

They're both in their nightclothes. Lena's hair is plaited in two long braids, and she wears a chemise just like mine. Maxine is wearing her monogrammed set of men's pajamas, her hair up in a bun.

Unceremoniously, the two of them throw themselves onto my bed, nestling in on either side of me.

"To what do I owe the pleasure?"

"We just want to make sure you're all right," Maxine says. She puts her chin directly onto my shoulder and looks up at me with her big, gray eyes. "And Lena's light was on and it was driving me bonkers."

"I was awake painting."

Maxine nods. "I could hear her charcoal scratching through the wall."

"Can I see the pieces you've been so hard at work on?" I ask.

Lena shakes her head no. "Not until they're finished."

I lean back against the pillows. "Thank you," I say. "For so many things."

Maxine hums. "You're welcome."

Lena bumps her freezing feet against mine under the duvet. "Stuck with us, you see. No more secrets."

"No more secrets," I agree.

I savor the weight and warmth of them next to me. Twin anchors in the darkness.

Well after the three of us have gone to sleep, in the floaty part of the night between midnight and dawn, I wake with a gasp.

There's a searing pain in the middle of my chest, as if I'm being stabbed in the heart. The feeling travels up, stinging and ripping through my throat, my tongue, my forehead.

I'm choking, unable to take a breath.

And then—as suddenly as it began, it stops. I fill my lungs and rest my head back on the pillow. My heart is hammering so loud, I'm surprised it hasn't awoken Maxine and Lena. But they're still asleep next to me, their chests rising in tandem slow and gentle.

I close my eyes. It's easy to pretend it was a dream, but I know better.

I wake with Maxine's hand in my face. I fling her off me just as Gabrielle, one of the lady's maids, enters with a tea tray and a chipper "*Bon matin!*"

We make a plan to see my father immediately after breakfast. I don't know his schedule, but I'll sit outside his wretched office all day until I get the answers I need.

The polished mahogany dining table is covered with fingerprints by the end of breakfast. I've spent the whole meal drumming my fingers against it restlessly, lost in thought. They've served omelets today. I miss the food at Haxahaven desperately.

At the far end of the table, Maxine's little sister, Nina, fiddles with the baby pink silk bow around the neckline of her dress. She's chattering away with Maxine, flipping between French and English so quickly I can barely keep up.

She wants us all to go to a carousel somewhere, I think. I'd like that. It's clear Maxine adores bright, little Nina but I've gotten to spend so little time with her.

Maxine's mother takes tiny bites in silence. Her stepfather is hidden behind a newspaper at the head of the table.

From behind the paper he clears his throat, then noisily flips to the next page. "Awful . . . ," he mutters to himself.

When he gets no response he says it again. "Just awful."

"What's awful, dear?" Maxine's mother asks, her delicate hands now wrapped around a bone china cup of coffee.

"There was a murder last night. Poor kid was only eighteen."

Slick nausea rises in my throat. I can't help but picture the family waking up in Paris today absent their son, their brother. I remember when the eighteen-year-old dead boy in the paper belonged to me.

"Can I read it?" I ask.

Walt, Maxine's stepfather, pulls the section of the paper, folds it in half, and passes it across the table to me.

The newsprint stains my fingers gray as I unfurl the pages. The newspaper is in English, but the advertisements are a mix of both English and French.

It's right there on the front page, underneath a banner advertising polo betting. BODY OF BOY FOUND IN SAINT-GERMAIN-DES-PRÉS ABBEY, HORRIBLE, SAYS NUN WHO FOUND HIM LAID ON THE ALTAR.

> The Saint-Germain-des-Prés church, the oldest in Paris, was home to a grisly sight this morning. Three nuns came upon the troublesome scene at six a.m. as they entered the main chapel for sunrise prayer. Instead of incense and holy water at the altar, they found the body of an unidentified young man. "It was horrible," says Sister Evangeline. "He looked so young. We thought for a moment he might be asleep, but as soon as we came closer, we saw the wounds." The police arrived by seven a.m. to transport the body to the coroner where a full investigation is anticipated. The police had no comment on Sister Evangeline's claim that ritualistic symbols had been present in blood on the deceased's torso. Father Olivier anticipates Mass will proceed as usual on Sunday.

My blood runs cold as the itchy sense of familiarity takes over. I tamp down the urge to pass the newspaper to Lena or Maxine with a meaningful look. Paranoia is the price I've paid for what happened with Finn in New York.

We're in a big city; horrible things happen. This has nothing to do with me. But the voice of reason in my head is weak and easily drowned out.

"How awful," I say, folding the newspaper in a neat crease and passing it back to Maxine's stepfather. He gives me only a grunt in return, too busy sipping his coffee and reading.

A fork clacks against a plate. My coffee has gone cold. Breakfast moves on, but all I can think of is the dead boy laid out on a golden altar, bathed in the rainbow light of a stained-glass window. How awful indeed.

Maxine and Lena ask me questions about my father the entire walk to Saint Bosco's.

"Do you remember him at all?" Maxine asks.

I shake my head no. "I have a memory of one Easter, a man sitting at our table laughing with William, but I think I may have made the whole thing up. It's hard to tell sometimes."

"Did he seem repentant for abandoning you like that?" Lena asks.

"Not at all. It's almost funny."

"I don't think it's funny," Lena replies.

"Enough about my father, tell me about yours."

Maxine takes a bite out of the croissant we snagged from the bakery across the street at the beginning of our walk. "Dead," she says in between bites. "He was an art dealer, though. Used to bring me home penny candies and take me to tea on my birthdays. He was kind, I think. I remember him being kind."

My heart aches for her. Her stepfather seems more boring than anything.

"You'd probably like my father," Lena says. "He's a carpenter. He's funnier than me."

"And your mother?" I ask. Lena doesn't speak often of her family back home and I fear it's because she doesn't think we'd understand them.

"Oh, she's very serious. A bit more like me. The toughest woman I've ever met. Taught me how to do proper beadwork and to always keep my knives sharp."

"She sounds terrifying," Maxine says.

Lena laughs. "She is. Loving though, too. She knows all about the two of you."

"What does she think?" I ask.

Lena laughs. "That you're bad influences. She's correct."

I love Paris in the morning. The whole city smells like baking bread. It makes it easy to forget why we're walking and who we're walking to.

Rue de Vis is just as sleepy as it was the last time I was here. Just rows and rows of still, storybook houses covered in vines.

Saint Bosco's sits right in the center of the street, the crown jewel of an idyllic neighborhood.

It's made of white limestone, blending in with the other buildings on the street. The eaves are decorated with weather-worn ornate carving. Set into the center of the facade is a massive arched window. Dark green English Ivy and pale purple wisteria crawl up the walls, draping themselves over the massive oak front doors.

The lawn is a perfect verdant green dotted with neatly trimmed hedges.

The building is beautiful in the ordinary way all buildings are beautiful in this city.

You'd never guess what resides inside.

The gate is locked. Maxine sees me tug on it and mutters "*briseadh*" under her breath, unlocking the gate with a thunk. I know she's trying to help but it's embarrassing that I'm incapable of performing the simple spell myself.

There are a few students milling about on the lawn. Their uniforms are a deep cobalt blue, the boys in suits, the girls in ankle-length skirts and white high-necked blouses with a blue tie around their necks.

One of the girls, the tallest one, with a hard line in her jaw, stops us as we approach and asks a question in French. Maxine volleys a response, just as quick.

The girl narrows her eyes as her friends stand behind her, but doesn't stop Maxine as she marches through the doors.

The morning is a brilliant blue, but stepping into the front hall of the school is like snuffing out a candle; all at once, the world goes dark and cold.

There are a few students in similar cobalt uniforms in the hall, their steps echoing off the marble floors, like the students out front. They stop in their tracks, a worried look in all of their eyes. One leans over and whispers to a friend behind his hand; another scurries up the stairs like a spooked animal.

"What did she say?" I ask.

"She said no visitors were allowed today and I told her we weren't visitors, that we were seeing family."

"Family" may be an overly generous term for my father.

I don't bother knocking on his office door. He doesn't deserve the deference.

We find him sitting at his desk, looking a little disheveled, hunched over a stack of papers with a coffee mug in his hand. There's another mug balanced on the edge of the desk and another discarded on the shelf behind him.

"Oh!" He jumps a little as we walk in. "Did we have an appointment?"

I frown. "Do I need an appointment to see my father?"

He opens his mouth like he means to say "yes," but shuts it before his bad sense wins. "I do apologize; I'm a little distracted this morning. It's not a good time."

Maxine muscles her way to the front. "It's going to have to be a good time."

"Who are you?" he asks her.

"I'm Maxine."

He looks a little afraid of her. He should be.

He glances between the pile of newspapers on his desk and the three of us. It's then that I realize he's got the pages open to the same story I read this morning about the murdered boy in the church.

He says, clearly distracted, "I have five minutes before I need to leave to meet a few colleagues."

"Meet them where?" I prod.

He leans down to shove the newspaper into his open briefcase. "No need to worry yourself." He dismisses me.

"But I am worried, so you might as well tell me."

He looks up, exhausted. "There was a murder."

"Are you a detective as well as a teacher?" Lena asks. My father doesn't know her well enough to hear the mocking in her voice, but under the panicked rushing of blood in my ears, I do.

"In some ways, I suppose. Frances, do you remember what I told you about New York and the veil? We fear the problem may have just arrived on our shores."

"Why are the events happening here instead of in New York?" I ask.

My father taps his desk with a pen. "No one can be sure. Are you familiar with the concept of referred pain? You injure yourself in the shoulder but it hurts down your leg? Magic is energy and it works very much the same. A rupture in power in New York could very well manifest abnormalities in Paris. Magical energies run across the globe in an interconnected web. What happens in Seoul echoes in Cairo, et cetera, et cetera. There's no such thing as a truly isolated event."

I nod curtly but fear my knees might collapse from under me. *No coincidences.*

"So the murder is related to the veil?" If he hears the panic rising in my voice, he doesn't say anything. If the disruption in the veil is my fault, and the murder is related to the veil, that means the blood is on my hands. I can't stand it. I've spent so much time trying to be good, but still I can't wash myself clean.

He latches his briefcase and sets his coffee mug down on his desk. It sloshes, dampening the rest of the discarded paper.

"No need to concern yourself. This is business for gentlemen."

My father's desk reminds me a little of Mrs. Vykotsky's. Like hers, it's covered in scattered papers and half-dried inkwells. Florence took over Mrs. Vykotsky's office after her death. The walls are now whitewashed, the door always open to the students who wander by. I wonder what Mrs. Vykotsky would think of the open tins of candies and the complete lack of blackmail material hidden in the desk's drawers.

"But—" Maxine interrupts.

"Now!" my father exclaims, paying no attention to our protests. "I'd really best be going. I'm already running late."

It would be easier if his tacit rejection of any fatherly warmth was accompanied by some great, big ocean of sadness.

I don't feel much of anything looking at him. I'm mostly just tired. Frustrated, too.

He's halfway to the door. There's no point in fighting with him. "I understand."

"Let me walk you out," he says.

I open my mouth to say "yes," but Lena speaks first. "I'd love to use the powder room before we go, if you don't mind."

My father nods. "Two doors down on the left."

Maxine and I follow him through the black-and-white-checkered entrance, our heels sliding on the freshly waxed tile, and out into another warm June day in Paris.

My father hops into a passing pedicab, hauling his briefcase in after him, and we offer him a cursory wave goodbye.

Lena comes walking out of the school a moment later, steps at a fast clip. She doesn't slow as she approaches us. "Let's go," she hisses under her breath.

Maxine and I share a confused glance but pick up the pace to keep steps behind her. It isn't until we're nearly home that she slows to a halt on a street corner while a Clydesdale towing a cart passes.

"You're certainly in a hurry," Maxine says.

"I prefer the term 'a quick escape.'" She opens her light overcoat and reveals a stack of papers tucked under her armpit.

"My, my, Lena Jamison, what do we have here?" Maxine asks.

There's a wicked glint in her eye as she explains, "If the killing is related to the veil, we can't just sit and wait until he decides to give us more information. I decided to be proactive. And really, he should be less careless with his research. It was all there, on his desk in his unlocked office. It could have been any number of Saint Bosco's students."

The wind ripples through the tendrils of hair falling in front of her face. She smiles. I smile back and it doesn't feel false.

"Let's go, then."

Back at Maxine's flat we run into her room and shut the door behind us.

Nina bangs on the door a few times begging to be let in, but Maxine bribes her with a promise to take her to the carousel later in the day.

Lena fans the stolen documents out on the floor in front of us, a variety of yellowing pages, freshly handwritten notes, and torn newspaper clippings.

The fight with Oliver in the train station still stings, like paper cuts all over, and I am grateful to have this distraction. I'm glad I told them all the truth about William and my father, but I'm unsure where Oliver and I currently stand. It feels as if we're fragile. Not broken, but covered in hairline cracks that could rupture at any moment.

The papers are hard to discern. They include articles about art exhibits, grainy black-and-white pictures of archeological artifacts, nursery rhymes, poems, firsthand accounts of historical events.

It's difficult to find a common thread between them, let alone a clue worth following. The ones that mention death at all are few and far between.

There are a few family trees that mysteriously end. Photographs of graves with the dates circled and annotated with question marks.

We work for hours to untangle it all, to find even a single thread of connection to pull on. But we don't get far. I have a headache and Lena has painting class, so we call it quits for the day, stack the papers up neatly, and hide them in the drawer of Maxine's desk.

I'm lying in my bed later that evening, thinking of the documents and trying to figure out next steps, rather than dressing for dinner, when a knock at the door startles me.

It's Greta, the DuPres' housekeeper with the perpetually stern look on her face.

"There's a guest here for you."

"For me?"

"Yes, Miss Hallowell, for you."

I force myself upright before my brain has the chance to shuffle through its desk of worst-case scenarios. I picture Finn, pacing and sharp-toothed in the finery of the DuPre receiving room. He'd charm his way in. I know he would.

But the guest in the parlor is not Finn. It's Oliver, in a neat blue suit, holding his hat in front of him, his long fingers fiddling with its brim.

"Hi," he breathes.

CHAPTER ELEVEN

We haven't spoken since our fight yesterday at the train station. But I should have known he'd be here today of all days.

"You remembered?"

"Of course I remembered."

I turn to Greta, who is standing in the doorway, probably attempting to chaperone me.

"Greta, please tell Mrs. DuPre I'll be dining out this evening."

She looks at me disapprovingly but nods anyway.

Oliver and I don't speak down the elevator or on Maxine's street.

It isn't until we're on the banks of the river, the breeze off the water cooling the summer evening, that he speaks.

"I'm ashamed for the way I spoke to you in the train station. My father is a yeller. I vowed to never raise my voice to anyone. I hate that I broke that promise to myself, and I hate even more that you were on the other end of it," he confesses.

It makes me a little sad that he feels it's his duty to bend first. I know full well that I was the one in the wrong. "No, no, Oliver, I'm sorry. It was my fault."

How do I explain this wobbly feeling in my chest, the one that has existed since I was a child, the one that tells me not to burden others with the ferocity of my emotions?

I don't want to be a wobbly person.

I want to be a steady hand in the dark like Oliver.

"I don't want to keep things from you."

Oliver looks down at me, light weaving golden through his dark hair. "Then why do you?"

I swallow my fear, will myself to be brave. I've already told him so much, I might as well tell him this, too. "Because I am afraid if you see all of me you will decide I am too difficult to love."

I blink and see Mrs. Vykotsky's body in the parlor of the Commodore Club, see Oliver and his parents tied in ropes, on their knees in their fine drawing room, see Maxine and Lena unconscious on the Haxahaven lawn. Sometimes I don't think I ever really left that night. I live it over and over again, the guilt at the destruction I caused eating away at me like termites at the foundation of a house.

I stop walking and press my fingers to Oliver's abdomen. Just above his belly button, a little to the left, right where the bullet pierced him.

"I've already caused you so much pain. I wonder if there is another girl, a nice, normal girl who would give you a better life than me."

He shakes his head. "Ahh, this is the crux of our misunderstanding."

"Oh?"

"There may be a quiet, normal life out there for me somewhere, but this is not your choice to make. I don't want that life. I don't want any life you're not a part of. My choice was made long ago. I chose you, Frances. I am still choosing you."

It flutters in my chest, this familiar feeling. A feeling that's been stuck between my teeth since I was thirteen years old and Oliver came to our apartment in a fancy new tweed suit and something in me went *oh.*

"All right, then."

"All right?"

"I choose you back, you know I do."

The corners of his mouth tug, revealing his dimples. I reach up and poke one. He laughs quietly.

"That's good," he whispers, and even on the crowded banks of the Seine, it is just the two of us.

"Good," I agree.

I've kissed Oliver before. In daylight, and in the darkest hours past midnight, and for the first time, in the glowing evening light of the Haxahaven solarium. It was last February, the day before my birthday. He'd come up to celebrate and brought a chocolate cake covered in pink icing from a bakery we used to visit together when we were young. We ate the cake straight out of the box with forks stolen from the kitchen, and I know now that Maxine bribed the little girls to leave us alone for one hour. They each got ten cents out of it.

I couldn't stop staring at his lips. We were sitting on the floor and I don't remember why now, maybe I thought it would be romantic. But the winter sun streamed in through the glass roof in golden beams. Oliver's green eyes considered me and I could tell he was thinking hard about something. His gaze was careful. Oliver is a careful sort of person, especially with me.

I wasn't thinking about anything other than how much I wanted him to lean in. I'm not a careful sort of person at all.

The carpet was itchy under the heel of my hand as I set down my fork and I waited for him to make up his mind.

"Will you stand up?" he whispered.

I nodded and he helped me to my feet.

He was so nervous then, I remember his hands shaking as he ran a thumb over my rib cage.

"Hi," he whispered.

"Hi," I breathed back.

I laughed against his mouth as he finally leaned in. It was such an inevitable thing, that kiss. His mouth tasted like pink icing.

Now, he dips his head and his lips meet mine. I sigh into the kiss and it is a relief. There's hot breath and a hand at my waist and a sound coming from the back of my throat.

He kisses me, really kisses me. He presses with enough pressure to swell my lips and we grasp for each other, sharing the same searing frustration of being apart for so many months.

There is so much we're still figuring out, but this makes sense.

He slips his tongue between the seam of my lips, and I press my hips closer to his.

He's the one to break it, pulling back with a gasp. "People are watching."

"It's Paris, the women here are freer," I joke.

Oliver nods over to a very stern-looking old woman twirling a parasol. "I think she would disagree."

"Fine," I relent.

While we walk along the banks of the river, I tell him about seeing my father today, about Lena stealing the documents.

"How can I help?"

I should have expected this from him. But it is another thing entirely to experience it playing out in front of me. I have handed him all of the things I am afraid of, and he has tucked them into his pocket and asked what else he can carry.

"You don't have to," I reply.

He looks down at me. "But I want to."

I stop and raise a hand to his cheek. He presses slightly against it. "I do love you." It's not a confession. He already knows. But it feels new in light of everything.

"I love you too, nothing could change that."

His hand is big and warm as he takes mine in his. "Let's go to dinner."

The café is quiet, set off the main street, with a dark-green awning. Green was his favorite color.

Here is the main event, the true reason Oliver showed up on my doorstep today, his hands raised in a truce.

"I can't believe he would have been twenty-two today." I sigh. It seems like an impossible age, so grown-up. What would my brother have been like as a man? He would have been a good one, I think.

For so long we were a trio, OliverWilliamFrances, said in a single breath. Oliver and I are still getting used to it being just the two of us when there should be three. The last time we were all together I was seventeen.

Oliver and I are now nineteen and twenty, but William will forever be nineteen, even now, on what should have been his twenty-second birthday. It's so cruel.

This mess I'm in is because of my deep, unending love for him. Was it worth it? Probably not. But I know in my heart I'd do it again.

Oliver raises a glass. "He was the best of us. Happy birthday, Will."

"I'll toast to that."

We order a slice of cake after our meal, and when the waitress asks us the occasion we say simply "a birthday."

In a world that's kinder than this one, my brother is standing over a cake, flames from the birthday candles dancing over his face, and he's laughing.

He was always laughing.

In this world, Oliver and I hold hands and walk along the Seine, William's ghost keeping pace beside us.

Maxine and Lena are still up when I return to the flat after dark.

They're sprawled across the drawing room floor, a game of backgammon between them. Maxine is levitating a black chip, twirling it between her fingers, so I don't know if it's going well.

"She's cheating," Lena says as I enter the room.

"Am not," Maxine retorts.

"No progress on my father's papers then?" I interrupt their bickering.

Maxine shakes her head. "We snagged my father's newspaper from this morning, but there were no additional details about the murder. We think we should go to the church tomorrow to investigate for ourselves."

I nod. "Sounds like an excellent idea."

Outside, a sudden summer rainstorm taps against the window, making the room feel like a cocoon against the cold and wet.

"Where were you?" Lena asks. I hate that she sounds worried for me.

"With Oliver. Today is my brother's birthday. We went for a walk."

Lena looks sympathetic, but Maxine lies back on the carpet and barks a laugh. "I hope you celebrated him better than you celebrated me."

Maxine has never let a single thing go. Me and the little girls making the world's least appetizing Pavlova last September for her birthday celebration is something she'll never let me live down.

"How could I have known little Flossie Packard snuck corn into the batter?"

"There were whole kernels, Frances! You think you would have seen them as you stirred!"

"I thought I'd overwhipped the egg whites!"

Lena laughs. "I sent you a lovely card and that's why I'm your favorite."

Maxine flicks the backgammon piece at her. "You already were."

We're startled by a rapping at the window, sharper than raindrops.

First short, a single *tap*. Then a rapid *tap, tap tap*.

"Did you hear that?" Lena whispers.

"Was it the rain?" Maxine offers.

As if it can hear us, it begins again, urgent and too precise. *Tap, tap, tap, tap, tap*.

"Not the rain," I say.

Lena pushes herself up off the ground, the bravest of us, and crosses the room to press her face to the window that looks out to the street.

"There's . . . a figure. A man, I think."

Tap, tap.

She turns to us and chuckles softly. "Good Lord, it's pebbles. He's throwing pebbles."

Maxine laughs and falls to the floor in relief. "Looks like your Romeo isn't quite ready to say goodbye."

"Quiet, the both of you!" I roll my eyes and rise to my feet, suppressing the smile on my face. A blush rises in my chest. "I'll go see what he wants."

I walk through the quiet halls of the DuPre family flat to the elevator, which digs just slightly off-key.

The ride down is jerky and slow. The doors squeak open.

The vestibule is empty, echoing with the sound of falling rain. The doors to the outside are tall, covered in molding and cast in white plaster. They stick a bit as I push them open. I have to really put my shoulder into it.

Finally, they open with a groan.

"Oliv—" I go to shout his name, a smile on my lips, but it dies in my throat.

Because the man standing at the door with a fistful of pebbles isn't Oliver.

It's Finn, soaked to the bone, his hair plastered to his forehead and an innocent smile on his face.

"Surprise?" He shows a dimple and I resist the urge to slam the door in his face.

"What are you doing here?" I do not give him the satisfaction of a reaction.

"You said you needed my help. I reconsidered."

The sight of him, on today of all days, makes me viscerally sick. "I told you to write me a letter."

I turn and attempt to slam the gate behind me. He stops it with his foot.

"You don't historically have a great track record of responding to my letters."

I open the gate a little wider just to slam it against his foot again. He winces.

"Leave me alone," I say.

He follows me, limping on the foot I just slammed in the gate. "Do you intend to let me stand out here and freeze to death?"

"I'm considering it," I reply. A ripple of discomfort moves through me. "How did you know where to find me?" There's no reason he should have known where we were staying.

He shrugs, as casual as ever. "I make it my business to know where you are. Maxine's parents' address is public record. I figured you were here or at Callahan's dormitory. How is he enjoying the Sorbonne?"

I look at him, disgusted. "You're stalking me?"

"'Stalking' is such an ugly word. I'm being practical. I can't very well help you if I don't know where you are."

If I had my powers, I'd do something like swipe his knees out from under him, leaving him sputtering on the pavement.

In response to my glare, he says, "I'll be of less use to you dead."

"Don't press your luck, you don't know that for certain."

He reaches into his coat pocket and pulls out a square of parchment. The rain leaves splatters on the thick, cream-colored paper as he passes it to me.

It's sealed with black wax that Finn has already peeled open. I unfurl the letter. In perfect calligraphy it reads:

The honor of your presence is requested by Duke Valentin Mourrir

Saturday, June twenty-first, nineteen thirteen

Thirteen Rue Blanche

At the bottom of the page is a seal. A skull surrounded by a halo of small flowers.

"What is this?"

"A meeting of the Brothers of Morte d'Arthur. If we're going to find anything about the veil, it'll be there."

"You just gave me the address. Why wouldn't I just go without you?"

He looks pathetic, waterlogged and cold. "Because they won't let you in. It's a gentleman's club."

"We have Oliver."

"He isn't a member."

I chew on my lip, thinking.

His long fingers unfurl from their fist and he drops his pebbles on the ground. With a grin I'm sure he has used his entire life to get what he wants, he shrugs his shoulders and asks, "Please?"

And here he is again, the vampire begging to be let in from the cold.

I do what all foolish girls do. I let him in.

CHAPTER TWELVE

We put him in an empty guest room as far away from the rest of the family as we can manage. Lena suggests tying him to a chair and I halfway consider it.

"A study group reunion," he jokes weakly, offering his wrists up to the curtain tie Lena holds in her hands.

She doesn't bind him, but she twirls the cord between her fingers as a threat.

Maxine juts out her arm and shoves her hand, palm up, in his face. "Give me the invitation."

It does feel a little like he's our prisoner, with all of us standing and pacing around him, while he sits at the ornate desk.

Finn sighs and passes it to her. With his wet hair and slumped posture he looks so young.

"It's a meeting of the Brothers of Morte d'Arthur. A gentleman's magic club not unlike the Sons but slightly . . ."

"Slightly what?" I prod.

"Slightly more obsessed with death. If anyone will have information about the veil, it'll be them."

"How'd you get this invitation?" Lena asks.

"I'm a provisionary member."

"Why would they let you in after what you did to the last club who admitted you?"

Finn doesn't wince or look away as I remind him of his crimes. He's completely nonplussed. "The Brothers of Morte d'Arthur are famously not . . . fans of the Sons of Saint Druon. What I did in New York earned me an invitation to the club over here. I laid low at Duke Mourrir's estate for a while before setting off on my own."

Maxine rolls her eyes viciously. "How can we trust you?"

"You can't, I suppose. Can I trouble you for a glass or water, or"—he gestures to his soaked-through clothing—"a towel?"

"No," Maxine says, but I toss him a spare blanket from the bed on instinct.

Maxine glares at me.

Sorry, I mouth. It's strange to be around Finn again. It's awful and itchy and nauseating, but he makes it so easy to forget what he's done with his easy posture and quick smiles. He's someone you want to believe. I want to believe him now, I always have, but that's my problem.

Am I just that easy to trick or is Finn an extraordinarily talented trickster?

He doesn't look extraordinary at all right now. He looks cold and damp and at our mercy.

"So what do you propose?" Lena asks. "We let you stay here and you go to this party and what . . . report back to us?"

"Yes," Finn says.

I shake my head. "Absolutely not. You need to take us with you."

"They won't allow women in."

"So take Oliver," I propose.

At the mention of his name, Finn's mouth turns to a grimace. "Is it my only option?"

"Yes," I say.

"Fine. Are we quite settled, then?"

"No. Why now? You were perfectly happy to ignore me back at the camp."

Finn sucks in a breath through his nose and looks down at the carpet. "You were right, my magic isn't acting right. And the murder I read about in the paper . . . I have a hunch it's related. I thought I could fix it myself. I'm beginning to think that might not be true."

I chew the inside of my cheek and consider his words. There's nothing I want less than to rely on him for help, than to have him under the same roof as me. But if what my father said is correct and the murder is related to the disruption in the veil, I can't afford to be selfish. Lives hang in the balance as long as the veil is still open, and it's my responsibility to close it.

It was my selfishness that killed Mrs. Vykotsky, that earned Oliver a bullet in the stomach. I don't want to be a selfish person anymore.

"You stay until the party and then you're out," I say.

"Deal," Finn agrees.

"And if you try to pull anything, we turn you over to the Sons. Let them deal with you."

Again, he grimaces. "Seems fair."

"House rules!" Maxine puts her hands on her hips. "No joining for family meals, Greta will serve you in your room. Keep quiet. If I see you speaking to my little sister, I will skin you alive."

"I missed you too, Maxine."

She strides up and smacks him on the side of the head. "Added rule: no saying stupid things like that."

"Four rules. Got it."

"I reserve the right to add more rules."

"I'm a quick study."

"Are we settled, then?" I ask.

Lena, Maxine, and Finn all nod.

"Then I'll be right back."

I rush to my room and throw an overcoat on over my dress. I still haven't had time to change since my evening with Oliver.

As quick as I am able, I lace up my boots and grab an umbrella from a stand in the hallway.

"Where are you going?" Maxine calls after me, poking her head out of the guest room door.

"There's a promise I have to keep."

I hail a pedicab outside of the apartment and ask the driver to take me to the Sorbonne.

I know Oliver's dorm only by the address I write on the fronts of the envelopes I've been sending him for the past three months, but I have a decent enough sense of direction. I'll knock on every door if I have to. The campus is ancient-looking, built in a square around an onion-domed center building. The whole campus looks like something from a painting tonight, dark blue and slick with rain.

I'm lucky. Oliver's dormitory is on the first floor, right off the main courtyard. I find it without issue, but I am soaked to the bone by the time I arrive at his doorstep. The umbrella was no match for the wind.

It's well past ten p.m. now and I know he'll be asleep. The glass is dark, the room behind it still and silent.

I knock once. Twice. Three times. No answer.

But I don't give up.

The door is hard against my knuckles. I rap so hard I'm sure they'll be bruised in the morning. Again and again I hit the door, the rain splashing around my feet as the storm carries on.

Finally, Oliver answers, wearing pajamas and rubbing sleep from his eyes.

"Are you all right?" He looks startled to see me.

"Perfectly. I'm sorry to scare you."

He waves me inside. "God, you're soaked, please come in, I'll make tea."

My wet hair whips around my face as shake my head no. "I'd love to, but not tonight. Can you come with me?"

He furrows his brow in concern. "You sure everything is all right?"

"I'll explain on the way."

I wait outside under the eaves while Oliver changes into something other than pajamas, and he meets me outside with an umbrella of his own.

He slips off his dry coat and drapes it over my shoulders. "If you catch a cold on account of me, I'll feel guilty for weeks."

I've paid the pedicab with the walking-around money Maxine's mother gave us. The automobile is idling at outside the gates of the school. Once in the warmth of the back seat, I do my best to explain.

"We think we need him to close the veil, Oliver. I'm so sorry. We wouldn't do this if we believed there was another way." *Him.* I don't even need to say his name.

Understanding dawns on him quick and terrible. "No," he says harshly. "Absolutely not."

"He's waiting with Maxine and Lena now. I'm so sorry, we didn't know what else to do. But I'm trying to be honest with you, Oliver. It's why I'm here."

His mouth is set in a fine line, but he nods once in understanding. He's angry, but he isn't angry with me. It's the best I could possibly hope for.

The DuPre flat is dark when we arrive back. My shoes make a squelching sound as I step into their marble entryway.

"They're down the hall."

Oliver nods wordlessly and follows.

The guest room they've put Finn in is evident by the sliver of light spilling from under the door. It's the only sign of life in the entire home.

I push open the door and find Finn over a piece of paper on the floor, the nub of a pencil in his hand.

"I didn't think you'd still be up," I greet them.

"Finn's drawing us the layout of the house where the party is being held," Maxine answers.

Finn tosses the blanket slung around his neck to me. "Rain got you, too?"

I take the blanket with a grimace, but use it anyway, eager to stop myself from shivering.

Oliver says nothing, but I can feel the rage radiating off him.

My brother and I used to say that Oliver grew too fast. One summer suddenly he was fifteen and banging his head into doorways. It was like he never quite got used to his larger body, and even years later he still enters rooms with his head slightly ducked. But he rises to his full height now, shoulders square and his breathing shallow.

"He's a rotten artist," Lena says of Finn's drawing.

Finn smiles up at Oliver, infuriatingly charming and at ease. "Callahan. Always a pleasure."

Oliver stares down at him, and balls his hands into fists at his side. Then, he strides across the room, towering over Finn. "Get up," he demands through gritted teeth. It was a bit of a running joke with Oliver and William, the fact that they were opposites, Oliver the lover, William the fighter. But Oliver looks ready for a fight now.

"As soon as I'm done with the third floor?" Finn doesn't lift his eyes from the paper.

"Now," Oliver snarls.

To my surprise, Finn acquiesces and pushes himself up off the ground. He follows Oliver into the en suite bathroom. The door shuts behind them with a click.

Lena and Maxine scramble from the ground, and together we rush to put our ears to the door.

From behind the thick plaster walls comes the muffled sound of voices shouting.

"—best friend." The voice belongs to Oliver. There's another word that ends in an "—er." It might be "murderer."

Finn's deeper brogue follows. I think I hear the word "sorry," but I'm not sure.

Oliver replies, his voice a rumble through the door. He's louder, angrier than Finn.

Suddenly there's the sound of scuffling, of an object being knocked over. Finn cries out.

Then, as soon as it began, it ends.

The door swings open gently and the three of us scramble back to our places on the carpet. We pretend to lounge casually, heads propped up in our hands, legs spread out long.

Oliver exits the bathroom first. His face is stony, and he's shaking out his right hand.

Finn walks out a moment later clutching his rapidly bruising eye.

I watch them in wide-eyed shock. My heart swells with pride as I watch Oliver check the joints of his fingers.

Maxine rises from the ground. "Need ice for your hand, Oliver?" she trills.

"That would be lovely, Maxine."

"I'd like some ice as well," Finn says.

"I'm sure you would," Maxine replies on her way out the door.

She returns a moment later, and Oliver, clutching an ice pack to his hand, joins us on the carpet. Finn grimaces, but finds a spot between Maxine and Lena.

"So, we're doing this together?" I ask.

"It appears that way," Finn answers, his eye an angry red and swelling shut as he speaks.

"All right, then," I say.

"All right, then," Oliver agrees, ice against his knuckles.

* * *

We leave Finn in the guest room, and I barely sleep knowing he's so near. I push the desk up against the door to stop him from coming to my room, even though I doubt he's brave enough to try.

Oliver caught a pedicab home, because it will be difficult enough to explain the presence of one strange boy residing in the flat to Maxine's mother and stepfather in the morning.

Well past midnight, I hear the soft padding of footsteps pacing in the hall. It could be any one of the members of this household or my own imagination, but there is only one face I picture lurking outside my door in the dark.

I feel as if I've only just fallen asleep when Greta knocks on my door with a silver carafe of coffee.

At breakfast Maxine announces to her family a new friend from New York will be staying for a few days. She can barely get out the word "friend," but her mother and stepfather don't seem to be particularly scandalized by the idea of a young man taking up residence in the flat.

I can't tell if it's because they're French or modern or simply don't take much of an interest in the finer details of Maxine's life.

The only show of emotion is from her stepfather, who asks hopefully, "A suitor?" to which Maxine grimaces and says, "I'd rather wed the devil himself."

Lena chokes on her orange juice. Under her breath she says, "Not far off."

"And will he be joining us for breakfast?" her mother asks.

"He's sleeping in."

The truth is that together the three of us woke before dawn and shoved a note under his door that said *Stay in there, we'll have meals brought to you.* To remind him of the deal he made last night.

We're well aware he could leave at any moment, perhaps we'd prefer it, but for now, he seems to be our willing prisoner.

I push back from the table, having choked down a few bites of egg, when Greta appears in the doorway to the dining room.

"A gentleman is here for Miss Hallowell."

For a second I'm terrified Finn is about to walk in.

But Oliver appears in the doorway a moment later, a summer straw hat in his hands, hiding his bruised knuckles, and a polite smile on his face. He greets Maxine's mother and her stepfather, who looks him up and down and says, "Maxine, why not a boy like this? He's so tall! So polite!"

"Thank you, sir," Oliver says, blushing. But beneath the polite facade he's spent an entire life curating, I see he is still unhappy about last night. His smile falters at the edges and he glances uncomfortably towards me. I don't entirely blame him.

Maxine rolls her eyes. "This particular boy is taken. Give me a fishing net. I'll go out on the corner and try to catch one of similar qualifications."

When Oliver is finished being flustered by Maxine's stepfather, he takes a curious look at me, halfway to the doorway where he's standing.

"Shall we?"

Oliver, Lena, Maxine, and I take a leisurely walk along the Seine, basking in the butter-yellow glow of the midmorning sun.

It's a particularly glorious day, which makes this feel less like a reconnaissance mission and more like a tourist excursion. It's nice to pretend.

Oliver navigates us through the streets of Paris for the better part of an hour. Eventually we reach a part of town where the houses are larger, more spread out. Gorgeous manors with perfectly square little shrubs and green lawns sit behind ornate gates, set back from the street.

The address on Finn's invitation is easy enough to find. The rest of the houses on the street are sleepy and still, but this one buzzes like a beehive. The gates are flung wide open, and staff haul in carts and carts of silver, linens, and wheels of cheese wrapped in wax.

A horse drawing a carriage whinnies and starts as yet another automobile pulls up and begins unloading what look to be tanks of live lobsters.

"Looks like it's shaping up to be quite the party," Oliver says.

My stomach is in knots at the thought already. "I don't like the idea of you being alone with him."

Oliver flexes his hand at his side. "I can handle Finn."

I hate knowing that without my magic, he probably stands a better shot against him than I do. I want to be able to protect him.

"What if you don't get the information you need at the party?" I look at the high gate. "This could be our only chance to get in."

"Finn is being awfully squirrely about what this party entails. I don't feel good about it," Maxine says.

"I agree," Lena says. "We don't know anything about the members of this club. It could be anyone."

"We need to come too. It's decided," I declare.

"How?" Oliver protests.

From across the street, I spy a trio of three maids dressed in identical black uniforms, carrying a wooden trunk into the service entrance.

I gesture to them with a jerk of my chin. "We'll become invisible."

Maxine grins. "Oh, I do love to play a role. What should my name be? My story? Can I be an heiress who has fallen from grace?"

"Sure, Maxine," I say with an eye roll.

We watch the staff from across the street for a moment more, lost in thought. "I have no doubt that the guests won't look at our faces, but what about the other staff? Won't they notice rather quickly we don't actually work there?"

Maxine shakes her head. "A party this big will have extra hands hired for the night. We'll blend right in."

Lena nods. "It's not the worst plan we've ever had."

"Oh, can we please not use that as a metric? When it comes to our plans, the bar is in hell," Maxine replies.

"I still think it's a good idea," I say.

Oliver frowns. "I don't like it."

Maxine laughs. "You don't have to."

I reach out and nudge his hand with mine. "It'll be fun. You'll see."

The rest of the day passes quietly. Finn joins the family for dinner against Maxine's will. Her mother set a place for him, insisting on meeting her daughter's mysterious guest. Finn, never one to turn down a dinner party, borrows a jacket from Maxine's stepfather and is seated directly between Maxine and Nina.

Maxine's mother and stepfather do not seem to be particularly concerned with Finn, who has taken up indefinite residence in one of their many guest rooms. This is something I'm learning about the wealthy: when you don't do your own housework, houseguests mean very little.

Finn breaks Maxine's fourth rule and delights Nina by pulling a quarter from behind her ear. Maxine levitates her steak knife just slightly off the table. It hovers there as a threat. Finn just laughs as if it's all one massive joke. It makes me lose what little appetite I had left.

We spend the day at the carousel with Nina. She laughs as it spins and spins, her skirts whipping around her.

Finn doesn't show up for dinner and I know I should be nervous about where he is, but I'm just glad not to have to look at him.

Later that night, I drift off to sleep with a book on my chest and the lights still on, waiting to hear his footsteps in the hall.

I fall into the dream like a bucket of cold water is being dumped on my head.

It takes a moment for my eyes to adjust to the darkness in this dream space. Slowly it comes into focus, lush tree branches reaching across a navy-blue sky, low bushes scratching at my legs. And all at once, I know I'm in the woods of Forest Park.

I hear him before I see him. I remember this part so well, the heavy footfall of his boots crunching through the underbrush, the way it used to set my heart fluttering.

"You could have just knocked on my door," I say. "You're only three rooms away."

He's holding a lantern, wearing hand-knit gloves. "The door was locked."

"So you did try?" The thought of him creeping through the dark hall and pulling at my door makes me want to scream.

He tilts his head as he considers me, like he's debating something internally. "I did try to visit you," he confesses. He must see the question in my face; why now? It's been over a year since I last saw him in my dreams, why wait until we're sleeping on the same hall to return? "But even after I got my power back, I couldn't seem to manage it. Maybe it was the distance or the magic itself, but . . . you must know I never stopped trying."

"Why?" I breathe. I don't know if I'm asking why he's speaking to me now or why he never stopped trying.

"I need to speak with you," he answers simply.

"Then speak," I snap. I don't have time for his moony stares.

"I'm not sure how much time we have, the magic . . ." He doesn't need to explain to me of all people just how difficult it's been.

"All the more reason to gets things corrected quickly and then never see each other again."

"Is that what you want?"

My answer is immediate. "Yes."

He has the gall to look sad, as if this a rejection.

"Is this what you wanted to speak about?"

He shakes his head. The lamplight is reflected in his eyes. "No. I wanted to tell you that you don't need to worry about me. I'm telling the truth this time."

I try to walk away, my boots crunch through the frost-slicked underbrush, but I don't make any progress. No matter how I move my feet, I stay stuck in the same spot.

"You know as well as I do I have no reason to believe that."

Finn is right beside me, despite my attempts to get away. "I can't stand the way you look at me like I'm someone you're afraid of."

I whip my head to face him. My hair is unbound, the tendrils tangle around my shoulders. I want to respond with fury, to tell him

I'm not afraid of him. But the truth is, I am. I'm terrified of him.

It scares me the way Finn can do horrible things and smile and move on with his life as if nothing is amiss. I'm scared by the way he lies as easy as breathing. What kind of person inflicts as much pain as he has and still feels entitled to move through the world with easy manners, performing stupid magic tricks at dinner?

With his golden curls and sparkly eyes and straight teeth behind a ready smile, Finn wears the disguise of a normal person well. But the smell of blood and gunpowder lingers on him. He can't wash himself clean, not to me.

The edges are rippling. We don't have long.

"Does it truly not haunt you? What you did?" I ask.

"What *we* did," he corrects me.

Aching for someone is a privilege, except when it's not, except when it's like this.

I see his face and my heart is all muscle memory, the ghost of a want I can't make go away.

The dream space collapses on itself and I wake up, sweaty and alone.

He's three doors down, in a bed that looks just like this one, alone as well.

CHAPTER THIRTEEN

Rue Blanche is bathed in the firelight and crawling with men in masks.

The stone mansion looks so much bigger in the dark than it did in daylight. Torches have been lit and placed along the perimeter of the grand entrance steps, but the flicking light bathes the imposing building in long shadows, making it look as if it isn't quite of this world. It ripples in the dark as if it's something from Finn's and my shared dreams.

There are perhaps two dozen guests milling about, laughing as they climb up the steps of the manor. Footmen stand stock-still in black silk uniforms and hold goblets on golden platters. They wear masks, simple and black, covering their eyes and noses.

The guests are wearing masks too, some ornate, dripping with jewels, others simple and make of silk, but no one's face is fully visible.

The anonymity makes me uncomfortable. I knew the Brothers of Morte d'Arthur had secrets, Finn made that evident, but this only confirms it further. If they're hiding their faces, what else are they hiding?

For a moment, Finn, Oliver, Maxine, Lena, and I just stand across the street and watch.

I turn to Lena. Since leaving Haxahaven and returning home, her magical training has waned and her visions of the future have slowed, but I still have to ask. "See anything for tonight, Lena?"

She closes her eyes and presses her thumb in the space between them. We stand in silence and watch her until she sighs and opens her eyes. "The collar of Oliver's jacket will get torn. I see Frances mending it."

"That's all?"

She shrugs. "All I see for now."

The service entrance is as busy as the main entrance. The side door that opens to the basement is propped open and currently in a flurry of activity.

From somewhere a few blocks away, church bells begin to chime, low and haunting, as if counting down to something.

"We need to go in," I say.

Finn pulls two masks from his inner jacket pocket and hands one to Oliver. Oliver looks confused for a moment, but it wouldn't be wise to draw attention to ourselves, even across the street like this, so he holds it up to his face.

Like the footmen's, their masks are simple, made of black silk, thinned to points at the corners of the eyes. It has the effect of exaggerating their features. Even in the dim light, Finn's eyes are brighter, Oliver's jaw sharper.

"Where'd you get these?" Oliver asks.

Finn just grins. "I never show up unprepared for a party."

"I'm not putting it on until you tell me."

"The host had them sent along with the invitation. Came in a fancy box and everything. It was all very la-di-da."

Oliver huffs, not happy, but apparently satisfied. I stand behind him and pull the velvet strings of the mask into a little bow at the back of his head.

Maxine does up Finn's mask, flicking him hard in the soft spot behind the ear as soon as her bow is done.

"That hurt," he mutters, rubbing the sore spot.

Maxine flashes him a smile. "Good."

Mist from the river rolls in, and the gas lamps set the whole street glowing golden against the black of the starless sky.

"Finn, we'd better get good information tonight or I swear to God I'll throw you in the Seine," I say through gritted teeth.

"If anyone will know about the veil, it's the Brothers of Morte d'Arthur."

"C'mon, let's not miss the party." Maxine takes off walking across the street and we follow her.

The boys take the main steps up to the grand entrance of the house, joining the group of identical-looking men in their fine tuxedos and masquerade masks. Their voices morph into one, like the buzzing of insects. Laughter spills into the night from the glow of the open doors, but I don't feel like laughing. My heart is in my throat as I watch Oliver disappear into their midst.

Maxine, Lena, and I circle the house and step right in through the open door to the kitchens.

A scullery maid takes one look at us and barks something in French. Maxine mutters something polite and timid in a very un-Maxine-like voice in return, and we scurry in through the door behind her.

"What did she say?" I whisper.

"She's upset we're late. The other help from the staffing agency arrived a half hour ago. I apologized. She said our uniforms are in the hall closet."

Lena sighs in relief. "That was easy."

We weave through the chaos of the kitchen, around steaming copper pots and harried boys carrying plates and plates upstairs.

The hallway isn't any less busy. The closet with the uniforms is half propped open. Maxine pulls three black pinafores off their hangers and passes them to us.

We discard the gray uniforms we stole from the DuPre laundry line this morning and tie each other's new disguises at the waist with quick hands. We finish by pinning on each other's crisp white maid's hats.

"You were good back there," Lena praises.

Maxine preens. "I know."

Another older woman, the housekeeper maybe, passes us in the hall and scolds us in French.

Maxine leans over and whispers, "Time for hors d'oeuvres."

We walk into the kitchen, grab silver platters of tiny little appetizers, and walk up the narrow basement stairs with them balanced on our hands.

There are so many extra staff members hired for tonight, it's easy enough to blend in. No one is on the alert for unfamiliar faces. Nearly everyone is unfamiliar.

We climb the stairs up to the butler's pantry, then out the pocket doors to the corner of the drawing room.

For a moment I'm nervous that someone will recognize we don't belong here, that we'll be kicked out or punished. But no one turns as we enter the room at all. A few hands reach out as I step into the room with my tray of caviar on little crackers. But I've never been looked at less. I didn't need a spell to become invisible. All I needed was a uniform.

The foyer is comically grand with sweeping ceilings painted gold and crystal chandeliers that throw rainbows over the marble statues lining the room. The parlor is built like an atrium, open all the way to the ceiling, all four soaring floors. It makes the parlor of the Commodore Club look like a poorhouse.

The men stand in groups or three or four, clutching sweating whiskey glasses and laughing uproariously.

It reminds me so much of the political fundraiser I attended with Helen at the Hotel Astor. My magic hummed in my veins then, begging to be released. I was scared of it then, but there was something exhilarating in knowing I contained so much. For months, there's just been a hollow spot in my rib cage where the power used to live, and I've felt awful and unmoored without it.

But tonight feels so much like that night, I can almost imagine the magic kicking, and alive. Like a phantom limb, I remember it so vividly it almost feels real.

I scan the room, searching for Finn and Oliver among the men. It's difficult to find them with the masks and the identical black tuxedos, but then I spot him. I'd recognize Oliver's back anywhere. It's in the particular way he holds everything that worries him in the space right between his shoulder blades.

I circle the room until the tray is almost empty to get a better look at his face. He's standing next to Finn and a few other men, smiling as if he's nothing more than delighted to be here tonight. Oliver has his own kind of magic, the ability to make anyone like him. On my quick pass by him, I hear one of the men call him "my boy."

We don't make eye contact, it would be too dangerous, but I feel him watching me as I pass. It's a relief to know he's all right.

I return to the basement kitchen and refill my tray. On my way back up I pass Lena on the stairs.

"Anything yet?" she asks.

"No. I found Oliver and Finn. It doesn't look like Finn is up to anything, but you can never be too sure."

She nods in agreement. "We'll keep an eye on him."

The magic flickers in me. I suppress a gasp. I can't draw attention to myself.

To test the feeling, I levitate the silver tray just a whisper over the palm of my hand.

I thought I was imagining the feeling, but it's unmistakable now. It's weaker than before, but the spark is there. I could cry in relief.

The tray lifts, as easy as breathing. For once, my magic comes when called.

It's not perfect. It still feels a little strange and sore, like pulling a muscle in a direction it doesn't want to go in. That strange, sharp, buzzing feeling is still present too. It's in the juncture of my jaw, right behind my ear, vibrating like I just touched an electric light that's been wired wrong.

But it's *working*. It's finally *working*.

I have to stop myself from skipping to the kitchen, I'm so *happy*. The relief has physically made me lighter, I think.

I pick up a full tray of salmon blinis and return to the drawing room, where the men are finishing their drinks in preparation for dinner.

Maxine and Lena are making their rounds as well, looking mostly bored. Playing Finn's jailers tonight isn't fun. It's mostly just tedious.

He and Oliver are by the massive fireplace with a man who looks to be about forty. He's handsome in an understated sort of way, the kind of handsome that is easy to be with money. He's skinny, with a long neck and a pointed little beard that reminds me of a picture I once saw of William Shakespeare in a textbook. He's gesturing to a portrait above the roaring fire. On second glance, it's clear the portrait is of him. This must be the man of the house then, the duke. He's younger than I thought he'd be.

It's a good sign Finn and Oliver have already cornered him. They appear to be in deep conversation.

I need to get closer to hear what they're saying. I don't know what is happening with my power, but there's something strange about this place. Finn may have been right, and I don't have the patience to wait for him to decide and tell me himself.

I tuck my elbows into my sides, and use magic to balance the heavy silver tray just a breath above my fingertips to ensure I don't drop it as I cross through the crowd and give my aching arms a rest.

There isn't much of the conversation I can make out over the din of the room, even this close. The duke gestures to the painting again. "It must have been done twenty years ago," he says. "You're kind to compliment it."

I look from the painting to the duke and back again. The duke is wearing a small black mask, like the rest of the party guests, so I can't be completely sure, but it looks as if it could have been painted yesterday. He has no lines around his eyes or mouth, and his hair is as brown as a young man's. The decades-old portrait's likeness to the duke is spot-on.

Oliver nods politely. Finn smirks, like there's a joke he's in on that the rest of us have missed.

I don't have any more time to eavesdrop. The bell calling the partygoers to dinner will ring at any moment and my chance will be lost. Something strange is going on in this house. I don't believe it's a coincidence that my magic has sparked awake after so many stagnant months. Finn's magic is connected to mine, connected to the veil as well. Is he feeling what I'm feeling?

I focus my power on Finn's hand. It hangs casually at his side, the blue veins of his wrist evident against the black cuffs of his tux. His golden cuff links glint in the firelight.

I close my eyes for a beat and gather all my concentration, the way he once taught me to in a forest thousands of miles from this fine room. With a flash of magic, I tug at his hand.

It moves barely more than a twitch, but he feels it, I know he does by the way his eyes widen briefly in shock.

Then his eyes find me. I raise my eyebrows and hopes he understands what I'm saying. He replies with a small nod.

I take a few steps before slipping the toe of my shoe under the edge of the heavy rug, dropping the tray on Finn's feet with a clatter.

Finn, Oliver, and Duke Mourrir jump into action to assist me. In the chaos, I seize my opportunity.

Finn ducks down to help me right the tray. "Do you feel it?" I whisper urgently.

He exhales, "I do."

CHAPTER FOURTEEN

The duke extends a hand to lift me from the ground. I widen my eyes in shock, then put my hand in his. He hauls me up to my feet.

He doesn't seem like the kind of man who would show kindness to the help, but there's warmth in his eyes. "My, what a spill," he says.

I duck my head, playing the part. "*Pardon*," I say in my best French.

"Mistakes happen." He shrugs, speaking to Oliver and Finn, not to me. "The salmon was subpar tonight, the floor is a better place for it anyway."

I scurry off right as the dinner bell chimes. I glance behind my shoulder as I'm nearly to the door to see the men following the duke into the formal dining room. Their matching masks and black suits give the whole thing the effect of a twisted funeral procession.

Lena and Maxine aren't far behind me. We're shepherded downstairs by a stern white-haired butler.

Only the male staff will serve at dinner. It's modern that the duke had women serving during the welcome reception, but for the formal meal, strict tradition will be observed.

A group of tall, masked footmen pass us on the stairs.

We gather with the other hired help and one by one are handed envelopes with a few bills from the housekeeper. She barks something in French, and most of the others head for the door.

"She said we're dismissed," Maxine says.

"What now?" Lena asks in a whisper.

I'd hoped we'd be allowed to linger for the rest of the night, find a pot to scrub or a vent to listen through. It seems like a childish plan, now.

But I can't leave Oliver alone with Finn. He may have said I can trust him, but I don't. I also can't go without answers. The magic buzzing in my veins tells me there is information to be found here.

"C'mon," I whisper, and jerk my head to Lena and Maxine, urging them to follow me down the dark hallway opposite the brightly lit kitchens.

With the party still in full swing upstairs, downstairs is in chaos. No one pays any mind to us as we walk away.

From her pinafore pocket, Lena pulls out Finn's pencil drawing of the house layout and studies it. "There's the other staircase. . . ."

Maxine looks over her shoulder and nods. "It goes up the east wing of the house. If it reaches to the service quarters, we should find an alternate staircase over here." She pokes the corner of the map.

We wind through another narrow hallway, which houses a few

doors I assume open to staff rooms. It isn't grim in the basement, it's just plain. The whitewashed stone walls make everything feel cold and stark.

We round another corner and we find it, the service staircase we were looking for. It's narrow and made of plain wood, so different from the sweeping red-carpeted staircases in the manor house above-ground.

But the stairs don't just go up, they also go down. I thought we were in the deepest recesses of the house, but I must have been wrong.

Maybe it's just a hunch, or maybe it's too many years spent reading novels about castles with secret passageways, but I start to climb down.

Maxine and Lena look on with confusion. "I need to know where it goes," I say.

I can't explain the tug I feel. I don't know if it's magic or pure desperation, but I follow it.

Lena pulls out the map to refer to it once more. "It should just be a cellar."

I look to them. I don't know how to explain it. "Can we please try anyway?"

Maxine narrows her eyes. I wonder if she feels the buzzing too. They both nod.

We climb down one story, ending up in a cellar that houses a few stacked wine crates and a discarded chair covered with a white drop cloth. A single light bulb hangs sadly from the ceiling.

Three of the walls are ordinary, made of stone as old as the city itself.

But built into the fourth wall is a golden gate, gleaming and out of place in this dusty basement. It reaches to the ceiling, made of ornate filigree that twists into patterns resembling human skulls. In the middle is a massive lock shaped like a human heart, four chambers re-created in sparkling gold.

"What is this?" I whisper.

We breathe in tandem, staring at it together. Lined up in front of it, like it might open for us, like we could step right through and find out what hides in its depths.

Ever-present is the same warm buzz of magic I felt upstairs.

"I feel something strange," Maxine says. It's nice to have confirmation it isn't all in my head.

"We have to find out." I approach the gate, hands outstretched, and whisper, "*Briseadh*."

The heart-shaped lock unclicks gently, like it's been waiting for us.

Without any push, the gate swings open on its own, revealing a pitch-dark passageway.

Our housekeeper's uniforms are made of thick cotton, but they are no match for the chill of the tunnel. We must be so far underground.

I look to my left and my right, Maxine and Lena beside me, and we push on wordlessly into the dark.

We mutter under our breaths, conjuring light between our hands to illuminate the passageway.

In silence, we walk.

And walk.

And walk.

The dirt floors crunch beneath our shoes and our breathing comes out in small puffs of vapor. I'm chilled to my very core, but still I press on. I have no other choice. I can't turn back when we've come so far, not when this might be my only chance.

We've been walking for close to ten minutes when the buzzing intensifies.

It starts in my jaw, sharp and high-pitched, before traveling into the tiny bones of my ear and then up and into my temples.

"Ah!" I cry out as the pain zaps behind my eyes. I stumble forward a few feet, placing my hands on my knees to steady myself.

"Are you all right?" Lena reaches out a hand and pulls me to my feet. "We should go back."

"No." I shake my head. Something in these tunnels is calling to me. I have to know what it is.

The buzzing reverberates through each cell of my body, mounting until it becomes a pressure behind my eyes so strong, I begin to tear up. It's like it's picking me apart from the inside out, delicate and precise and devastating.

In the low light, just in front of me, Maxine doesn't seem to be faring much better.

"Shit," she curses as she stumbles forward, clutching at her ears.

"You feel it too?" I ask weakly.

She nods, grim. "Must mean we're close." It's close to *what* that remains the question.

We follow the hallway left. The tunnels smell of fresh rain and something dead.

The light from Lena's spell illuminates something on the wall. I stumble with a gasp, nearly falling to my knees.

"I—" I clutch my chest in shock, my heart pounds beneath my palm. "Did you see that?"

I lift the light I've conjured between my hands closer to the wall, and what I see is so terrifying for a moment I think I may be sick.

Staring back at me, large sockets devoid of eyes, mouths permanently open, is an entire wall of human skulls.

Lena swings her hands to the opposite wall, illuminating an elaborate crisscrossing pattern made of arm and leg bones.

This is hell. That's the thought that first enters my head. *I've walked into hell itself.*

Maxine huffs out a laugh and shakes her head. "It's the catacombs. We've found an entrance to the catacombs."

"The *what*?" I ask, nearly on the verge of tears in fear.

"A few hundred years ago, Paris ran out of cemetery space," she explains. "They relocated all the bodies down here to make room for new ones. I've heard there are entrances all over the city. The tunnels stretch on for miles, allegedly."

"Miles . . . ," Lena marvels. "We should probably turn back then, before we get lost down here forever."

I want nothing more than to return to the surface of the earth, away from the bones and the sharp buzzing, but I can't go yet, not until I know what this is.

"Please," I beg. "Just a little farther, then we'll all go up together."

Lena and Maxine look to each other, then nod.

We turn another corner, on and on through this labyrinth of bones.

The buzzing continues, awful and scratchy under my skin, but if I have destroyed the veil between the living and the dead, if my magic and the lives of others hang in the balance, I have no choice but to press on.

The light changes so subtly I think I'm imagining it at first. No longer pitch dark, there is a weak silvery-blue light, barely visible along the seam where the earth meets the bones.

Then we turn the corner and I see it.

The light ripples like we're underwater. I can't breathe for a moment, like suddenly I'm underwater too.

My heart catches in my throat.

Because we've found it. I didn't know what we were looking for, but this is unmistakably it. The next hallway is a dead end. The wall is made up of a solid panel of light, the source of the strange blue-silver hue. It moves like the surface of the ocean, like something alive, like it's breathing.

I've seen it once before, just a glimpse in the scrying mirror before I spoke to my brother that final time.

But the way it calls to me is unmistakably familiar. It tugs at a deep spot in the center of my rib cage, pulling me closer, begging me for something I don't know if I can give it.

I curse under my breath and squeeze my eyes tight to hide the pain. Lena gasps sharply. Maxine just laughs.

I'm about to take another step to approach it, when a fist at my collar yanks me back.

Maxine pulls me around the corner, and the three of us press our backs to the wall. The dirt is cool against my shoulder blades. Maxine widens her eyes. "Shh," she whispers. "Do you hear that?"

It's difficult to make out over the sound of our breathing and the hammering of my own heart, but floating from out of the darkness come voices. Low, male voices.

We wink out the lights between our hands, and we wait.

It doesn't take long for the men to appear. They come from an adjacent hallway, blessedly missing us. I don't know how I'd explain myself if found. The thought terrifies me.

They stream out into the rotunda of space in front of the veil. I peek my head out a fraction of an inch to get a better look at the scene.

All of the men from the party seem to be there, led by the duke, who is standing directly in front of the veil, facing the party guests, each of whom holds a candle, flickering against the dark, their faces still masked.

The scene reminds me of a Christmas Eve church service. The air down here bites like December in New York.

With the masks and the low light it's nearly impossible to find Finn and Oliver, but after scanning the group for a moment, I spot them. They're standing in the back of the crowd next to each other. Oliver is bouncing one heel against the dirt floors. He's anxious. Finn stands perfectly still, which is more unsettling.

"Gentlemen," the duke declares. A hush falls over the crowd. "It's time to begin."

Each man lowers his candle, holding it still at his chest, as if singing a hymn. Oliver looks around, confused, then follows suit.

The duke extends his hand to an older man in the crowd and pulls him into a warm hug, clapping him on the back. "Henri," he says, placing his hands on both his shoulders. "It is time."

Four footmen emerge from the same passageway the rest of the men came from holding something between them. At first, I think it's a trunk, but as it comes into the candlelight, I realize I'm mistaken; it's a body.

The body of a young man is laid out on a golden stretcher. His chest rises and falls slowly, so I know he's not dead, but he is unconscious. He's dressed in shabby clothes, but two glistening rubies are placed on his closed eyes.

I watch in horrified silence.

The footmen lay the stretcher and the boy at the duke's feet, directly in front of the veil. It ripples, alive and hungry.

The buzzing in my head grows louder, like something under my skin is alive and desperate to crawl right out of my body.

"What a gift tonight has been," the duke declares. "What a gift the veil is to us all." He's speaking in English. It makes me wonder if the Brothers of Morte d'Arthur traveled from England and the United States for this event. Whatever this is clearly reaches beyond the shores of France.

The duke continues, "We have sat in front of this veil for centuries waiting for it to open, and only twice in the past five hundred years has it revealed itself to us. The last time was over one hundred years ago, when I myself was granted the eternal gift, and now, it is my honor to bestow it unto you, my beloved brothers."

He places his hand on the man named Henri's shoulders and presses, forcing Henri to kneel at his feet. Henri goes willingly and closes his eyes in reverence.

"Tonight, we grant the gift of eternal life to our brother, Henri Saint Germain, who has loyally served the Brothers his entire life.

He stood guard at this very gate as a young man and has dedicated his adulthood to the pursuit of triumph of life over death. The funds he and his estate generously provide us allow our operations to function, and after tonight, we will ensure the longevity of both Henri and his generosity."

I turn to Maxine and Lena, who are watching the scene with horror-struck faces. I don't dare whisper, it isn't worth the risk of being found out, but what the duke is saying sounds like madness. Living forever is a myth, something silly children's tales are spun from, but then I think of what he said of the portrait upstairs and the smallest part of me wonders if he might be telling the truth.

"A small life, in exchange for a very big one." The duke levitates the stretcher and the body on it to waist height using magic and places his hand on the boy's forehead.

My knees threaten to buckle under me. I'm light-headed and the buzzing, the awful, incessant buzzing grows louder. I look to where Finn stands. He closes his eyes and sways just a little, then reaches out to grasp on to Oliver's elbow for balance. Oliver recoils, but lets him hold on.

The duke begins to chant. It starts as a low rumble in his chest, then it gets louder, until he's shouting. It's in a language I don't understand, maybe Latin? I'll ask Oliver later.

The veil flickers, shifting more and more rapidly, like the surface of the sea in a storm.

The noise in my head roars. A voice in the back of my head screams at me to run.

The duke pulls a sword from where it hangs at his belt.

He raises it above his head. The point glints in the firelight, poised directly over the sleeping boy's chest.

And then—it's as if I'm being stabbed. As if every part of me is being torn apart. The soles of my feet, the back of my knees, my hips, the space behind my rib cage, my fingernails, my wrists, my collarbones, the crown of my head—all being ripped apart by white-hot fire.

I open my eyes just in time to see Finn collapse.

Then everything goes black.

CHAPTER FIFTEEN

I come to, still in the basement, my back propped up against the stone wall of the cellar, with Maxine and Lena standing over me, out of breath and sweaty.

Maxine braces her hands on her knees and huffs in and out, her cheeks flushed. Lena doesn't look much better. She leans against the stone wall and tilts her head back as she struggles to catch her breath.

The golden gate is hanging open, the heart lock still unlatched. The single light bulb above us flickers and swings back and forth.

"What—" I say weakly.

I've never seen Maxine look so scared, not even the night Finn and the Sons of Saint Druon attacked Haxahaven.

"Not now," she says. "Can you move? I don't think we're strong enough to carry you any farther."

"You carried me?"

"You can thank us later," Maxine replies between gasps.

I wiggle my toes. I feel weak, but the searing pain is gone. I push myself up. "What about Oliver?" I won't leave without him. This is another mess I've drawn him into; I won't leave him alone in it.

Lena shakes her head. "He's with Finn."

Panic rises in me. "That doesn't mean he's safe!"

"Yes, but we don't have time," Lena argues.

I open my mouth to fight back, but before I can, the door to the cellar swings open.

We freeze. My heart is in my throat. I feel so weak, I wonder if I have it in me at all to fight.

Illuminated by the swinging bulb is a girl. She leans against the doorjamb casually. The toe of her satin heel taps against the floor.

"*Qu'est-ce qu'on a ici . . .* ," she says with a smirk. Her dark hair hangs loose around her shoulders, cut bluntly, as if she did it herself in a hurry. Her hair may be a bit of a mess, but set atop it is a coronet of sparkling diamonds.

She's wearing a gown of midnight black, adorned with a thousand jet beads. It hangs off her thin frame like she's wearing a costume.

Maxine responds in rapid French.

I reach for the magic flickering inside me and debate seeing if I could take hold of the girl's body. Everything feels so shaky, I'm not sure if I could. But I'm not above trying.

"Did you like the party?" the girl asks in French-accented English, saccharine sweet and dripping with sarcasm. She sucks the inside of her cheek as she considers us.

"Not particularly," Maxine quips. "We'd really ought to be going.

Got lost. Forgot our manners. We apologize—" She makes a move to go around the girl, but she juts out her arm, blocking the doorway.

Maxine has a few inches on her, and I think if it came down to a physical fight, she'd have the upper hand, but there's something about the girl's self-assured condescension that makes me hesitate.

"I'm forgetting my manners. I'm Anais. Anais Mourrier." She smiles, full lips around white teeth.

We don't give her our names. In response to our silence, she continues. "Does Saint Bosco's know you're here? Or is it the Sisters of Saint Joan who sent you? God, they do love to meddle."

"We're staff from the agency brought in for the party," Maxine says.

Anais laughs. "Don't insult my intelligence."

I'm shaky with fear and nauseated from the blow to my head as I fainted, but Maxine just smiles, undeterred. "We don't look like scullery maids?"

Anais clucks her tongue and shakes her head no.

"Fine. We're from Haxahaven," Maxine says. I'm surprised she gives in so quickly, but she's biting back a smile in that confident Maxine way. Anais is terrifying, but she may have met her match.

The girl chuckles and lowers her arm. "I knew a girl who went to Haxahaven many years ago, Ruby something. God, she was horrible. What brings the witches of New York to my great-grandfather's basement?"

"We got lost," I say.

"You look sick," she replies, looking at me with disgust in her catlike eyes. "Should I call for the infirmary?"

"No, no, we'd really best be going," Maxine insists. Lena watches silently. I resist the urge to look behind me, to search for any movement in the tunnels. Is Oliver still trapped down there?

"If I were a good hostess, I would take you upstairs, insist you join me in the lounge for a glass of port."

"I hate port," Maxine replies.

"So do I," the girl smirks.

"Rain check, then." Maxine takes another step toward the door. This time, the girl lets her pass. We scurry behind her, out into the hallway.

"You are lucky I am not a good hostess. My great-grandfather would never forgive me if he knew I let guests leave without coming upstairs to say goodbye. You are also lucky my great-grandfather and I are very different people." She takes a few steps so she is in front of us and jerks her head forward. "Come along then, I'll show you out."

The other staff give us questioning looks. We're all covered in dust and I'm bleeding from my knees where I hit the ground, but with Anais as our guide, no one dares question us.

We make it to the door that leads to the outside, and Anais nods to the footman guarding it. He clears the way and holds the door open.

We step out into the thick night air.

I want to run as fast as I can away from this place, but Maxine pauses at the top of the steps, looking down at where Anais is haloed in the light of the kitchens. "*Merci*, Anais."

Anais bites her lip to suppress a smile. "May I know your name?"

I tug at Maxine's elbow. She shakes me off and bites her lip. "I'm Maxine."

"May I be lucky enough to see you again, Maxine," Anais replies.

Maxine pauses and shakes her head with a small smile, then follows Lena and me across the wide cobblestone street.

The night is cloaked with fog. In the warm June air, I feel as if I am choking on it.

"I won't leave Oliver," I say.

Lena nods. "We'll wait for him over here. It'll be fine, Frances, you need to breathe."

Maxine agrees. "Is your head all right? We can call for the doctor once we've returned to the flat."

"My head?"

Suddenly two figures emerge from the mist, tripping across the wide cobblestone street.

Oliver is dragging Finn as quick as he can, with Finn's arm slung around his shoulder.

"Oliver," I sigh. Relief floods through me at the sight of him.

"Go—" he demands.

We stare at them, frozen and confused. "*Go,*" he says again, and this time we do. He nearly trips over Finn's dragging feet, as his weight shifts and the hand around Oliver's neck slips.

The fabric of Oliver's jacket collar tears as Finn grabs half-consciously at it in an attempt to stay upright.

Maxine, the tallest of the three of us, grabs Finn's other arm, supporting him between her and Oliver.

We turn the corner, off Rue Blanche and out of sight of the hulking mansion, and down another residential street.

Finn's lips are parted and nearly blue. His breathing is shallow and his eyes are closed. He's conscious, but just barely.

We're moving as fast as we can, but it's difficult hauling Finn, and I'm still shaky on my feet. Lena takes my hand in hers to steady me.

"What happened?" I ask between gasping breaths.

"He hit his head when he fell," Oliver replies.

Maxine nods. "So did Frances."

With my free hand, I reach up and gingerly press on a sore spot directly in the back of my skull. It's swelling into a goose egg, but I'll be fine.

"What happened after that?" I ask.

Oliver sighs and readjusts Finn's heavy arm over his shoulder. "Another man helped me carry him upstairs. I told him Finn had a weak stomach and there was all that blood. . . ." He shudders. "I volunteered to lay him down in a guest room to get some rest, and instead I ran right out the front door. I don't think the guests saw us, but the butler sure did."

"It doesn't look like you were followed," Lena says with a glance behind her shoulder.

"I want to get as far as possible before they realize we're gone," Oliver huffs.

"No one questioned the fainting?" I ask. "What happened after?"

I'm still not sure what I witnessed in the catacombs. It's all coming back to me in flashes, like a dream I only half remember. There was the duke and the boy on the golden table and the sword and the veil and the spell—it's all in pieces.

"Frances, you don't remember?" Lena asks gently.

I hate the way she, Maxine, and Oliver look at me with identical expressions of pity. "You might as well go ahead and tell me."

Maxine makes eye contact with Lena, who nods gently. "They

killed the boy. We started running the minute the sword went into his heart."

Oliver is quiet, remembering the horror. "The duke said a spell. They did something to the body. I was hauling Finn away before they got to the end of it. Everyone was too preoccupied to notice us leaving early."

"I'm sorry," I whisper. What they witnessed was all my fault. What happened to the boy was all my fault too, and the other body in the church as well. This confirms it.

I've spent the past year trying desperately to be good, to not cause any more destruction, but it seems I cause harm no matter how hard I try.

Maybe something about me is inherently bad. Maybe I really am irredeemable.

My stomach turns. I nearly trip over the toe of my boot as I stumble and throw up all over the sidewalk.

"Frances!" Lena exclaims.

"I'm sorry," I heave, fighting back tears. "I'm so sorry."

Every step we take away from the mansion, away from the veil, I feel my magic weaken. What was once a blaze is now a candle, flickering weakly in the wind. I'm grateful to be away from the Brothers of Morte d'Arthur, but I grieve for my power. It hurts worse to lose it now that I remember how alive I feel when it's present.

Finn comes to enough to walk for himself a few blocks later and in silence, we make our way back to the DuPre flat. Finn is the slowest amongst us, hobbling alone behind the rest of the pack. Oliver keeps pace with me, a protective arm slung over my shoulder.

In thick silence, we ride the elevator up, and march through the abandoned, dark halls. The heels of our shoes click against the checkerboard marble.

We follow Maxine to her room without question, and collapse on the floor as she lights a kerosene lamp.

Oliver brings me a crystal glass of water from the washroom. I take it and gulp it down. It washes away the sour taste from my mouth, but my stomach still rolls.

"I knew the duke was interested in dark magic, but I didn't know—" Finn says from where he lies on the floor by the window. He's illuminated in moonlight, flat on his back under the fluttering white curtains.

"About the human sacrifice?" Maxine finishes his sentence venomously.

"Is the duke really immortal?" I ask. "Is that what tonight was about?"

Finn sighs heavily. "The Brothers of Morte d'Arthur are obsessed with overcoming death, I told you that. They spent centuries trying to find the Fountain of Youth and then the Holy Grail. Most regarded them as zealots. But there have always been rumors."

"Rumors of what?" I say. I don't have it in me to be angry. I'm too hollowed out.

"That they could use the veil between the living and the dead to perform forbidden magic. It's made them a laughingstock in the magical community. I didn't think much of it until tonight. I was hopeful they'd know about the veil. I never dreamed they'd use it like that."

"Does the spell work?" Lena asks. "Did that man truly make himself immortal?"

Immortality. I shiver at the thought. I wish my brother had gotten more time and I certainly hope I have more years left on this earth, but *forever* is a terrifying prospect.

"Anais did say she was his great-granddaughter," Maxine says.

"Who is Anais?" Oliver asks. He's unbuttoned his tuxedo, and laid his head on the jacket. The black silk tie hangs loose around the hollow of his throat.

I extend my hand and he understands immediately. He sits up and hands me his jacket. I run my fingers over the collar and find the place where Finn ripped it as he stumbled. I pull a needle and black thread from the sewing kit in Maxine's desk and begin to sew as the others speak. It is comforting and familiar to have a needle and thread in my hand. Lena's visions are rarely wrong.

"We were caught leaving the catacombs. She let us go," Maxine explains.

"And there was the creepy portrait," I add. "He said it was painted decades ago but he looked exactly the same."

"Both of those could be lies," Lena considers. "There's no way to prove it."

She's right. Maybe the Mourrier family is conducting an elaborate ruse, maybe it's a way to con people out of money or magic, or maybe it's just a sadistic joke and Anais is sitting in front of the fire laughing with the duke right now.

I don't know what it is the Mourriers are about or if it's possible to live forever.

But I do know that a boy is dead and that we have to do something about it.

"It doesn't matter, does it? We have to stop them."

"As long as the veil is open, they'll keep killing," Finn agrees.

Oliver props himself up on his elbow. "At dinner, the duke made a joke about the Sons of Saint Druon and their key, tucked away in the Louvre. He made it sound like the key could close the veil."

Finn sighs. "It's just a rumor."

I sit up to look at him properly. Just moments ago I felt so dead inside, but now the smallest bloom of hope grows. "The last rumor proved to be true. We'd be foolish to dismiss this one too. Did he say anything more?"

Oliver shakes his head. "He didn't give details, only that the Sons had a key."

"Wait!" I exclaim. I bounce to my feet, ignoring the way my head pounds, and rush over to Maxine's desk. I jerk open the drawer and grab handfuls of the papers I stole from my father. I kneel on the carpet and fan them out in front of me until I find the one I'm looking for.

"Aha!" I hold the yellowing page above my head triumphantly.

It's a fading yellow photograph from a museum collection of a simple golden key. It's labeled LOUVRE, PERMANENT COLLECTION. ANONYMOUS DONOR, 1813.

I remember thinking the picture was odd, even amongst all of the other odd papers. The key appeared too simple to warrant being displayed permanently at the Musée du Louvre.

"It seems too easy," Maxine says.

"Perhaps that's the point," Lena replies. "They needed something they could access in case of emergency. Hide it in plain sight, always ensure it's protected."

"What will we do once we get it?" I ask. It didn't look like the veil was equipped with a lock.

"Perhaps the key will have more information," Lena offers, but she sounds unsure.

Oliver sighs. "There's something else the duke said at dinner. It could mean nothing."

"Spill it," Maxine prompts.

"He implied only those who opened the veil can close it. Said something along the lines of them not having to worry about the veil ever being closed because those who opened it probably had no idea they'd done it at all."

"He sure let a lot of information fly freely at dinner. Could it be a trap?" I ask. I'm uneasy but I do feel some level of relief wash over me. I may have opened the veil, but there's a possibility I can make things right and close it too.

"Or maybe a few hundred years of life make you feel invincible," Lena offers.

"Is there any way for us to find out?" Maxine asks.

I suppose he's right. Either the key is real and it can close the veil, restore my magic, and stop the killings, or we're being set up. But leaving the veil open isn't an option, so I will tug on the only lead we have and hope something unravels. "We'll find out once we get the key."

Finn toys with the edge of the curtain, sitting a ways from the rest of us across the room under the window. "So it appears we're stuck with each other until this mess is cleaned up."

"How do you know he'll help us? He's betrayed us before," Oliver asks, refusing to ask Finn directly, but instead directing the question to me.

I can't bear to look at Finn, so I look at the wall instead. "Because he can't close the veil on his own. He needs us if he has any hope of holding on to his power." I don't know much about Finn—he feels slippery, impossible to grasp—but I do know he'd do anything for his own magic. For once, I have the upper hand. The darkest parts of me relish the control. The terrible tether still stretches between us, but the leash is firmly in my hand. I want to *tug.*

Oliver grabs a shiny silver pen from Maxine's desk and chucks it at Finn. It clatters into his shoulder and he winces. "I didn't deserve that."

Oliver just rolls his eyes.

"Stop it, the two of you. Let's focus on fixing this," I scold. "We need the key."

"It's well guarded," Finn protests.

I'm struck with a memory, Finn and me, younger than we are now, sneaking into the Commodore Club to steal Boss Olan's dagger. He called me his Watson. I really believed we were partners.

The memory hurts like a scab I shouldn't have picked at.

"Anyone have any better ideas?" I ask. I'm met with stony silence.

I flop back on the floor. If I moved my arms and legs, I could make a snow angel out of the papers. "Fine." I sigh. "Let's rob the Louvre."

CHAPTER SIXTEEN

Nina accompanies us two days later for a perfectly respectable, perfectly innocent trip to the most renowned art museum in the world. What else would three tourists on summer holiday from New York do while in the City of Lights?

We debated asking my father directly about the key, but that would require admitting to stealing his paper or breaking into the meeting of the Brothers of Morte d'Arthur, and we don't trust him yet. The fewer people we can involve in this, the safer we are.

Maxine's mother herself told us it would be a crime not to see the *Mona Lisa*.

We cut the very picture of three upstanding members of society as we enter the marble halls of the museum, clad in near-identical high-necked white tea gowns, large sun hats poised on our swept-up hair.

Lena hauls her art kit by her side, an easel and paints that fold cleverly into a carrying case.

Nina runs in front of us, skittering like a duckling on an icy pond, the pink sash of her dress flowing behind her.

"I want to see the ballerinas!" she shouts.

Maxine's stepfather was annoyed to see us leave without an escort, as the city is on edge. Another murder was reported in the paper this morning. Like last time, they left the body in a cathedral. Maxine's stepfather offered the article to me, extending it over a steaming carafe of coffee this morning. "Another body," he said.

"I'm sorry," I said, shaking my head, refusing the paper. "I have a weak stomach."

I don't need to read the details in the paper to be on the edge of vomiting. My head has been pounding all day, which hasn't helped things. Lena has checked my pupils at least three times. I insist I'm fine, but I may be lying to myself.

We follow her to the Impressionists Hall, their blurry colors dancing over walls. Degas's ballerinas in their pale blue and baby pink seem to dance right over the walls.

In the center of the room is a statue in bronze of a young girl posing in her tutu. Her hands are clasped behind her back, her head arched to the ceiling.

I wander over to her and re-create the pose, lacing my hands together at the base of my spine. And for a moment, I just breathe.

Nina skips over and pokes me in the side, snapping me back to reality. "Your feet are in the wrong position," she corrects me. "Like this." She does a perfect impression of the statue, right down to the way the satin ribbon at the end of her braid hangs down her back. One flawless pirouette later, she skips away again, leaving me laughing.

We stroll to the next gallery, filled with washed-out, dreamy watercolors. "These are my favorites," I declare.

"They say Impressionists painted rain as a metaphor for washing the streets of the blood of the Revolution," Maxine says beside me. I consider the painting. "Hmm," I reply, noncommittal.

What if they just liked the rain, I want to say. What if they thought it was pretty and it was as simple as that? I'm so tired of trying to decipher meaning, of trying to decode secrets. Rain is never just rain. A key is never just a key. Death isn't death. It's exhausting. I'm exhausted. It would be nice to be washed clean.

I blink to clear my head and move through the gallery.

We pass through the Renaissance next, Maxine and Lena trying to swallow their giggles at all the truly hideous Baby Jesuses, haloed in gold, beatific in the arms of very stern-looking Marys. "Why does he have the face of a grown man?" Lena laughs. "You're going to hell for that," Maxine replies, but she's laughing too.

Next is the hall of Greek statues, standing above us, tall and chalk white.

There's a laughing group of schoolchildren in matching straw hats and wide-collared little blazers, weaving between us and the busts.

In the hall of Dutch still lifes, Lena sits down on a bench and unpacks her paints. She pulls out a canvas only a few inches wide and squeezes out globs of oil paint onto a tray for mixing. Bright red, sunshine yellow, vibrant blue, titanium white, and from them, she creates magic.

We watch in silence, the sun streaming in from the skylight, as she re-creates a pale pink peony on a dark wood table. In one clever stroke, she's created a perfect shadow; in another, a drooping petal. I could watch her work for hours. We sit there until Nina tugs us along and Lena declares the painting "decent enough." I think it's more than decent, and tell her so. "Can I have it when it dries?" I ask. Lena wraps the canvas in cheesecloth and tucks it back into her bag. "Let me paint you something better than this."

I throw an arm around her shoulder, despite her being taller than me. She laughs and ducks down to put us on an even level. "Nope, I want that one," I say.

This would be a nice day, if not for our true mission.

The key we seek is in a deceptively simple glass case, off to the side of the room in a dim gallery of eighteenth-century European realists.

The room is empty of schoolchildren and nuns and tourists like us, and I understand why. It's by far the most boring gallery we've been in so far. Paintings are arranged from floor to ceiling, in similar hues of dark reds and forest greens. Nearly all depict bowls of fruit or flower arrangements in varying states of decay.

Except for one. It's tucked most of the way up the wall, like a secret. It's of a man hunched and clutching a sheet over his face. Above him fly three figures wearing pointed hats, holding the body of a writhing man between them. The sky behind them is pitch black.

I check the placard: WITCHES IN FLIGHT, FRANCISCO GOYA, 1798.

"It's in here," Maxine nearly whispers from where she stands at the case.

It's set quietly, in the green velvet of the case, nearly comical with its incongruity.

"Why don't we just steal it now?" I ask.

Maxine narrows her eyes in consideration, then extends a hand and whispers, "*Briseadh.*"

The lock on the case does not budge.

I don't know if it's because the lock is enchanted, something from the Sons, or perhaps the magic going haywire from the open veil has something to do with it.

Suddenly Maxine stumbles backward, snatching her hand to her side as if she's been burnt.

I know without having to ask that she's just felt it too, the horrible shocking. Her eyes are frightened as they meet mine.

The three of us jump as a man in a black guard's uniform appears behind us. "Can I help you ladies?"

"No!" we all say at the same time.

Nina scurries into the room, a giant smile across her face. "You have to see this one!" she exclaims. "There's a mermaid!"

We should have known it wouldn't be that easy.

Lena and I share a glance once out in the hallway. I know she's considering our options too. I could control the body of one guard, assuming my magic is working, but more than one and we'd be out of our depths. And then we'd have to get out of the museum without getting caught, and we have Nina with us.

It's impossible.

I spend the rest of the museum trip lost in thought, considering my options. We could break into the Louvre at night, but I'm sure there are guards patrolling then, too. We could come back with disguises and weapons and a getaway driver, conducting a smash and grab like proper criminals. I could ask my father, but I'd really rather do anything but that.

We're nearly to the exit, making our way across the shimmering main entry hall, when a voice snaps me out of my own head. "Maxine, *cherie*!" an older woman in an elegant purple hat covered in silk rosettes calls. She rushes over to us and greets Maxine with a kiss on both cheeks.

"My schoolmates, Lena and Frances. We're all studying art history at Barnard." She feeds her the same fake story we devised on the boat. "This is my mother's old friend Mrs. Grenoble."

The woman smiles at the introduction. "Oh, it is lovely to see you, Maxine, and how delightful you are a student of art history. Your late father would be delighted."

"Thank you, ma'am."

Mrs. Grenoble gasps as a sudden realization hits her. "Will you girls be joining us at the fundraising gala? As art history students, you simply must attend! They're building a new rococo wing and charity is so important for a young girl. I sent your mother the invitation, but you should all come."

"It's a generous offer, Mrs. Grenoble," Maxine responds politely. I catch her eye and widen my eyes. She understands immediately. "We'd love to attend."

Maxine is thinking what I'm thinking: a crowded gala is the perfect place for a robbery.

We bid our goodbyes and step out into a glorious blue day.

"We'll need a plan for the night of the fundraiser," Lena says low so Nina won't hear.

I nod. "The guards will be distracted then, I hope."

"We'll need more than just the three of us."

The pit in my stomach tells me she's right.

It's windy in Paris this morning. The city sprawls out in front of us. Leaves race down cobblestones, followed by flurries of dust and pollen. I sent Oliver a message via courier last night asking him to meet us, and he arrived right after breakfast.

Lena, Maxine, Oliver, Finn, and I have ended up at the café across the street from Maxine's flat, at the largest table they have. It's in the back, near the swinging door to the kitchens. Every time the waiter has to come out with a new tray of something it knocks into Finn's elbow.

At one point nearly an entire glass of ice water is spilled on his shoe. "Can we move, perhaps?" he asks.

"No," Maxine cuts him off. "As I was saying, we'll need to get the blueprints."

Lena has seated herself as far from Finn as the table allows, leaving Maxine and me next to him. He's hunched over the notepad he's pulled from his breast pocket.

"I can do that," Oliver says.

Finn scribbles something down. "We can't rely on Frances's magic to get in and out, it's too unpredictable."

"I agree." It makes me feel useless that I'm the one who got us into the mess and the one least able to help.

Oliver is still scowling like he has been since we walked into the guest room this morning to find Finn reading Emily Brontë in the window seat. The maid brought him clothing from Maxine's stepfather, and the fine white shirt and linen suit jacket hung a little big off his shoulders.

"Oliver, lad, good morning." He greeted Oliver as if he hadn't given him the black eye he was currently sporting.

Oliver said nothing. If I had to guess, he physically bit his tongue to stop himself.

He's been frowning since, looking alternately between Finn and me, a look on his face like there's a math equation he can't get right.

"My stepfather won't let us go to the gala without escorts. But he'll be thrilled to give us the tickets if it means an evening with an eligible suitor," Maxine explains.

"Pascal will come," Oliver says. "I'm sure of it."

"And I know Pascal," Finn retorts. "It works out perfectly. You'll take Lena, Pascal takes Maxine, I'll take Frances."

I kick him hard under the table.

A muscle in Oliver's jaw flexes. "I'm not dignifying that with a response."

"It's not a terrible plan," Maxine considers. "Well, not the escort part, but the gala part."

Oliver nods toward Finn. "Behave yourself or I'll black your other eye to match."

Finn just chuckles. The tips of Oliver's ears go red, and I place my hand on his knee to soothe him.

I'd also like to punch Finn, but it's hardly the time to be fighting. Once the veil is closed, I'll let Oliver do whatever he wants to Finn. I'll tend to his bloody fists when he's done, then take a turn myself.

But for now, I pass Finn the carafe of coffee and play nice.

Slowly, over the course of croissants and so many espressos my stomach aches, a plan comes into focus.

Finn comes to me in my dreams that night. We're standing in a rain-soaked field. The sky is rolling and angry, the soft grass beneath our bare feet is drenched, but we are dry. It's so green here, it even smells green. I don't know this place. I wonder if it's Ireland.

"You really won't leave me be, will you?" I greet him.

He shakes his head and laughs quietly. "Oh, love, we both know you don't want that."

"Did you interrupt my rest to say stupid things?"

"No." He shakes his head and his face turns grim. "I came to tell you if we're caught by any Sons at the gala, pretend you don't know me."

"Do you expect them to be there?"

Finn sighs. His curls blow gently across his forehead. "If the key is real, I can't imagine they'll leave it unguarded during such a public event."

"Will they hurt you?" I ask.

"Yes." His response is simple and immediate.

I laugh, but there's no joke here. "You're trying to protect me?"

He furrows his brows. "That's what you don't understand, Frances. I'm always trying to protect you."

I wake with tears running down my face in rivulets like raindrops, but I don't remember beginning to cry.

CHAPTER SEVENTEEN

The last time I went to a gala in a fancy dress, the night began with a murder and throwing the commissioner's body in the river, and ended with me sobbing at Maxine's bedside accusing her of killing my brother.

She's laughing now as she passes me a ruby-encrusted headband. "Don't hurl this one at me, I beg you."

"I thought you'd said all was forgiven," I joke, but the guilt that rests inside me blinks awake at her jab. There's a sick feeling in my stomach tonight, heavier than just nerves.

"Ahh, but not forgotten."

I laugh along with her, but still feel a little like crying.

She hands Lena a pair of emerald earrings next. "Perfect against your hair. Don't tell Maman I stole them off her vanity."

It would be easy to pretend we were getting ready for a party if not for the small, sheathed blades Maxine and Lena have pressed to their thighs under their skirts.

They offered me one as well, but the idea of stabbing someone sent me reeling so horribly I had to excuse myself and put my head between my legs to get my breathing back to normal. In the end, Maxine accepted my simple "no, thank you" without further debate.

Maxine's mother and stepfather were easily convinced to secure us tickets to tonight's gala after Mrs. Grenoble paid a call. "I should have thought of it earlier," Maxine's mother replied. "As long as you have escorts," her stepfather replied.

"Very acceptable ones," Maxine replied with a self-satisfied nod. Oliver and Pascal will be here to fetch us soon. Finn, I assume, is somewhere down the hall getting dressed by Maxine's stepfather's valet.

I haven't seen Finn in nearly twenty-four hours, except in my dreams. We've told him to make himself scarce, but what does that matter when he's always *there* in my head. He's like a shadow I can't shake, he flits just out of vision, always behind me, always watching. I used to relish the weight of his eyes on me, but now I wish I could free myself from them.

Greta startles us with a knock at the door. "They're here, girls. You look lovely."

Maxine and Lena are breathtaking in gowns made by the DuPre family's Parisian couturier. Lena swishes her silk emerald-green skirts to the door and asks, "Are you ready?"

"Frances looks as green as your dress, but I have never been better," Maxine replies.

Oliver and Pascal are standing in the drawing room, their shiny shoes sinking into the thick carpet, nervous smiles on both their faces.

From the outside this moment must look sweet. It's easy to squint and imagine my life reflected through a mirror. This moment should be pretty, instead of warped and fake.

Oliver draws in a soft gasp when he sees me. "You look beautiful." The cuffs of his jacket brush gently against his wrists. I want to place my fingers where the fabric meets skin and see if his pulse is hammering like mine. But Greta would never approve of such an unladylike show of affection, so I clutch my beaded bag instead. It matches my dress exactly, the same shade of purple so pale it's nearly gray. Silver beads swirl into flower patterns around my neckline and waist.

"You as well." I turn my head to hide my blush and accidentally meet Lena's eye. She swallows a laugh.

Oliver takes my arm. "I can nearly imagine this is a normal evening."

"But it's not." The words are sharper than I mean them to be.

As if to remind us, Finn comes padding into the room, grinning and infuriatingly casual. He's made no attempt to tame his curls and is clearly wearing a tuxedo borrowed from Maxine's stepfather. The valet has done his best to tack up the pant legs, but the shoulders are visibly too big. It has the effect of making Finn look gangly and young, so different next to pristine Oliver. There's a shadow of purple around his right eye, fading to sickly green, still healing from where Oliver punched him.

"Shall we?" Oliver looks as if he still wishes to hit him.

Oliver's driver is idling outside, so he takes the boys, while

Maxine, Lena, and I pile into the back of the DuPre family's vehicle.

The back seat is tense with nervous energy.

"Are you sure about this?" I ask.

"No," Maxine and Lena answer in chorus. I do appreciate their unwillingness to lie to me.

The drive isn't long, but each pitch of the vehicle over cobblestoned streets has me threatening to spill my guts.

Maxine places a hand on my bouncing knee. "It's going to be all right. We have a plan."

"We have half a plan."

"I think at least two-thirds of a plan," Lena replies. It does nothing to quiet my nerves.

Paris prides itself on their adaptation to electric lights, but the Louvre Museum looks like something from a medieval painting tonight. The steps are lined with torches that look like person-sized golden goblets. The flames flicker against the pale stone of the building and in the eyes of the upper echelons of Parisian society.

Maxine looks at home among them in her midnight-blue House of Worth gown, but I know her well enough to know, like all of us tonight, she's wearing a carefully crafted disguise.

The beads of my earrings clink in my ear with each step up, like sleigh bells or prisoner's chains.

"Ready?" Lena asks. Her dark hair is wound on top of her head tonight, a coronet of emeralds set against it, matching the earrings.

"The answer has to be yes, doesn't it?"

"We've planned for this."

But not enough.

We don't have enough information about the key, the veil, or museum security to give me any real confidence we'll be able to pull it off.

But I remember the dead boy in the catacombs, and I know I have no other choice but to try. Every day the veil is still open means another person potentially lost.

I wish desperately we could just tell the Sons and my father what is going on and ask for their help. We know the location of the veil and they have the key, but if they have the key and know about the murders, I fear they could be a part of it. I won't risk them taking the key to somewhere we can't get it. We can't tip our hands this early lest we be outplayed.

And there is the tiniest, weakest part of me that fears what they'd do to Finn. Relying on them for help almost certainly means turning him over.

The bells of the church down the street begin to peal the moment our heels hit the stone steps.

They clang, one after the other, echoing off the night nine times. Each hit of the bells reverberates off the bones of my rib cage, and I know in my bones we have a long night ahead of us.

The boys meet us at the base of the stairs standing close together like real friends. I'm probably the only one who notices the way Oliver's hands are balled into fists inside the silk-lined pockets of his tuxedo pants. I can't quite hear them from this distance, but Finn has said something to make Pascal laugh. Oliver glares down at him and Pascal's grin falls. Finn shrugs, undeterred.

We reach them and Oliver threads his arm through mine, the picture of a respectable escort. Lena takes Pascal's arm with a grimace. Finn attempts to take Maxine's hand in his but earns himself a sharp jab to the ribs.

"That'll bruise," he hisses.

"Good." Maxine smiles.

The crowd envelops us, and soon we are mere pieces of the sparkling, silk landscape. When we went to the Musée D'Orsay last week, I saw a painting made up of thousands of little dots. From far away it looked like a seascape, but the closer you got the less it made any sense.

I imagine us now as single dots in a painting. Blurry and inconsequential on our own. Hopefully, no one will look too closely tonight. The plan depends on it.

Maxine presents our thick invitations to the doorman, who looks them over with white-gloved hands and waves us inside. I don't know why I'm already nervous. We are invited guests. Nothing about what we're doing now is a trick.

The marble entryway of the Louvre buzzes like a beehive. I take a moment to really feel the ground beneath my fancy borrowed shoes. I savor the peace that comes with being in the eye of a hurricane before steeling myself to join the storm.

Oliver must sense my panic because his warm hand finds mine and squeezes. "Shh, I've got you."

A hand appearing as if from nowhere passes me a glass of champagne.

Oliver and I pour our flutes into a massive arrangement of white lilies.

Finn raises his to his lips, but it is promptly swatted away by Maxine, who finds a potted plant to dump it into.

We made an agreement tonight. We need to have our wits about us.

It's easy enough to get through the terrible banquet dinner. Oliver quiets the incessant shaking of my leg with a gentle touch of his hand. Finn complains about not being able to get a drink. Pascal makes jokes in French that only Maxine laughs at. And Lena just watches, her eyes wide, like she's seeing somewhere beyond this room.

It's after the delicate porcelain dessert plates are cleared that our work truly begins.

There are easily three hundred people here tonight and our main task is simply not to draw attention to ourselves. It's why we came with male escorts. Three unaccompanied ladies would have drawn too much attention, and our work is easier to get done without the son of a steel magnate asking if he can call on us at the flat tomorrow.

Oliver leans down to whisper in my ear. "Two dances, then up the stairs." I nod.

The front hall of the museum has been turned into a ballroom. A stage has been set up on the far wall and is currently playing host to an entire orchestra and a corps of twirling ballerinas.

Lena appears at my side. "Five minutes until Pascal and I go up."

"You sure you can get it unlocked?" Oliver asks. We didn't have great luck before, but without Nina present as a distraction, we're hopeful we'll be successful tonight.

Lena looks unbothered. "If I can't, Maxine will have a shot after I am through."

She doesn't say it out loud, but Finn and I know as well as she does that we are all but useless tonight. Our magic is too erratic to be relied upon for something this important.

Above our head, chandeliers sparkle, and I imagine how good it must feel to be one of tonight's guests. One of the people who know nothing of magic or what lies beyond death or how it feels like to take another person's life. How warm and comfortable it must be to dress in fancy clothes and have the candlelight filtered through a crystal chandelier turn the irises of your eyes golden. I meet the eye of a girl who can't be much older than me on the arm of her handsome husband and feel the uncomfortable roil of envy.

The band strikes up a waltz, and Oliver takes me in his arms.

"Have you been practicing since our last dance?" he jokes at the way I confidently press my hand into his, the way he taught me.

"Maybe I'm just a prodigy?"

I remember the year Oliver turned fifteen, he was growing so fast it was as if he barely had control over his limbs. My mother threatened to ban him from our home, he'd bumped into and broken so many things. I can still picture the exact cornflower-blue vase that was nearly the final straw. There's nothing of his once-incoordination present tonight. The pressure of his hand on my back is steady. He holds my hand so firmly I forget to be afraid of tripping over my own feet.

He's so steady now. My brother would have liked this grown-up Oliver, I think. Though I'm sure he would have made fun of all his fancy suits.

It would be easy to get lost in this moment, twirling across a ballroom, flowers around us blurring in and out as I spin. Candlelight reflects in Oliver's eyes and I ache for him, I always do, but this moment feels like a window into a life we could have had. A life where my brother was alive and Oliver asked me to court him on a sunny Sunday afternoon in the park after William ribbed him for it. A life where Oliver slipped a diamond ring on my finger in the quiet of his dorm room and my brother walked me down the aisle. I think I would have been happy. I don't think I would have been bored.

My fantasy falls as quick as a curtain at a play as my attention snaps to a man. He's a face in focus in the middle of a blurry crowd. He's smiling, holding a crystal glass of red wine, and wearing a wrinkled suit. He's deep in conversation with another middle-aged man, and I pray he stays distracted.

"*Shit*," I whisper.

Oliver's eyes go wide with fear, and the moment between us is snapped like a fraying thread.

"What is it?" he asks. His hand is still steady on my back. We have to keep dancing as to not draw attention to ourselves.

"My father. Two o'clock. Brown hair. Talking to the white-haired man in the pinstripes."

Oliver searches the crowd, but I can tell when he finds him by the way his face crumples. "He looks like Will."

"I know."

"So what do we do?"

"Pray he doesn't see us. Get upstairs as quickly as possible."

Just then, Finn comes into view, crossing the ballroom alone. It is a relief not to see Maxine by his side. My father has met Maxine, and it would only be polite for him to stop her and say hello.

But Finn is blessedly alone. He crosses so near my father they could reach out and touch. But neither pays the other much mind. And why would they? Finn has no idea it's my father, and my father has no idea he's breathing the same air as the boy who killed his son.

I hate and pity them both in such different, confusing ways.

The orchestra lowers their bows, the waltz ends, and Oliver grabs my hand and tugs me toward the grand staircase that leads to the second floor. Lena and Pascal should already be upstairs. Maxine and Finn should follow soon after. But if Finn was alone, where is Maxine? Uneasiness takes root in my throat, slippery and sick.

My foot is on the first step when Finn rushes by us, pulling Maxine by the hand. Gala attendees must assume they are lovers looking for a dark corner, or particularly enthusiastic art lovers looking for the galleries, but I know it means something has gone wrong.

It's imperative Oliver and I remain casual. We can't turn back now that we're already on the stairs. It would mean facing the whole of the room, letting them get a good look at our faces, a young unmarried couple opening themselves up for the gossip of the rich and bored. We need to remain as invisible as possible, so slowly, we climb.

At the very top of the stairs, we pause and tilt our heads up to the statue on the landing. *Winged Victory.* Carved from cream-colored stone, radiant and broad-shouldered and headless, she takes my breath away. I try to summon some of the bravery imbued in the wings that stretch proudly behind her.

I want to fly away tonight. I don't want to have to do any of this. But I have no wings. My only choice is to stand and face it.

We turn into the gallery of the Impressionists, close to the meeting spot, when the movement of a figure in the shadows startles me.

Standing in the corner of the near-empty gallery is my father. And he's not alone. He's surrounded by four other middle-aged men who look to be discussing something serious.

Oliver and I stop short at the top of the stairs, watching them.

I startle as Maxine appears behind me. She opens her mouth to say something, but I bring my fingers to my lips and gesture with my head toward the group of Sons.

My father and the other men nod, then rush off in two groups, down two different hallways, their urgency unmistakable. Are they going for the key too? My panic heightens.

Oliver, Maxine, and I walk away as quickly as we're able without drawing attention to ourselves, and then, finally upon turning into a dark, empty corridor, we begin to sprint.

The gallery where the case is displayed is completely dark. Maxine conjures light between her hands, illuminating our way. The statues cast long shadows, giving them the effect of being alive, watching us.

The case is sitting pristine and untouched, right where we left it. We're out of breath by the time we reach it.

Lena, Pascal, and Finn enter the gallery right after we do. "No security in the gallery to the left," Finn confirms.

"Nor the right," Lena says.

Finn huffs, "Though it would have been nice to investigate with the help of my date."

Maxine rolls her eyes at him. "I am not your date."

"Do you have another? Is it that pretty girl you abandoned me to go talk with downstairs?"

Maxine flushes red and looks to the carpet. "She is pretty, isn't she?" she says.

"Who?" I demand.

"Anais," Maxine answers.

That is bad news. If Anais is here, then any number of Brothers of Morte d'Arthur could be present, and we already have our hands full avoiding the Sons.

"We don't have time to waste then."

Maxine approaches the case, lays her hands on it, and tries the unlocking spell once more. She jerks her hands back as if she's been burnt and curses under her breath.

Lena tries next, with more powerful spell work than we tried on the trip with Nina, conjuring a small flame between her hands and holding it to the glass. Like Maxine, she is nearly thrown backward as the glass repels the spell.

"It's warded," a voice comes out of the darkness. The six of us jump.

Standing in the doorway, silhouetted by moonlight, is Anais with her dark hair done up and covered with pearls. Her dark satin gown glistens, even in this low light.

I take a few steps back and ball my fists at my side, ready for a fight. But Anais strides into the dark gallery room as casual as you please, her gown swishing behind her.

"Your spells won't work."

"Why are you here?" I demand. I look between the six of us and Anais. We could take her on our own, but if she's brought the duke or other Brothers of Morte d'Arthur with her, we might be in trouble.

Anais's glance flits to Maxine. "I wanted to keep talking to her, and then she snuck off, so I followed. Above all things I am . . . curious."

"You're not here to stop us?" It feels stupid to ask out loud.

"No." Anais smiles and strides closer.

"So what do we do?" Maxine asks Anais, gesturing to the display case.

Anais shrugs. "*J'ne sais pas.*"

Just then—the sound of male voices and rapid footsteps come echoing through the halls.

I look frantically between my friends. "We don't have much time."

"What do we do?" Oliver asks.

Maxine looks to Anais, then back to us. Then she levitates the entire glass display case and whispers, "Run."

Maxine's steps are jerky—levitating the entire case must be taking immense effort—but we go as fast as we're able, down the hall, away from the approaching voices.

We studied the maps of this floor of the museum for days. We take one turn, then another, then one more, leading us to a hallway mostly used for service.

It's dark and still and in the middle, there is a door. Lena flings the door open and we scurry inside.

The room is so dark it takes a moment for my eyes to adjust. Six figures file in behind me, all breathing heavily. Maxine drops the display case in the center of the small room, and we shut the door.

I prop a bucket and a mop under the handle as a makeshift lock, but it won't hold much at bay.

We're in a glorified supply closet. It was the biggest workroom we were able to locate on the blueprints Oliver found at the Sorbonne's library last week.

I attempt to make my way across the small space, but bang my knee terribly against the corner of the display case.

There are no windows in this room. The only light available is what is filtering in through the bottom of the door.

Lena sparks a small golden globe of light between her palms.

I jump, finding Anais to my left. The hall was dark. I didn't realize she'd followed us in. "What are you doing here?"

She laughs, "You really don't like me much, do you?"

"I don't know you. I don't trust you," I answer honestly.

Anais leans against the display case. "Fair is fair. This is certainly more exciting than the dog and pony show going on downstairs."

"She's not going to rat us out," Maxine says confidently.

"How can you say that? You've known her for five minutes." She's the great-granddaughter of the duke we all witnessed murder a man in cold blood. I know well enough we are not the actions of our relatives, but this feels extreme.

"I'm a good judge of character."

"Maxine . . . ," Lena cautions.

"We can't very well let her out now," Finn reasons. "She could go and tell them where we are. It's best to let her stay."

Anais smirks at Maxine. "So am I your prisoner?"

Maxine arches a brow. "Seems that way."

"What now?" I ask.

"We stick to the plan," Finn replies. "There's nothing else to do. We can't go out there."

"With the case gone, will the museum be locked down?" Oliver asks. We planned for this possibility.

"The entrances and exits will be monitored for the rest of the night, certainly. We'll simply have to hope they don't have enough staff to do a full sweep. The halls of this museum span miles. It's unlikely they'll check every closet and workroom," Finn replies.

"And if they do?" Lena asks.

"We run," Finn says.

And so begins what we all know will be one of the longest nights of our lives.

We all stand against the wall while Pascal levitates the display case to the front of the room, blocking the door. It's better than the mop and bucket I attempted.

Lena and Maxine try a few more times half-heartedly to unlock it with magic, but the lock doesn't budge. It doesn't much matter. We have hours ahead of us now.

Finn sinks to the floor first, then Lena, then Maxine, until we're all lying down on the cold marble. Oliver takes off his suit jacket and bunches it behind my head as a pillow.

Maxine forcibly tugs Finn's off his shoulders and wraps herself in it. "What if I wanted that?" he asks her.

"That makes it better," she replies.

"Should we sleep in shifts?" Oliver asks.

"Is there any point?" Maxine says. "We'll hear them try to move the case and if they find us, additional time won't help."

She's right and we know it.

"So we try to sleep?" I ask. "Deal with the case in the morning?"

"I think so," Maxine says.

Oliver is sitting with his back against the wall and his legs stretched out in front of him. I pull the jewels from my carefully pinned hair and lay my head in his lap.

His hands find all the sore spots where the pins were just digging in. He presses his fingers, not too hard but with real pressure, and I sigh. After a few moments he stills, but leaves his fingertips resting against my skull, warm and heavy.

From across the small, dark space, Finn scoffs. Or it might be a cough. I don't care one way or the other.

I don't think I'll get much sleep, but I must drift off at some point because I wake to the sound of hushed voices.

The room is pitch dark, cold and hard. My hip is sore where it is pressed against the floor. I'll be bruised in the morning.

Maxine is asleep on Anais's shoulder. They whispered to each other long into the night, so quiet I couldn't follow their conversation.

Lena has fallen asleep on my stomach. There's something heavy in the air, and even in this windowless room. I am certain it is the dead of night.

"You won't even look at me." The deep Irish brogue is Finn's.

"You killed my best friend," Oliver whispers back. "I wish you were six feet deep. But unfortunately, you're breathing, so I wish you were anywhere on earth other than this room with—" Oliver pauses like he's thinking.

"With her, you mean?" Finn asks.

"With all of us. I'm halfway waiting for you to finish the job and kill the rest of us. You'd probably like that."

Finn's answer comes in one quick breath. "I wouldn't."

"Wouldn't like it or wouldn't do it?"

"Both. I wouldn't hurt you."

"I don't believe you," Oliver says.

"I wouldn't hurt you because it would hurt her. Do you believe that?" Finn says.

Oliver thinks for a moment. "I'm not sure how to believe anything you say."

I want to cry out, to open my mouth and say *something.* But I don't have the words. So I just listen and ache.

For a few minutes there is only the sound of our breathing, and I think the conversation must be over, but Finn speaks again.

"I am sorry. I told her but I never told you. I am sorry about William."

Oliver sniffs. I can't see his face but I can picture it, his pretty mouth turned down in a frown. "You don't deserve to say his name."

"I know." Finn sighs. "I just wanted you to know."

There's a soft thunk as Oliver leans his head back against the wall. "You've got a lot of nerve coming back here, I'll give you that."

"I'm trying to help. She asked me to help." Finn's whisper is slow and steady. There's no malice in his words.

"I know she did. I just wish she didn't need you."

"But she does, so I'm here."

"And what will you do when we're done?"

Finn pauses. "I'm not sure. I'm not sure about anything anymore."

Oliver sighs. He's tired but not defeated.

"What would you do if she left with me?" Finn asks in a whisper so quiet I wonder if he means for Oliver to answer at all.

"She won't."

"But what if she did? Would you try to kill me?"

Oliver laughs softly. "We're not all you, Finn. Regardless, you know as well as I do, she's not something to possess."

"Don't make me out to be the villain here," Finn says.

"You are, quite literally, the villain here."

"But I'm helping, aren't I?"

"That's what I'm trying to figure out. I don't know why."

"Because she asked me to. Because I care. Because I'm trying to be . . . ," Finn trails off.

"To be?" Oliver prompts.

Finn is quiet for so long I don't think he means to answer him. But then he says, "Better." It comes from the very back of his throat, like it pains him.

"Jesus." Maxine's sharp whisper pierces the darkness. "If you don't shut up, I'll kill the both of you. Maybe I should seduce Frances away from the both of you just to prove a point. She's fine, I love her, but good Lord . . ."

I nearly laugh but then I remember I'm supposed to be asleep.

I wake again what must be a few hours later to the sound of shattering glass. I'm gasping, blood thrumming with nerves, up and on my feet before I realize what's happening.

Maxine is standing in front of the now-shattered glass case, a ball-peen hammer slung casually in her hand.

"Good morning," she says to me cheerily. "We forgot we could break things without magic."

Anais is awake, standing next to Maxine and grinning widely. The pearls in her hair are askew and her dress is wrinkled. "Hammers, who knew, such a useful tool."

I laugh and laugh until the rest of them are all laughing too, all of us delirious from lack of sleep. Leave it to magicians to get so hung up on using magic for everything, they forget about the simplest solution. We were guilty of it, and it appears the Sons were as well.

Lena grabs Finn's discarded suit jacket from the floor and wraps it around her hand and up her forearm before reaching into the glass case to withdraw the key.

"What does it feel like?" I ask.

She weighs it in her hand. "Like a key." She tucks it inside the beaded emerald-green bag that matches her dress and nods toward the door. "We haven't heard anyone in hours. If the glass breaking sent anyone looking, we should get out now, while we still can."

"Agreed," Oliver says. He wipes sleep from his eyes and extends a hand to Maxine, who pulls him up from the floor. "Let's go."

The hallway is washed gray in the watery light of dawn seeping in from the skylights overhead.

The six of us peek our heads out the door but are met only with the sleepy silence of a city before its residents have risen.

Maxine looks to the right, then the left, then back to us. She nods once. We follow her.

We do our best to quiet the clacking of our footsteps against the stone floors, but Maxine, Lena, and I are wearing spindly, delicate little heels, so our efforts don't do much.

My heart is on the verge of jumping out of my skin. I once cried when a teacher scolded me for writing my cursive *D*s incorrectly. I don't have much of a stomach for openly breaking the law, no matter how many times I've done it now.

I know the story we've rehearsed. If we run into any guards, we'll simply pretend to be drunk and young and lost.

We're nearly to the exit when we hear the footsteps. Panicked, I glance to Maxine and Lena. "Do we run?" I whisper.

Male voices float down the hallway, angry male voices. "We've searched all night," one of them says.

"There are miles of galleries, they very well could still be here," another responds.

Finn curses under his breath.

They'll round the corner any moment and see us. We're in a hall of white marble statues with no hallways to duck down. Our only option is to fight or hide.

"Go," Anais hisses.

"What?" Maxine replies.

Anais takes her by the chin and kisses her on the cheek, leaving Maxine stunned and blushing. "I'll distract them. Better they suspect me than you. My great-grandfather can get me out of any trouble. I fear you may not share such luck. Take the key, and go." Anais takes off running before we can stop her.

Seconds later, one of the voices yells, "Wait! Stop!" and I know they've spotted her. We take our opportunity and run for the exit.

We crisscross through the corridors we studied so diligently on the map until we find the steel double doors that lead to the back service entrance.

Oliver extends both arms to push them open, and they swing out onto a back alleyway.

"Will Anais be all right?" Lena asks once we're out into the fresh air.

Maxine nods, unbothered. "I have no doubt."

We share looks of disbelief between us. Then I start to laugh. Maxine follows, then Lena, then the boys until we're nearly doubled over, tears in our eyes, like we've just heard the funniest joke ever told.

I realize it's probably just the sleep deprivation, but it is nice to feel light after a night that's been so heavy.

We walk back to the DuPres' flat as if we're floating on air. It would be easy to mistake us for a group of friends returning home after a night that went too long. At one point a baker unlocking his shop for the day is so charmed by us, he passes Maxine a paper bag of day-old *pains au chocolat*.

The sun rises over the Seine a soft, butter yellow, and the first morning summer rays feel like an embrace.

Oliver slings an arm heavy around my shoulder, and my joints feel loose with relief. I let myself imagine, for the first time since I arrived in France, that things may truly turn out all right.

We have the key to close the veil. Soon this nightmare will be finished and I can return to my perfectly pleasant holiday, wandering Paris hand in hand with the boy I love most.

Lena fears the key may be too simple. I don't think I deserve much from the universe, but perhaps it has decided to gift me this, finally, an easy solution.

Hand in hand with Oliver, I tilt my head up to the sky and let the sunrise warm the tired spot between my eyebrows.

It's good. This is good.

But then—

It isn't.

An ear-shattering pop bursts the precious bubble of joy. At first, I think it's a machine backfiring, but then I hear the screaming, see the blood.

Finn is still upright, but he's stumbling, hunched so far over his fingertips are nearly dragging on the ground.

Just when I think he's about to fall, Oliver scoops under his arms and pulls him upright. My breath catches in my throat at the sight of him. The entire left side of Finn's body is covered in blood. It's dripping all over Oliver, marring his white tuxedo shirt with a rapidly spreading stain. Blood drips from between Finn's fingertips where his arms lie limp at his side.

"Run," he gasps. "*Run.*"

CHAPTER EIGHTEEN

And we do. Oliver hauls Finn along with him, and we sprint, tripping over our own feet, going as fast as our legs will carry us until our lungs are screaming for air.

From behind us I hear the sickening *pop* again as whoever is chasing us shoots once more.

I whirl my head around to look behind me, my carefully pinned chignon from last night unraveling with every step. It is not easy to run in a heavy silk gown and heels, but we manage somehow.

We turn the corner and burst onto the next quiet street like an explosion. Maxine's building is in view now. We're so close.

Maxine pulls the key out of her handbag and with astonishingly steady hands, she unlocks the gate that leads to the front door of the building.

Lena and I barrel in after her. Oliver and Finn aren't far behind.

Finn is still conscious, which is a good sign, but he's gone so pale and has a hazy look in his eyes.

The gate swings behind us with a clang and locks automatically. I place my hands on my knees and suck in a breath.

Cautiously Lena looks through the bars of the locked entrance. "There's no one coming, I don't think they followed."

"Let's not wait around to find out," Maxine says.

The flat is quiet as the elevator dings and we step out. Oliver shoves his jacket against where Finn's shoulder is bleeding to keep his blood from making a mess of the floors.

We collapse into the guest room at the end of the hall where Finn has taken up residence.

Oliver, who is still half supporting Finn's body weight, shoves him hard off his shoulder and onto the floor. Finn winces as he falls.

"You're going to get blood on the carpet," Maxine says, and wastes no time grabbing fresh towels from the bathroom.

I don't want to be the person to check on Finn. He's breathing heavily, but we all are. There is an enormous amount of blood, but it all seems to be coming from his shoulder, which is a good sign. I tamp down the instinct to kneel at his side and play nurse.

Maxine tosses him the towels. He strips off his shirt, soaked through with blood, and presses one of them to his shoulder.

We take a moment to catch our breaths. After a short while he says, "I think it just grazed me."

"All right," Maxine says.

I can't say I want Finn dead, but the three of us refuse to show him any real sympathy.

"I can give you tips on gunshot wound recovery if you'd like,"

Oliver snipes. I wonder if Finn even remembers one of his men from the Sons shot Oliver nearly two years ago.

Finn steps into the bathroom. "I'll clean the wound myself, thank you."

We're startled by a knock at the door. Oliver ducks behind the bed. Before we can panic, Greta appears in the doorway with her morning sterling silver carafe of coffee.

"Oh!" She jumps at the sight of us sitting on the floor. Lena pulls a silk throw pillow over the bloodstain on the carpet.

Just when I think we're about to be scolded a small smile appears on her face. "I was young once. Don't let your mother see, Maxine darling. I'll leave you to it."

She shuts the door behind her as Finn strolls out of the bathroom, shirtless with a towel wrapped around his upper arm and tied across his bare chest.

"I'll live," he announces. "Much to your displeasure, I'm sure."

"Oh, Finn, we don't think enough about you to be displeased. Don't flatter yourself," Maxine replies.

Oliver stands and walks to the window. "No one out there. I don't think we were followed."

"So who shot at us?" I ask.

"At Finn," Maxine corrects.

Finn sucks back on his teeth. "It was the Sons. I'm sure of it."

"How can you be so sure?" I ask.

"They've wanted me dead since New York."

"But that means they saw you at the gala. It could mean they know we have the key now. It can't be that hard to put two and two together."

"All the more reason to fix this quickly." We have nearly everything. All we need now is the spell to close the veil and it will be finished and Finn's enemies will no longer be my problem.

Finn sighs and lowers himself onto the carpet, joining our circle. "So, shall we see what all of this trouble was for?"

Maxine levitates her handbag across the room and pulls out the key. It's about the length of her palm, gold all over, and faded with age.

"May I?" Oliver extends his hand, grasps the key, raises it to his lips, and *bites*.

There's a chorus of confused cries, but he pulls the key out from between his teeth and says, "It's real gold." He points to the tiny dent in the key where his incisor just was. "This is how you tell."

"And this helps us how?" Lena asks.

"I don't know, I just thought having as much information about the key as possible would be helpful."

Oliver talks with his hands. The key grasped between his long fingers reflects the sunlight streaming in from the window.

"Wait!" I cry out. "Wait, let me see."

Oliver passes me the key, and I tilt it on its side. On the small side of the shank there is an engraving. In elegant script, shining as if it could have been done just yesterday, are the words *Si Sin Morte.*

I whisper them under my breath.

Beside me Oliver goes completely still. "We will be deathless," he mutters.

"What?"

"That's what it says. It's Latin. *We will be deathless.*"

* * *

Oliver slips out the door and down the elevator before breakfast, and Maxine, Lena, and I go to our respective rooms to dress.

I have Maxine's mother's lady's maid, Gabrielle, this morning. She combs the snarls out of my hair with a gentle touch and removes the heavy rubies dangling from my ears.

She doesn't speak much English and I don't speak French, but she gives me a conspiratorial smile in the mirror like she thinks my night was much more fun than it actually was.

She dresses me in a gauzy white tea gown that has me feeling like a ghost haunting the halls of this house.

Finn is already at the breakfast table when Lena, Maxine, and I walk in arm in arm not looking at all like we committed several crimes last night.

"How was the gala?" Maxine's mother asks.

"I can't believe you didn't take me," Nina adds with a pout.

"Lovely," Maxine says after a sip of orange juice.

From the head of the table, her stepfather swears behind his morning paper.

"*Qu'est-ce que c'est, chéri*?" Maxine's mother asks in her lilting voice.

"There's been another murder. The body of a young boy has been found in Église de Saint-Germain-des-Prés. Mutilated. What sort of monster is roaming Paris?"

Finn pushes back from the table in a sudden rush. "You'll have to excuse me."

"Where are you going?" I ask.

He glances up at the grandfather clock in the corner of the fine dining room. "To church."

He must be speaking in some kind of code, wanting me to follow him out the door. "I'll come too," I say, but Finn doesn't look relieved. He just looks confused.

I rush out the door behind him before Lena and Maxine have a chance to formulate their own lies and follow.

The elevator dings shut behind us. "What did you need?" I ask him.

He looks at me like I've grown a second head. "What do you mean?"

"You asked me to follow you."

"No, I did not. I said I was going to church."

"Yes, exactly, I thought that was code for something."

He chuckles. "What would it be code for? I'm truly going to church."

"I—" Words escape me. "But . . . why?"

He runs a hand through his curls and looks at the ground. "Because I used to go with my mam and it reminds me of home. And because I'm a sinner in need of redemption." He gestures between the two of us, to the invisible ties that bind us. "Isn't that the whole thing here? Redemption?"

The elevator dings as we reach the first floor. We step out onto the quiet street.

Maxine and Lena burst out from a side door. "Sorry! Had to take the stairs!" Maxine huffs.

"Oh Christ, not you, too," Finn mutters.

"Took us slightly longer to get away from the table," Maxine breathlessly explains. "I haven't been to church since I was nine and spit in the communion wine."

"And despite the Thomas School's best efforts, I am very pointedly uninterested in the Catholic Church," Lena says.

"So, my mother didn't believe our lies when we too tried to leave the table. Anyway, what is this about?"

I look Finn up and down. "He said he really is going to church."

"But . . . why?" Lena asks.

Finn throws his hands up in the air and winces at the movement in his wounded shoulder. "Can't a man go to church without being interrogated? Everyone in this city is going to church today!"

"An ordinary man can, but you cannot."

"I'm not your prisoner," he laughs.

"But you aren't our guest, either," Maxine says.

"So, what would you have me do?" Finn asks.

I sigh. "I'll go. I'll go to make sure he doesn't do anything else."

"You want to be my jailer?"

"You can hardly blame me for not trusting you."

"All right, then." He jerks his chin in the direction of the street. "Let's go to church."

"We don't have to go, do we?" Lena asks.

"Not if you don't want to," I say. It's not as if I could beat Finn in a physical fight, but I doubt it will come to anything of the sort. I just want to ensure he's not sneaking off to meet with someone or return to his strange settlement by the lake. We still need him to close the veil, even if we don't quite know how yet.

"Fantastic, let's go buy pastries," Maxine says. "Pray for me!" she calls over her shoulder on her way across the street. None of us are talking about the way Finn was shot just hours ago or what happened last night at the Louvre.

I've been accused of keepings things too close to my chest, but the others are just as guilty of it as I am. Why is it we're capable of facing down death together but so terrified of admitting we're terrified?

"Mass is at ten, fancy a stroll?" Finn asks.

I huff out something noncommittal but follow at his heels.

"I'm surprised you tagged along, I imagine you're tired after last night," he says after two blocks, casual like we're friends on a walk.

I don't want to answer. I don't want to be doing this with him at all. "I am. I'd rather be back in bed at Maxine's but I'm here instead, playing nanny to you."

"I didn't ask you to come," he laughs. "Perhaps you just wanted time with me?"

I punch him in the shoulder, right where I know the bullet grazed him.

He winces and I smile.

It isn't long before we reach the river. It makes me sick to walk with him alongside its banks.

Do you remember him? the most spiteful parts of me want to ask. *Did you walk alongside the river with my brother before you threw his body in?*

I hold the thought for a moment, pressing on it like a bruise, just to make sure it still twinges.

Finn makes it easy to forget he's hollow inside. Curly hair and a lopsided smile, quick to laugh. Yes, it's easy to un-focus my eyes and see him as the boy I once thought I loved. It would be so easy to hold his hand.

But he isn't that boy. That boy never existed.

My hands hang by my side, cold and trembling.

He's taken us to a church that could be one of any dozens in this city. Hewn from ancient-looking stone, it's made up of a rectangular main building and a tower topped with a sharp spire.

The small sign out front is barely visible, obscured by the parishioners streaming into the cathedral.

ÉGLISE DE SAINT-GERMAIN-DES-PRÉS.

"It's the oldest church in Paris," he says as if I asked.

Discomfort ripples through me. "Of all the Catholic churches in the city, why this one?"

He shrugs. "Because I wanted to see it."

I don't fight back, but he has the slippery "trust me" look in his eyes that I know means to do the opposite. Every nerve in my body is on high alert.

We join the stream of people and step into the halls. The temperature drops noticeably despite the crush of bodies. I crane my neck up to look at the ceiling, crisscrossed with flying buttresses and painted a navy blue almost the exact shade of the night sky.

"Beautiful," Finn mutters. "Makes our parish back home look like a sheepherder's cottage."

We shuffle into a pew, finding a space between two white-haired ladies speaking rapid French and a couple in their fifties not speaking at all.

It isn't long after we're seated that the priest walks down the center aisle, swinging a golden ball on a chain, pouring sickly sweet incense smoke into the worship hall.

He's wearing robes and saying something in a language that

might be French or might be Latin, but Finn's head is bowed reverently, regardless.

Catholic Mass is even longer than the quiet, homily-filled sermons I used to be dragged to at our small neighborhood church back in New York. I feel as if I am eight years old again, fidgeting, picking at my fingernails, counting the angels sketched in the tall stained-glass windows.

Their beady eyes stare back at me. I'm not sure if I believe in God, not in the literal sense anyway, but if there is a higher power to judge me, I do not think they would judge me favorably.

The priest drones on in French, but Finn watches with the reverence of a choirboy. His eyes are wide, the hard line of his jaw is relaxed, unclenched. A beam of light through the stained glass sends a slash of blue light across his face.

The congregation moves to their knees and Finn joins them. He bows his head and he prays.

There is a twinge of fondness in my heart, like a ghost coming back to wander the halls of the home it once inhabited. It's not real, it's not really here. But it used to be.

Finn is on his knees and he's praying, and there's no part of me that still believes in miracles, but still I have the urge to join him.

What would I pray for? For redemption? For peace? For him to be a better man?

I don't pray. There's no point. I stare at the altar and try to remember what my brother's face looked like.

When the final organ note is played and the long service is over, Finn doesn't rise immediately.

The congregants shuffle out the other end of the pew, leaving us alone.

Finn's eyes are wide and wet as he rises from his knees and looks over at me.

"Are you ready to leave?" I ask. I'm annoyed I've spent my whole morning with him rather than with Lena, Maxine, or Oliver.

"Not quite. I'll need to go to confession."

I swallow down a laugh, even though none of this is funny. "And will the priest forgive you for what you did to my brother?"

He nods. "That is his job."

"What will your penance be?"

He gestures between us. "It's this, I think."

I'm so disgusted I can no longer stand the sight of him. That vague stabbing sense of fondness is gone, lost like a wisp of incense smoke in the rafters.

"I don't intend to waste my whole day sitting around waiting for you, so please, keep the descriptions of your crimes brief."

He nods. "Will do."

The confession booth is across the main floor of the cathedral. Finn joins the small line and I stand behind him, shuffling my feet against the stone floors.

We stand in complete silence like strangers. I wish we were strangers. It would be simpler.

He walks into the booth with his head down. Good. I hope he is ashamed.

I sit in one of the pews and count every cross I can see. I'm at 113 before I run out.

I don't have to wait much longer until Finn comes out of the confessional. His face is a little red, but his eye is already swollen from Oliver's punch, so it's unclear if he's been shedding tears.

"What did the father say?"

"He told me to come back on Wednesday."

"That much to forgive, huh?" I joke but Finn doesn't smile. He's deadly serious as he replies, "Yes."

The flat is quiet when we return. Maxine has taken Nina to the carousel at the Jardin des Tuileries, and Lena is meeting with her art teacher. I make a mental note to ask the cook where best to procure a cake to celebrate her later.

Greta has left a note on my bed. On the front is my name, scrawled in Oliver's neat penmanship.

I unfold it.

A night just for us. Then you'll go back to saving the world. I hope you like opera.
—OHC

I bite my lip to hide my smile, but there is no one here to see me alone in my room.

I fall into the feather pillows of my bed and nap off last night's long hours sleeping on a marble floor, only waking when Gabrielle knocks at six p.m. to dress me.

Tonight, I'm in a borrowed gown of champagne gold duchess silk. Maxine leans in the doorway as Gabrielle laces me up. "You look like a Romanov."

"Thank you?"

"He's going to die when he sees you." Lena appears next to Maxine.

"I prefer Lena's compliment."

My hair is in an updo woven through with small pearl pins. The gown is boat-necked, exposing a wide swath of my chest, and cinched in tight at my waist. The bustle is small, modern, even. The fabric nearly glows from within.

I've spent my life making garments half as nice as this, sewing until my fingers bled in the dark. It will never stop feeling like a dream each time Maxine hands me over a gown worth more than my old apartment as if it is something I deserve.

I meet my own eyes in the mirror and hate my own face, hate the terrible things I've done.

I extend my apologies to Maxine's mother and stepfather for once again missing dinner, but they seem delighted by my courtship with an Ivy League–educated son of a judge. "Maybe she'll be a good influence for Maxine," her stepfather says after a sip of whiskey.

The flat is so quiet tonight I think Finn must be out, but I'm wrong. I catch a glimpse of him in the hall, right before the elevator dings open. He's standing like a ghost in the hallway, dressed in a borrowed suit for dinner. His eyes are big and bruised. His mouth is open like he means to say something but it dies on his lips. Our eyes meet and for the space of a heartbeat I stare back. I hope it hurts.

I step in the elevator and exhale.

Oliver's driver is waiting out front and swings open the door to the back seat, where Oliver sits in a tux, elbows on his knees, looking a little nervous.

"Thank you for coming. I'm sorry it was such short notice. My mother sent the tickets and I'd completely forgotten what with everything going on and I didn't want to go with anyone who isn't you."

I hold up a gloved hand to pause his babbling. "Of course I came, Oliver." Of course, I would rather be banging down my father's door for answers, or further researching the key. I don't want to waste any time. But I also can't stand disappointing Oliver. He deserves a girl who can go to the opera and not think of death the whole time.

Lena, Maxine, and Finn have promised to stay in tonight and comb through my father's papers for more answers, but it doesn't assuage my guilt.

Oliver lets out a breath and relaxes back into the tufted leather seat. "All right, then. Good. That's . . . good."

He's gentle as he takes my hand to help me out of the machine and leads me up the stairs of the Palais Garnier.

The sky is clear tonight, stars reflect off the river, the Eiffel Tower is lit against the dark, and Paris feels like it's sparkling. An entire city, dunked in a champagne glass.

Statues of golden angels stand watch on top of the green copper roof of the opera house, and we join the crowd of people below, streaming into the opulent lobby.

There's the whine of strings from inside the theater as the orchestra warms up and the hum of voices of opera lovers and lovers of being seen at the opera.

A blood-red poster set on a golden easel near the doors to the theater tells me that tonight we will be treated to a show of *La Bohème*.

I turn to Oliver. His eyes glint green in the firelight of the opera house. They haven't converted the sconces on the wall to electricity yet, and the flames dance across the red velvet drapes.

"Now is probably the wrong time to tell you I know nothing of opera, but this one is supposed to be quite good."

"I'm sure I'll love it," I say, but the truth is the curtains could stay drawn on the stage tonight, the lights could remain cold; the main attraction is Oliver's warm body next to mine, his hand held in the dark.

We take the stairs up to a box—of course his mother has a box—and take our seats. The inside of the theater takes my breath away; it is somehow even more opulent than the lobby.

Oliver laughs good-naturedly at the way I crane my head up to see the circle of gold inlaid into the ceiling.

The cavernous space is two-tone, red and gold. So visibly expensive, I feel almost embarrassed that they've made the mistake of letting a girl from the Lower East Side in.

Sadness tugs at me as I identify why it feels familiar. The first place I saw that was this opulent was the Commodore Club, the headquarters of the Sons of Saint Druon. It was on a smaller scale to be sure, but it too was paneled in golds and red velvets. It too made me feel an aching sense of longing and the discomfort of knowing I didn't belong. The last time I was there was the same day I killed Mrs. Vykotsky. I blink away the image of her face.

The orchestra hums to life. The lights dim. Oliver puts his hand on my knee and I settle, heavy, back into my chair.

The curtain whooshes open and the whole theater looses a breath. The opera begins with two men in a dark, dirty room. They sing a mournful song in Italian.

A woman knocks on their door, the burnt-out stub of a candle in her hand. She's shivering under a threadbare shawl. She, too, sings something sad.

And I barely pay attention. All of my focus is on a singular point, the place where Oliver trails his fingers, featherlight, along the cream silk of my dress against my thigh.

His long fingers move in swirling patterns, delicate and distracting. It's silly, how the brush of his thumb against the side of my knee has my breath catching in my throat.

Yesterday we could have been killed. We're still risking our lives. What will happen when we close the veil or if Duke Mourrier finds us out?

Tonight could be all we have.

He takes my hand in his, but his fingers don't stop moving. His thumb strokes the inside of my palm. His other hand reaches over to brush the back of my hand.

It's been so long since I've been touched in the dark.

A blush rises in me.

If he stops touching me, I might cry.

He doesn't.

Losing the spark of my magic has made me feel hollowed out, but Oliver's hand on me makes me feel solid and real. It's as if by touching me, he reminds me that I exist. I am a physical thing, worthy of kind hands and attention.

I can't quite follow the story. I'm too distracted by Oliver's touch.

The shivering woman from the beginning of the opera marries a rich man and strides across the stage dressed in a fine gown. She dies a horrible death not long after. I'm the only one in the theater who has to stifle a laugh. Art so does love to punish women who dare to rise above their station. I suppose the world does too.

I let the weight of Oliver's hands brush away my darker thoughts.

I'm so sick of thinking. I don't want to think anymore. About death or magic or Finn or what a massive mess I've managed to make of everything.

Just for tonight, I give myself this.

The curtain rises and the theater lights flick on.

"Will the DuPres miss you if I don't have you home straightaway?"

Whatever boldness has taken Oliver tonight, I like it. "I doubt so, what do you have in mind?"

"I never did get to show you my room at the Sorbonne properly. Would you like to see it?" He can't hide that he's blushing too.

I want to say something clever. Instead, I give a simple "yes."

I let him lead me by the hand down the stairs, out the door, and into his awaiting vehicle.

It's silent on the drive. I don't think either of us knows quite what to say. But his hand is still on mine, a warm pinkie trailing over the back of my hand, and that is enough.

Next to me, his body is warm, stifling, solid, and real. His fingers trail up my hand to play with the golden bracelet around my wrist, and such a simple gesture has me aching.

It's not raining like it was the first night I came here, but the night still feels thick and heavy. Stars blot out the moon, and the campus is so quiet it is easy to pretend that in this moment, we are the only two people on earth. A planet of only two, how simple would that be?

Our footsteps echo through the empty courtyard. No part of me wants to turn and run.

Oliver's hand trembles as he puts his key in the lock and turns.

His lips find mine the moment the door shuts. He doesn't

bother to click on the lights. We both knew this was coming. We've known since his hand found my leg in the opera house, or perhaps long before that, when his eyes met mine in the woods outside of Haxahaven or the first time they lingered too long on Delancey Street.

His mouth moves against mine and heat rises in my chest, and I just *want.* That's how it's always been with Oliver. He makes me *want.*

"Please," I gasp. I don't know what I'm asking for.

"Do you want me to slow down?" he asks.

"No." *No, no, no.*

I went to church with Finn, but this feels more holy, hands pressed together, every place he touches like a prayer.

His breathing turns desperate as we trip to his narrow bed. Or maybe it's me, it's hard to tell with the blood rushing in my ears. But there's something trapped in my chest and I need him to keep touching me.

I ache for him, every part of me, and that ache is soothed with every brush of his hands. His thumb across the hollow of my cheekbone, the jut of my ribs, the dip of my hip.

He's touching me like he means it.

A finger presses in the tender spot behind my ear, loops around my wrist, brushes at the back of my knee as he picks me up and lowers me to the bed.

The fire is everywhere, like a trail of gasoline and Oliver is the match.

"You're perfect, this is perfect, I—"

I put a hand up to his mouth, he kisses it messily. "You're

babbling," I laugh. He runs a thumb over my swollen bottom lip and looks at me in that bruising, wide-open way of his.

Then he closes his eyes and moves his mouth to my neck. "But I mean it. You—" He breathes in, his lips press against my jackrabbit pulse. "I waited so long for you."

My heart is in my throat, I'm nearly dizzy with feeling. His hands are so warm on my spine. He presses there, but I know it won't leave a bruise. Oliver doesn't feel the need to mark me up, to possess me. "I waited for you. I'd keep waiting." I mean it, I would.

"You don't have to. I wouldn't make you. I'm yours, Frances." His hands trail up my vertebrae, thumbing at the buttons there. With shallow breaths, he gasps, "*Yours, yours, yours.*"

I touch him back, hands scrambling for purchase across his broad chest. Recklessly I tear the tuxedo jacket off his shoulders and for one moment he stills. "Are you sure?" he asks weakly.

I am. I am because it's Oliver.

I nod and his eyes go wide. "Me too."

With careful fingers, I unbutton his crisp white shirt, and arch my back off the bed to kiss the scar just to the right of his belly button, where the bullet pierced him. He threads his fingers through my hair and sighs.

I'm blushing all over but there is no shame in letting Oliver see me as I am. In the warmth of his embrace, I am as safe as I always am.

He bends again, his mouth finding my collarbone.

It's Oliver and he's *everywhere.*

His hands are still so light. They don't hurt, instead they ghost over me, like he's amazed he gets to do this at all.

He presses me into the mattress, shoulders wide, silhouetted against the dim ceiling, waves of brown hair falling over his face. His mouth is open, swollen a bit, and he's looking at me like he loves me.

This want isn't a wildfire. It's a warm hearth. Something to build a home around.

I love him and he loves me. In the end, it is simple.

CHAPTER NINETEEN

Finn comes to me in my sleep. We're alone on the shores of the lake of his camp. Behind us, the white tents flutter in the dark like ghosts.

I deflate upon seeing him. "Not tonight, Finn. Please just leave me alone."

He looks wounded, his hands shoved in his pockets. "You didn't come home. I wanted to make sure you were all right."

"More than all right," I say.

"Are you with him?" There's no venom in his words, just sadness.

I don't answer. The dream fades, leaving Finn alone in the dark.

I wake to Oliver's hands drawing slow patterns on my shoulder. "I didn't know you had freckles here."

"You do too," I reply. I reach up and brush my pinkie against the bridge of his nose, where a wash of summer color has created a small constellation of them. "Right here."

He grins, illuminated in the soft pink light of morning, and I wish there were magic that would allow me to bottle this moment so I could return to it when things get heavy again.

"Thank you," I say, dipping to bury my head in the warmth of his bare chest.

"For what?"

"Everything." I mean it. He's been so patient this trip. He's been so patient in general.

"Don't thank me until I have you home. Maxine is going to murder me."

I blink more awake now and calculate how much light is streaming in from the dim curtains. We've certainly slept too late. I want to stay here forever, in this bubble of two. There is nothing I want to do less than face the world outside the warmth of these four walls and the flannel sheets tangled in my bare legs.

But Oliver is right. Lena and Maxine will be worried about me not coming home.

I rise from bed and take stock of my discarded clothing on the wood floors. My dress is in a heap by the bed, my corset thrown over a desk chair. One of my elbow-length silk gloves is on a lampshade; the other is near the closet.

"You're going to have to help me back into this gown," I say.

Oliver rises dutifully from bed.

"And then, we can work out when you want to go to my father to secure our official betrothment. I am, after all, a young woman of high moral regard."

Oliver knows I'm joking. I expect him to laugh, but not even a smile crosses his face. Instead, he shrugs as he bends to pick up my gown and says casually, "You know that I would, if I thought that's what you actually wanted."

Together, we wrestle last night's evening gown into submission and he sends me out the door with one last longing kiss.

I walk to where his driver waits across the street, dangling my silk gloves in my hands, feeling completely unchanged but also missing him already.

Maxine hurls a halved grapefruit at me as I walk through the door and into the dining room where the family, Lena, and Finn are eating breakfast. I duck to the left and the grapefruit hits the wall with a splat and then thuds to the ground.

"We thought you were dead!" she shouts.

"*Mon Dieu*, Maxine!" her mother shouts, and clutches her chest.

I'm so impressed by her fastball arm I'm more stunned than anything.

"I'm sorry!" I say. "I should have called. Oliver and I spent the night at his parents' home. It was nearer to the theater and we lost track of time after a nightcap."

It's a believable lie. His parents do keep a home in the city. It's still not entirely proper, but it is less ruinous than admitting to spending the night alone in his dorm room.

"I do apologize," I go on. "I'll go change into something more appropriate."

At the end of the table, Finn's crystal glass full of orange juice shatters in his hand.

He swears under his breath and holds his hand aloft. It's already bleeding, a big cut down the center of his palm. The blood drips all the way down his arm, off his elbow and into the white tablecloth.

"My, isn't this a morning of excitement," Maxine's stepfather deadpans from behind his ever-present newspaper.

Greta runs into the room with a dish towel to wrap around Finn's wound and shepherds him into the kitchen.

One of the lady's maids is sent to my room. She giggles as she unpins what's left of my ruined hair.

"*Toute en nuit, eh*?" She blushes.

I don't understand, so I smile back at her in the mirror as innocently as I am able and nod.

We haven't made any progress with the key and I refuse to wait at another dead end, so Wednesday, I walk to my father's office.

My magic has barely more than flickered since the night in the catacombs. There have been no more bodies, but each morning I scan the newspaper with panic in my fingers and guilt heavy on my heart.

My father is sitting at his desk, looking as disheveled and startled to see me as ever, despite the fact that this meeting was prearranged.

"Ah! It's you!" he exclaims as I walk through the door.

I sink down into the hardwood chair across from his desk, teetering so high with stacks of paper, I fear we may end up buried under them.

"I am looking forward to our discussion. You'll have to excuse the mess," he says.

I nearly tell him that I've never seen his office look less messy than this, but I keep my mouth shut.

"There was another murder last week," he says. "Still haven't identified the body, but he looked young."

My stomach rolls at the memory of what happened in the catacombs. "I saw in the papers," I reply as casually as I am able. "The city is in a tizzy."

My father nods, grave. "Don't you worry, we'll find the culprits soon."

"And when you do?" I prompt.

He glances out the window, then back to me. "Did you ever write to Haxahaven's headmistress?"

"Yes, but I doubt the letter has reached New York yet."

My father leans back in his chair, looking uncomfortable. "It really is time-sensitive. I apologize for asking, but could you write again?"

"All right. I'll send a telegram this afternoon," I reply hesitantly. "But I must insist you tell me why."

"Information about death magic is forbidden," he explains. "I've dedicated my career to research, and even I know very little of it. The only two people who are supposed to know how to open and close the veil are the leaders of the Sons of Saint Druon and the witches of Haxahaven. Since it was their pupils who opened it last, they took it upon themselves to be the keepers of the true events of the story, and therefore the arbiters of the information on how to close the veil. It seems, however, that the leaders of both organizations have died unexpectedly without identifying successors and passing the information on. What rotten luck. I'm hoping your Florence Poole may have more information."

Mrs. Vykotsky and Boss Olan died and took their secrets with them.

"What do you mean it was their pupils who opened the veil last?"

"It's just a story."

"Please." It comes out begging. This was what he began to tell me the first day I arrived in his office, before backing off and running out the door. I can't let him leave again without knowing the truth.

My father sighs. "I really shouldn't be telling you this."

"I won't write to Florence until you tell me why."

He considers me. He must take my threat seriously, because he begins. "The last time the veil was opened was about one hundred years ago. A young witch from your very own Haxahaven Academy fell madly in love with a dashing Son of Saint Druon and they ran away together, or so the story goes." He sort of sighs like it is a funny way to begin a story and takes a sip of coffee. But I think of my mother meeting my father at the Haxahaven garden wall. I think of myself climbing over that same garden wall twenty years later to meet Finn. No, a witch falling in love with a Son isn't funny at all.

"Ingrid was a Haxahaven student, besotted with a Son named Conrad. He asked her to run away with him, and she did, and when he asked her to marry him, she did that, too. But not long after the wedding, her beloved Conrad was overtaken by a rheumatic fever, and all the love and magic in the world could not save him, and she watched her beautiful husband, so young and full of life, fade away to nothing." He takes another sip and I nod, encouraging him to continue.

"But Ingrid was determined. She was not the type to take this kind of loss lying down." Ingrid sounds like someone I'd like. My heart aches for her, this stranger from a century ago.

"So, she did every bit of research she could, into forbidden magic, anything that would bring Conrad back to her. She performed a spell to try to reach him beyond the grave and it mucked everything up. Magic is, above all things, energy, and by disrupting the veil she disrupted the flow of energy across the globe." Ah. There it is. The answer I've been looking for. I don't feel relief, I only feel rising panic.

"For nearly two years, the magic went haywire. People died as a sect of radical magicians attempted to use the magic for their own gain. The last that was heard from Ingrid was a note, left on the altar of Saint Patrick's Cathedral, explaining and apologizing for her crimes, addressed to the then headmistress of Haxahaven Academy. Then she disappeared forever and magic returned to normal. No one knows what was in the letter except for the headmistresses of Haxahaven Academy. The contents are passed down between them."

I remember what the duke said in the catacombs about being made immortal one hundred years ago. I can still see the boy with the rubies over his eyes taking his final breaths. He has joined the others in the parade of ghosts who live in my head: Mr. Hues, Mrs. Vykotsky, Boss Olan, the Commissioner. My father may think this is just a story, but I know it's the truth.

"What happened next?" I whisper.

My father shrugs. "The murders stopped and everyone moved on. There's very little documentation of the event at all."

"But—" I have so many more questions. *Disappeared forever,* that's what he said happened to Ingrid. Did she disappear to protect herself or was it something more sinister? Was she punished?

He glances at the clock and pushes back from his desk. "I'm sorry to cut this short, but I have a one o'clock class."

I've gotten so much more than I hoped from him this afternoon, but it is still nowhere near enough.

"Please can we talk more, I can meet you after class, I—" I beg as he herds me toward the door.

"Not today, I'm afraid," he chirps.

"But—" I protest.

My father takes off up the stairs with a cheery "Goodbye!" Leaving me alone in the hallway with my hammering heart and racing thoughts.

My head buzzes the entire way home. The solution feels so close, so graspable, but there are still so many unanswered questions. The biggest looms heavy in my mind: *Can I trust my father to protect me?* I don't know the answer. *Disappeared forever.* Would my father be willing to let me meet the same fate Ingrid did?

We have everything we need to close the veil except for the thing we need the most: information on how to use the key. It's infuriating to feel as though the answer is just out of reach when we've come so far. It sounds as if by killing Mrs. Vykotsky I may have ruined any chance we have.

Every second that ticks by feels like borrowed time; eventually, another boy will be killed. I am sure of it. I just wish I knew how much time we had. The other bodies appeared about ten days apart. If the next sacrifice follows the same schedule, we have two or three days at most.

My father is hopeful about Florence, but I'm not confident she'll have the answers. She is an immensely talented witch, but Mrs. Vykotsky was threatened by Florence's powers and constrained her to the kitchens on purpose. It wouldn't have been like her to share her secrets with anyone, let alone Florence. She wasn't her choice of successor. If anyone were to know, it would be Helen, but she disappeared the night Mrs. Vykotsky died and hasn't been heard from since. I wouldn't even know where to begin looking.

All the walk home, I try to slow my breathing, think rationally. The last time I reacted on pure instinct, I ended up in the basement of the Sons of Saint Druon.

I open the front door of the flat to find Finn pacing in the entryway, a low cap pulled over his curls.

"Where have you been?" he greets me. I resist the urge to shove him out of my way and walk directly to my room.

"Why do you look so cagey?" I reply with a roll of my eyes.

"We're late?"

"Excuse me, *we*?"

He nods. "Yes, for confession."

I suddenly remember the church service from a few days ago. Finn said the priest told him to return on Wednesday for confession.

"Did you commit more sins you need to confess to?" I snap. It's so pathetic to watch Finn's little performance of redemption when we don't have a moment to waste closing the veil. The duke could be finding his next victim at this very moment.

"Yes."

Our spell in New York caused a rupture in the veil in Paris. Who is to say there aren't more ruptures around the world, more men like the duke using it for their own terrible gains?

"Am I truly to be your jailer, then? It's my job to accompany you? I have to send the telegram. We don't have time for this."

He shrugs, his hands in his pockets. "Or I can go alone. I thought you'd prefer to supervise."

I'm annoyed that he's right and confused that he waited for me. He could have easily snuck off.

I'm holding a simple straw hat in my hands. I'd ripped it off my pinned-up hair in the elevator, but I place it back on my head in resignation.

"Hold on a moment."

He waits like a puppy by the door as I go to my room and get a notebook and a pen. If I'm going to wait for him in the pews, I'll draft my telegram to Florence as I do it. Where do I begin? IMMORTAL DUKE PLEASE ADVISE.

The walk to the church is awkward. I still don't know how to be around Finn when it is just the two of us. There is the part of me that wants to extend an arm and shove him into the Seine, but the louder part of my brain knows we need him. I haven't ruled out pushing him into the Seine once we are done.

"Where were you?" he asks after a few blocks.

"It's none of your business," I say. The truth is, after my father's story, I'm terrified. But Finn is the last person I want to share my fears with. He has an uncanny way of picking at the things that scare me and using them against me, to draw me closer to him. I can't give him the ammunition, not when I already feel on the verge of breaking into a million pieces.

He scoffs, "Ah, so with Callahan, then."

"I said it's none of your business."

"He's got fancy suits and money to burn. You'll have a nice life. You'll be bored in three years."

"Go to hell."

He claps his hands together and furrows his brows. It takes me a moment to realize what he's doing, but then it dawns on me. He's trying a spell that won't come. "I'm already in hell, darling."

"Call me 'darling' one more time and I'll blacken your other eye. I'll match the one Oliver did."

"Your beloved has a weak right hook."

"Would you like to see if mine is stronger?"

Under his breath he mutters, "I know it would be."

"I'm starting to believe you like getting hit."

He rolls his eyes but doesn't push me further.

The ancient church is much emptier today than it was on Sunday. Perhaps a dozen parishioners trickle through the door, mostly older. A few ladies mingle in the back corner by a pot of tea set along a banquet table holding flyers.

A hunched man and a small boy light prayer candles in little amber glass jars.

I walk Finn over to the confession booth. He's awkward all of a sudden. He runs a hand through his curls and looks at the ground. "I'll, uh—be a moment, I suppose."

He's nearly to the open door of the confession booth when I stop him. "Finn?" He turns to look at me, his eyes big and questioning. "Just know, when you're in there, that stranger may say you are forgiven, but I will never, *ever* forgive you."

His face falls, but he doesn't respond. In silence, he bobs his head, an attempt at a dignified nod, and enters the booth.

I go to sit on the hard pew and pull out my notebook and pen. I watch a small group of nuns, three of them, sweeping the front altar as I debate how to begin the telegram to Florence. They move with such quiet precision, their attention to detail evident as they run a cloth over each ridge of the golden altar.

It's meditative. There's a quiet beauty in their work.

I take my pen to paper and write Florence the clearest telegram I'm able.

DEATH MAGIC STOP DO YOU KNOW ANYTHING STOP DID MRS V SAY ANYTHING ABOUT A VEIL.

It'll cost a fortune to send across the Atlantic but it's the best I can do.

Finn's confession takes longer than the telegram draft. I bounce my leg, antsy and sick to my stomach. The sooner we get to the telegram office the better. I wait for what feels like a very long time. I can't make out Finn's exact words, but his voice is humming low and steady from the direction of the confessional. There is so much to confess to.

Did he start with my brother, I wonder, or Boss Olan, or his own father? Maybe he started with me. That would be so like him. To center the story around the two of us like we belong to each other at all.

There's a small commotion as the doors to the church swing open, shattering the quiet calm inside. The little boy with his prayer candle jumps as three police officers enter the sanctuary.

They march down the center aisle, the patent leather of their shiny shoes nearly the exact same color as the black-checked marble floors.

And it hits me like a runaway train, why the name of this church was so familiar when Finn first brought us here: it's where the Brothers of Morte d'Arthur are leaving the bodies.

I move a few pews closer to the altar, and bow my head in a fake prayer. It doesn't help. The officers don't make an attempt to quiet their voices, but I don't speak French.

They traipse over to the altar, bending down to look at where I assume the body was laid. The nuns have stopped their work, but don't move. They stand, watching silently. It's unnerving.

Just as soon as they came in, they leave, seemingly annoyed with what they didn't find.

I jump as the door to the confessional swings open with a thwack.

Finn's face is a little puffy. I'd mock him for it but I don't want to give him the attention.

"Ready?" I ask.

But Finn doesn't answer. He's staring just beyond me at one of the nuns sweeping the altar. She makes eye contact with him and something passes between them. My blood runs ice cold, right down to my fingertips. Something isn't right here.

She straightens her hunched back and crosses over to us with quick, careful steps. No one in the church looks over at us, but I feel as if I am being watched.

Silently she jerks her chin in a "follow me" motion.

Finn takes a step.

I grab his upper arm. "Wait," I hiss.

"Do you trust me?" he asks.

My answer is an emphatic "*No*."

"Well, you're going to have to."

He follows the nun. I trip after him because I feel as if I have no other choice. I cannot let him go alone. I need to know what he is up to.

The nun leads us down a side staircase into a cold basement significantly less grand than the main hall upstairs.

"Do you know her?" I whisper.

Finn doesn't answer. He just keeps walking.

We reach a basement room filled with broken pews. We've turned through so many serpentine hallways I don't know if I could find my way out if I tried.

The only light is from a sliver of a window set high up on the wall. Dust flecks swirl in the dim beam.

In the corners are piled-up boxes and statues with chipped faces or missing hands. And on the far wall is a door with so much junk heaped in front of it, it's barely visible.

"Finn, what is going on? Tell me *now*," I demand. My blood is boiling.

I want to lash out at Finn. I want to freeze his body with my mind and slam the doors open and create a ball of light so large it illuminates all the shadowy parts of this awful basement.

But I can't.

I'm powerless.

The bruising, hollow loss of my magic has me feeling desperate and out of control.

"Finn!"

I will not say please. I refuse to beg.

"*Merci,* Sister Evangeline," he says, quiet and calm.

She nods, still unnervingly silent, and walks him to the nondescript door.

She pulls out a key, and Finn pulls a piece of paper from his breast pocket.

"Here's the address. You'll find her there."

I look between them. They're both so calm. I feel like a ghost, unseen, howling in the hallways desperate for someone to just *look* at me.

"FINN. TELL ME NOW." I haven't shouted like this since I was a child throwing a tantrum over William getting more penny candy than me.

Why did I ever stop? It feels so good to let the screaming inside me out into the world. I relish the shocked look on Finn's face.

"Jesus, Frances, give me a minute, I'll explain."

"No, explain now."

He sighs like I've annoyed him by mucking up whatever slick plan he's been concocting for God knows how long.

"She's looking for someone. I helped her, so she's helping me."

As I should have expected, his explanation begs more questions than answers. "Who?" I demand. "What is she doing for you?"

He looks to the nun, who nods, giving him permission to go on. She's not old, maybe forty, with unsettling sea-glass-green eyes.

"Sister Evangeline is a member of an ancient order of nuns, the Sisters of Saint Joan. A sister recently went missing. I told her where she was."

I remember my very first day at Haxahaven so long ago when Maxine told me the school used to be a monastery. The students, rather than playacting as tuberculosis patients, pretended to be young nuns. I supposed Haxahaven wasn't the only sect of witches to try the ruse. Women aren't stupid, and there are a limited number of places men leave us alone.

A chill spider walks down my spine. It was so warm aboveground, but this basement has me shivering in my gauzy tea gown.

"How did *you* know where she is?"

"She's with Les Selectionnes, near Fontainebleau."

Ah. Finn's creepy little commune by the lake. I wonder if they are missing their leader. "You sold her out?"

"It was a necessary trade." He doesn't look remorseful. He looks fine, perfectly relaxed. My heart is beating a mile a minute in my chest, but his breathing is steady.

"What did you trade for, Finn? If you lie to me, I swear to God I'll kill you."

He scoffs, "I wouldn't lie to you, Frances. That's not something I do anymore. I traded for this." He nods at the nun, who walks to the door, pulls out a golden key, and unlatches it with a small click.

"What's behind the door?" My voice comes out small, faraway.

He takes a step closer and puts both hands on my shoulders. "You already know."

CHAPTER TWENTY

The door opens to a stairwell black as death. The nun gestures with a thin hand for us to go ahead.

There is that smell, wet earth and decay. He's brought me to the catacombs. Maxine said there were entrances all over the city, that the tunnels crisscross underground for miles. The duke's cellar was one entry point; this cathedral must be another. It makes sense that this is where the bodies are being disposed of. They can bring them up from the tunnels undetected and disappear back underground.

"Absolutely not," I say.

"We have to," Finn says.

"It's too dark down there. I don't trust you. We don't even have the key."

He pats his chest over the same breast pocket where he just had the note and says, "But I do have the key."

We'd locked it up in Maxine's room, which means . . .

"You stole it?"

He raises his brows. "Can you steal something that was already stolen?"

I throw my hands up in frustration. "Yes!" Behind the fury is something more unsettling, disappointment and shock at being betrayed like this. I should have known better.

I recognize the look of frustration on his face so well. Finn wishes I was comfortable with lying and scheming like he is. "Please," he whispers. "We may not have another chance like this."

"How do you know?" He knows what I'm really asking: *What else are you keeping from me?*

There are footsteps from the hall; they're getting closer. "It has to be now," he insists.

"But why? We don't even know how to close it," I say. We have the key and we know where the veil is, but there's a massive missing gap of information.

Finn is undeterred. "The Brothers of Morte d'Arthur could seal off this entrance at any moment. Or I could be killed. You were there when the Sons of Saint Druon shot me. What if they don't miss next time?"

There are too many unknowns and what-ifs. It doesn't make sense.

The nun's wide doe eyes flit between the entrance to the room and us.

I hate this, that I am once again in a situation where Finn has left me with no choice.

Finn takes one step into the dark.

I ball my hands into fists at my sides, steel myself, and step in after him.

I don't have time to turn around before the door is shut behind us. It slams heavily, like it's made of steel. The darkness swallows us like a physical object. I can no longer see Finn. The primal part of me wants to reach out to feel for him, but I don't know if I'd be able to resist the urge to shove him down the stairs.

There's a shuffling sound, a thump, and then the snick of a lighter. Finn's face is illuminated as he sparks to life a lantern that he's pulled down from the wall. He brushes the cobwebs from the glass and looks up at me. "Shall we?"

"If you get me killed, I will haunt you forever."

He smiles, pleased. "An eternity with you? Deal."

God, I hate him.

I let him lead. If one of these rickety stairs gives out from under our feet, let him be the one to fall.

The soft hissing of the lantern and the padding of the soles of our shoes are the only noise for a long while.

The stairs go straight down for a bit, deep into the damp, dark heart of the city, before zigzagging and finally spiraling. We circle down and down and down until I am dizzy.

Just when I am sure we cannot possibly go any farther, the stairs stop. We've landed at the entrance to a dark hallway with a dirt floor.

I'm on edge, waiting for someone from the Brothers of Morte d'Arthur to pop out at any moment.

Finn chuckles softly at the way my head whips back and forth frantically. "We're safe. You think I'd let any harm come to you?"

No. "Yes."

"Well, then you're wrong. Come along, it won't be far now."

I keep my eyes focused on the dirt floors. Anywhere to keep from looking at the bones.

The muscle in my jaw twitches and my teeth begin to chatter from some combination of nerves and cold.

He shrugs off his jacket and hands it to me.

"No, I won't take it."

"Don't be proud, you're freezing. And anyone who means to do us harm could hear your chattering from a mile away. Go on." He shoves it toward me once more and I give in.

It's still warm from his body heat, so immediately soothing, I no longer have the willpower to complain. I tug it tight around my center and we carry on.

With each step, I feel my magic hum. It glows brighter and brighter in my chest the closer we get to the veil. And although I am terrified, I relish its presence, feeling at home in my body once more.

The catacombs may be a maze, but Finn and I can both feel the tug of the veil, unmistakable and strong.

The buzzing is there too, strange and head-splitting, but I'm too happy about the return of my magic to mind much.

I'm about to round the corner, to charge full speed at whatever waits at the veil, but Finn stops me with a strong hand wrapped around my shoulder. He tugs me back so hard I nearly fall. I'm about to exclaim in confusion when he claps a hand over my mouth.

"Shh." His breath is hot in my ear. "Look."

I was so focused on the veil, I didn't see the figure sitting in front of it.

It takes a moment for my eyes to focus in the new light, but he's so obvious it's a wonder I didn't see him before. He's sitting cross-legged in front of the veil, wearing a high-necked coat and plain trousers. His hair is cropped close to the skull, like a soldier's. But what strikes me the most is how young he looks. He may even be younger than Finn and me.

Something stirs in the dark. Another boy, leaned against the opposite wall, his eyes closed.

They haven't yet noticed we're here.

Finn snaps and a spark appears between his thumb and forefingers. He smiles and it lights up his whole face. He grins wide like he used to when we'd practice magic together in the woods.

"I can have a go at him from the left. Or you can do that clever trick with the neck you used to take out Vykotsky . . . that would be quick. I can take the one on the right . . . ," Finn whispers, thinking out loud. It takes me a moment to realize what he's suggesting, but I should have seen it sooner.

"You mean to kill them?" I whisper back in horror.

Finn's eyes go wide at my reaction. "What else do you suppose we do? We don't know how much time we have until his friends join him. This is an extraordinary stroke of luck, to find only two of them, unarmed and unprotected."

"No—" My answer is immediate and as sharp as I am able to make it and still keep my voice low. My eyes well hot with tears. "I won't do it. I won't, I can't, *I can't.*" The tears fall despite my best efforts to stop them.

My chest seizes up, my heart feels as if it is struggling to beat, all at once moving too little blood through my body. I feel as if I might pass out, as if I might die.

I cannot add another ghost to the parade of them that haunt me late at night. I cannot have another's blood on my hands. I cannot take another life.

I'd rather be dead myself than have to live a life with the knowledge that I have killed yet another.

I bend, placing my hands on my knees, and attempt to suck in a full breath, but my lungs are stuck too.

"Shh," Finn soothes me like a spooked horse. "Goodness, Frances, calm down. What has gotten into you?"

"I can't, I can't," I cry.

"Shh, you have to be quiet. He'll hear us."

"I don't care. Let him kill me, I'd rather be dead than do this."

Finn bends down to my level, peeking up to see my face. His face is soft, kind, even. "You can't truly mean that."

My gaze is hard as polished steel where it meets his. "Do they not haunt you, too?"

He lets all the air out of his lungs and threads his arm through mine, pulling me upright and down the hall, away from the veil.

"Fine. We'll find another way."

I can't stop crying. My eyes are so thick with tears I can barely see. There's no way I would be able to walk if not for Finn's steady steps and solid shoulders keeping me upright.

Echoing sobs threaten to escape my throat, but I swallow them down one by one just like I swallow the poisonous guilt.

I'm so stuck in my own head, I don't see it until it's too late—until the boy is standing right in front of us.

"Hey!" he shouts.

Finn curses and uses his power to send up a spray of dirt from the ground, concealing us effectively enough to run away.

A dagger zooms by my head and I trip, falling to my hands and knees. The sting is immediate as the skin breaks.

Finn hauls me to my feet just as the other boy rises and comes barreling at us.

It's so dark in the catacombs, the only light a single flickering lantern and the eerie blue luminescence of the veil, it's difficult to tell who is who.

I search desperately in the dark for the location of the two boys. If I could take hold of their bodies with my power, I could stop the fighting—suddenly someone lands a blow to my stomach, a fist right to my diaphragm.

I sputter for air as tears spring to my eyes.

Finn cries out and something wet splashes onto my shoes. Blood?

I reach out and take hold of one boy's body, my magic roaring to life under the surface of my skin. He thrashes against me, attempting to use his own magic to break away, but my power holds.

Then the other boy takes a handful of my hair and yanks hard, jerking my head back. I cry out. In my distraction, I lose my grip on the second boy.

Finn shouts and punches the boy who grabbed me squarely in the face. He crumples as his nose breaks.

I'm panting, frantic and panicking.

I ball my hands into fists, ready to land another blow, magical or otherwise, when a brilliant white light pours out of the tunnel behind us.

I turn to face the source of the light and find two nuns: Sister Evangeline, who led us to the entrance of the catacombs, and another young woman, not in a full habit, but a shorter black dress and small white headscarf.

They wave their hands, and immediately our two attackers fall to the ground, unconscious.

"Come with us," the younger nun demands.

"What—" I look between them and the boys, baffled at what I've just witnessed.

"Come along, Frances and Finn," she says once more. Because I fear we have no choice, we do.

We follow them through the corridors, their bright lights leading the way. I turn to Finn, concern in my eyes. He doesn't look scared; he just looks bruised from the fight. There's a nasty cut on his forearm where the dagger got him, the source of the blood all over my shoes. He holds his arm aloft to try to stanch the bleeding, but we'll have to get him bandaged soon.

I flit my eyes to the nuns in a silent question: *Should we fight them, too?*

Finn shakes his head. "Sister Evangeline is a friend," he whispers.

The nuns lead us up and out of the catacombs, through the back halls of the church, and up another rickety staircase behind the sanctuary.

The staircase lets out into an airy loft space. It must be the attic space of the cathedral. The flying buttresses on the ceiling go right into the line of the roof. The front wall is one massive stained-glass rosette. In the center of the room is a large gathering table, and a few worn sofas are set around a stone fireplace. There's a narrow hallway that must lead to the living quarters.

There are a few other women, some young, some old, all in nun's habits, milling around the space, reading Bibles or taking notes or with their eyes closed in prayer.

The odd thing is the complete and utter silence.

"What is this place?" I ask. I'm ready to cry, to fall apart, but I need to hold it together, at least for the next few minutes. "Who are you?"

The younger nun guides us to the table. She crosses the room and rifles through a cabinet producing medical supplies. "We're the Sisters of Saint Joan," she says. "I'm Sister Marguerite, a novitiate."

The rest of the nuns don't pay us much mind.

Sister Marguerite pulls up the bloody sleeve of Finn's shirt and pours alcohol on his cut. He gasps at the sting.

Sister Marguerite carries on. "We are a sisterhood of witches dedicated to Our Lord and the protection of His Kingdom. We've guarded the veil for thousands of years."

"How'd you meet her?" I ask Finn. I think back to the community at the lakeside, to the Brothers of Morte d'Arthur. Finn's ability to make friends and make others trust him is unmatched.

"Sister Marguerite lived with Les Selectionnes last summer before returning to the city to take her vows."

She nods in confirmation.

"What about the Brothers of Morte d'Arthur?" I ask. The nuns know where the veil is, they clearly possess powerful magic, they know of the murders. Why aren't they stopping them?

"Our Lord gives us free will," she sighs. "We are not responsible for the sins of men."

"But do you know how to close it?" I prompt.

She wipes away the residual blood from Finn's arm and shakes her head. "I do not. The abbess may, but like all sisters here, she has taken a vow of silence."

"You haven't yet?" I ask.

She shakes her head. "Not yet. When I take my full vows next year, I will."

I try to picture a life of silence. The sister is certainly stronger than I am.

"Thank you for helping us," I say.

She places clean white gauze over Finn's wound and begins to wrap it around and around. "Finn asked me to make sure you were safe." She looks at him with such reverence. I wonder if she's a little in love with him too, and suddenly I pity her. "I try to keep my promises."

Once Finn is bandaged, Sister Marguerite leads us downstairs and through the back entrance of the cathedral, bidding us goodbye at the door.

I memorize the back route she takes us through. I don't think I'll get any more information from her today, and I'm shaky and bruised and eager to return home, but if the nuns have answers, I must come back soon and demand to learn more.

We cut a path across the street, both limping a little. Finn's arm must hurt like the devil. His knuckles are busted open, and it aches every time I try to take a full breath.

Finn sits me down on a park bench and kneels down in front of me, placing both his hands steady on my knees.

Shaken from the fight and the thought of more death, I begin to cry. Sobs rack my whole body.

"Breathe, Frances, Jesus, you need to breathe."

But I still can't stop the tears. I wish I knew how to explain, but I don't expect Finn, of all people, to understand. "I meant what I said. I'd rather be dead than kill someone again. I wouldn't survive it this time. I'm barely surviving it now," I admit.

Finn's eyes are big and wide as he absorbs what I've just said. This is the closest I've been to him since we once shared a bed. I'd once memorized this face out of love. It is odd that the face didn't change even when the love did.

He's looking at me like he loves me now. It only adds to the guilt.

"I need to know it haunts you, too." My voice breaks. "I see Mrs. Vykotsky's face every night before I go to sleep. I can't see water without picturing the commissioner's hands floating just below the surface. I even feel bad about goddamn Mr. Hues."

Finn is silent. He just lets me cry. Watching me in that strange, soft way.

I don't think he's going to respond at all, but then he opens his mouth. "Of course it haunts me too. Of course it does."

He rises from where he's kneeling in front of me and joins me on the bench. I feel small and broken as he wraps his arms around me. He lets my tears dampen the shoulder of his shirt, and he strokes my back in small circles as I sob.

"I am sorry," he says against my hair. "If you think I'm not haunted by all of it, you're wrong."

I lift my head from his shoulder and push him away. I can't handle the sensation of touching him when he's so warm and so willingly offering me the comfort I desperately crave.

I do not need this moment, not with him. Any warmth, any closeness we once had was snuffed out unceremoniously like a burnt-down candle that awful November night at Haxahaven.

There are some things you can't come back from.

I push him away from me, and he slides willingly across the bench.

At my show of visible disgust, he speaks once more. "I'm sorry." I'm not sure if he's apologizing for the crime of killing my brother or touching me. "I don't want to fight anymore." His whisper is gravelly, the confession ripped from the back of his throat.

He crowds into my space again, soft curls and soft eyes and a sharp jaw, and it would be so easy to taste candy floss on a boardwalk instead of death in a river. But there is no taking back what Finn did. That's the whole thing. That's the point of all of this. I taste it, sour in the back of my throat like smoke from a gun.

I've only gotten fragments of Finn, never the whole thing. Is this him now? A boy, twenty and broken and full of fire looking for something to smelt into steel? There is something inside of him, a yawning pit that *wants and wants and wants.* I recognize it because I have the same one in me.

But there's a difference between me and Finn.

Finn wants, so he *takes.* He took my brother. He took the lives of Boss Olan and the other Sons. He took my very soul, scooped it right out of my chest like it was always his for the taking.

When Finn wants, he takes.

When I want, I *ache.*

I'm aching now, staring at the constellation of freckles scattered across his perfect nose. How is it that no one has broken it yet?

I push away from him.

If he's dead to me, I need to stop laying flowers on his grave.

"This isn't a fight. That implies there'll be an end to it." The seesaw between bruising longing and white-hot rage flips as anger rises in my throat. I scrub the tears off my face with the heel of my hand. I press so hard I'm afraid I've bruised the stinging skin under my eyes. I don't want to hit him, but I hope my words land like a blow. "And I'm going to hate you forever."

From the back of his throat comes a breath, like the very beginnings of a laugh.

"What?" I demand.

"I—"

"Were you going to say you're going to love me forever?" I taunt.

"You know me so well." He opens his mouth to continue, but I shake my head, silencing him.

"I have to leave," I say.

He looks at me through his thick lashes. His eyes well, but no tears fall. "Home?"

"No."

"Let's go, then." He goes to rise from the bench, but I shake my head no.

"This is something I need to do alone."

CHAPTER TWENTY-ONE

Finn, to his credit, let me go. He watches me with narrowed eyes as I rise from the bench and take off down the cobblestoned streets.

By the time I arrive at Saint Bosco's my legs are burning, but I barely feel it. I barely feel my body at all.

My father isn't in his office. I pace the small space back and forth, back and forth, feeling like there's something awful crawling through my chest and up the back of my throat.

I keep my eyes upward, staring at the ceiling as I pace, relishing the way staring at the overhead electric light leaves spots as I blink. Every time I close my eyes, I see the skeletons of the catacombs, piled on top of one another. I want to burn them out of my corneas.

After what feels like a very long time, when I am sure I have worn permanent marks in the floor, my father finally walks in.

He jumps at the sight of me and clutches his chest in surprise.

"Oh, Frances!" he exclaims. "Did I misremember a scheduled meeting?"

"No," I pant. "But I needed to see you urgently."

My father blinks in surprise, but sinks down in his chair and looks at me with his full attention.

Everything hurts because I'm nineteen and life is long. I don't know how to keep living like this. But I know I won't make it much longer if I don't change something.

Maybe I've learned something from Finn after all: the importance of a confession.

I stay standing, not able to bear looking at his face. I don't know what my father will do with the information I am about to give him, but I do know that I do not care. I'd rather be in prison, a captive of the Sons of Saint Druon, than try to live this lie another day. It's eating me alive, I can admit that to myself now. There is relief in that, as well, the confession to myself.

There is no great father-daughter affection between us, and perhaps that will make this easier. I'm not shattering his image of a perfect daughter. He doesn't know me at all. But it also makes it harder. I know the man across the room from me will offer me no comfort. He will not pat my back and tell me everything is going to be all right.

I don't trust my father. He may be working with the Sons who tried to kill Finn. He may punish me for stealing the key. Worse, he could turn on me and betray me to the magical community at large for opening the veil in the first place.

All of these seemed big enough reasons to do this on my own, keeping my secrets from him.

But something inside me has snapped. I can't do this on my own. I want his help, no matter the cost.

I'm staring at a cliff, but it's one that's loomed large in my mind for a while now. There is nowhere else to run; I have no choice but to jump.

So I take a breath.

And I tell my father everything.

There are so many places to begin the story: the day a pair of scissors flew into a man's neck, or the day I spoke to a dead boy in a basement, or the day my feet hit the shores of France. Perhaps it began the day I was born, that I've always been hurtling toward this very place in time, on a track I can't turn off of.

But I begin the night my brother went missing. The night my own soul shattered completely. I've tried so hard to glue it back together. It's shameful to lay it out in front of my father, evidence of what a poor job I've done of it.

"He didn't come home from work like he promised he would. . . ." My voice is small. I sound so young.

My father's eyes are wide, and it is the first time I truly see the resemblance between us.

For once, he pays attention to me. He doesn't glance at the clock or fiddle with a stale cup of tea.

The words come easy; it is the first time since that horrible night that I feel *sure.* I need to tell him this. He's failed me in every way a parent can fail a child, but I will be brave enough to give him the chance to finally protect his daughter.

My father doesn't have much of a poker face, but he nods along patiently as I spin the whole sordid tale. The day they dragged William's body up from the river, and just how much of me died right along with him; Mr. Hues; the scissors; Haxahaven; the secret lessons in the woods; and Finn. *Finn, Finn, Finn.*

He takes up much of the story, this dream boy with pretty eyes and big promises he never had any intention of keeping. I hate seeing myself through my father's eyes, a foolish girl taken in by a handsome face. But he bears the blame too; if he'd stayed in New York, or in my life at all, I would have had someone else to teach me. I would have had someone else to love me too. Maybe I wouldn't have sought it out so desperately somewhere else.

My father's face crumples as I describe the basement scene, how Finn and I laid out the scrying mirror, the pocket watch, the graveyard dust and the dagger. How Finn took my hands in his and promised to be mine forever, right before he stole my magic. How William flickered to life in the mirror and for one blessed, awful, final time I was able to speak with him.

He shakes his head sadly, disappointed. He has the nerve to be disappointed in me, a person he did nothing to raise.

I tell him about Mrs. Vykotsky and the way her neck snapped and I left the Sons to dispose of her body like a coward. The room melts away and I am no longer in Paris; I am back in the Commodore Club in a starless night that never really ended for me. I'm still there, in my head, watching her die.

I tell him about the magic going wrong months ago, how I've barely felt it at all since I've been here.

Sometimes words are just words. I try not to feel them as they leave me. I'm not strong enough to take the force of their blows.

I tell him we robbed the Louvre, stole the key right out from under the Sons.

I describe what happened today, as Finn and I climbed down the stairs into what felt like the heart of the earth and saw the veil itself.

"And now I'm here," I finish. "Because I don't know what to do and I'm tired of pretending that I do." I am tired. I am so, so tired.

When I am finished, he doesn't say anything. He lets the silence hang heavy between us, and in the quiet I begin to panic. Perhaps I have made the wrong choice by coming here. Making the wrong choice does seem to be a talent of mine. I wonder if it is something I inherited.

My father's face is usually so difficult to read, but right now he's horror-struck. "Oh no," he mutters to himself. "Oh, Frances, oh no." Tears well in his eyes and fall down his face, splattering all over the papers on his desk. "Oh, Frances. Please forgive me," he cries.

I'm taken aback. I expected anger, but not this.

"What is it?"

"It's the reason I left."

"What?" I recoil.

My father shakes his head. He looks so profoundly sad my heart breaks for him. "There's a myth about the veil, that only two fated souls can open it together. When I was twenty-two, a clairvoyant told me the Hallowell name was cursed, that she saw me in front of the veil. It scared me so badly I packed my bags and left the next day. I thought it was your mother and me. It was you and Finn all along."

I'm too numb to feel much of anything, but here it is, what I've been searching for, the reason he left us. A braver man would have stayed, would have told the truth, wouldn't have taken the easy way out. But the smallest bit of my heart twinges for him. I wish for a lot of things, for a brother who is alive, for a mother who could love me in the way I desperately wanted to be loved, for a father who is less of a coward.

If Finn were here, he'd laugh and say, *I told you so*. He was so insistent the universe wanted us by each other's sides, in each other's heads. Maybe I never could help the way I feel about him, maybe this feeling in my chest that I can't seem to excise was never my fault. Does that absolve me or make me just as cowardly as my father? Fate may incline us, but we control our actions.

"It's not fair," I say.

"What isn't?" my father asks.

"You were the one who got to do the leaving. I was the one who got left."

He takes my words like a blow, physically recoiling. "I'm sorry."

After nineteen years, I get the apology I've been craving all my life. It doesn't make me feel any better. I don't feel much of anything at all.

He wipes the tears from his cheeks and pushes back from the desk decisively. The legs squeak against the cold tile floors, the facade rising once more. He claps his hands together. "I will handle it. It is my duty."

"I—" I pause to gather myself. Surely there are follow-up questions I should ask him. "You will?"

My immediate reaction is to feel foolish. Could all this have been avoided if I was honest with him from the beginning?

I blink away the thought. I know better now than to get caught up in games of *what if* with myself.

My next thought is suspicion. "Surely, it's not that easy."

"Well, no"—my father considers—"but you are a child. The adults will handle it. I am your father. This is my job."

I almost correct him, tell him that I'm nineteen. It's been so long since someone looked at me and thought I needed taking care of. It is a relief. I lean into the feeling. I feel so young, still.

My father paces for a few moments, thinking, before walking to the coatrack by the door and pulling off his hat and overcoat. "I need to go now, people to meet with. I'll let you know soon. You have the key?"

"Yes." I'll fight Finn any way I can to get it back.

My father nods. "Come back tomorrow. We'll talk more about what needs to be done. But please, go home, get a good night's rest. We will fix this, Frances. You don't need to do this alone."

There is a part of me that wants to ask questions or insist I follow him. But I am so, so tired. The kind of tired that has turned my bones to jelly and stuffed my head full of cotton. I want to rest, I need to, before I shatter completely.

I do what is hardest for me to do. I accept his help.

"Thank you."

He nods, not unkind, but certainly not with any parental warmth. "Of course."

We walk to the front doors of the school together. He shrugs on his coat and hat as we walk; I never took mine off.

As if an afterthought, he calls after me as I'm halfway out the door. "Do you know Finn D'Arcy's current whereabouts?"

"No." My lie is immediate. I don't want any more blood on my hands. That includes Finn's. When it comes time to close the veil, if it's something we have to do together, I'll make sure no harm comes to him.

He bids me goodbye and we walk off in different directions. I do not watch him leave. I do not spare a single thought of distrust or uneasiness. It is done now.

Once back at Maxine's flat, I ask Greta to bring me dinner in my room.

I eat soup, wrapped in a goose-down duvet alone, and savor the small peace blooming in my rib cage.

I hear Finn come in sometime after dinner, his boots and accent echoing down the hall as he makes one of the lady's maids laugh at something.

Tonight I give myself this gift, the gift of quiet.

I wake with the early light of dawn, blinking awake as the sun catches something on the floor. Glinting up from the carpet, as if he pushed it under the gap of the door while I was asleep, is the key to the veil.

Finn has returned it to me.

I rise in the morning and eat with the rest of the family, even Finn, who makes Maxine's stepfather laugh uproariously from the other end of the table. I mostly ignore him, but I feel such relief from the meeting with my father yesterday that his presence isn't sickening, it's just annoying.

Today no grapefruits are thrown at my head. There are no secrets whispered or questioning sidelong glances. I eat an omelet next to Nina, who tells me about how desperately she wants a puppy, that she'll walk it every day. "Get the poor girl a puppy!" I say with a smile to Maxine's mother. "*Je'n parle pas anglais*," she says back, smiling.

"Yes, you do!" Nina whines. "You do speak English! You know exactly what Frances said!"

The warm summer sun pours in from the windows, and I brush aside the dull ache in my chest. Maybe good things are simply good things.

After breakfast, Maxine, Lena, and I take Nina to the carousel at the Jardin des Tuileries and make a picnic of crusty bread and soft cheeses on the grass surrounded by midsummer roses.

I'll stop by my father's office tomorrow and give him the key. For now, it jingles loose in the bottom of my handbag.

"You're in a good mood today," Maxine observes, passing me the butter knife across the checked blanket.

"Is that so remarkable?"

Lena and Maxine share a glance and utter, "Yes."

"I spoke to my father about . . ." I eye Nina, chewing happily on the heel of a baguette. "About *it,*" I continue. "He says he'll handle it."

Their eyes go wide. "You *what*?" Lena asks, horror-struck.

"I was honest, isn't that what everyone has been telling me to do? It's a good thing. He wasn't mad at all." I know that I'm being a bit of a coward, but is that the worst thing in the world? I am so profoundly exhausted from being brave. If my father has said he will handle it, I will accept his gift. He abandoned me my whole life. If he can give me this, I will let him.

Lena looks baffled. Maxine looks mad. "But we don't know if we can trust him, that's why we went to all this trouble," she hisses.

I shrug and pop a wedge of brie into my mouth. "I decided we could. Now we can enjoy our holiday. I still haven't seen the Eiffel Tower. We should climb to the top."

"Yes!" Nina shouts from beside me. "Please, Maxine, *please*?"

Maxine looks between us, but knows there's nothing she can do, especially not with Nina here.

"Fine," she says, not at all happy about it.

In the back of my head something nags. I'm waiting for the other shoe to drop, for another body to show up, for my father to betray me, for Finn to disappoint me.

But I smile for my friends because they deserve a day that isn't so heavy.

We walk to the Eiffel Tower. I've seen it from afar all trip, standing proud over the city like a sentinel, but up close it's breathtaking.

The maze of metal reaching into the sky exists in such contrast to the other buildings in the city.

We climb and climb up the stairs of the Eiffel Tower until our legs are burning and Maxine is cursing us for talking her into this.

Once at the top, I breathe in the sight of the city below me as the wind whips around my face. The roads sprawl out in a neat grid, dotted with rows of low buildings. Sometimes it feels like New York is growing so fast, skyscrapers popping up quicker than the island can keep up with. Paris feels peaceful, feels *done.*

I feel done too.

We descend the stairs and at the base, I buy a postcard from a woman selling them out of a cart and resolve to write home to my mother tonight. I do miss her.

Once back at Maxine's flat, the lady's maids arrive dutifully to dress us for dinner. I have Greta arrange my hair into curls gracefully pinned at the nape of my neck. She threads pearl earrings through the holes in my lobes and dresses me in a baby-blue gown of duchess satin with matching pearls embroidered along the neckline. She dabs rouge along the tops of my cheekbones. Suddenly, I feel like crying. I'm still so scared. I wish I knew what my father was doing.

Outside, the sun is beginning to set, sending the sky into a riot of pinks and oranges and purples dancing along the fluffy clouds.

I should walk to the dining room with the rest of the family. It would be the polite thing to do.

But as I slip on my shoes, grab my evening bag, and call the elevator, I know I will be forgiven. I've left a note on the edge of my bed, nestled in the duvet. *Off to see Oliver, don't wait up.*

Sweet Oliver, who has been unfailingly kind and patient as I've ruined what was meant to be a vacation for the two of us to connect. I've mucked so many things up so horribly and he just keeps on loving me like I'm worthy of it.

The elevator is slow to come, which is unusual. It dings from the ground floor as if someone stepped in right before I entered the hallway.

Once on the ground level, I scan the street and sure enough, I see Finn's broad-shouldered silhouette walking away, most of the way down the block.

If I were the girl I was last week, even two days ago, I would chase him down, demand to know where he was going. But I am not. My father is handling it. Tonight, I will see Oliver and we'll kiss in the low light of his dorm room and his hands will press all the bad thoughts out of my head. Let Finn have his fun, I don't care. He'll be dealt with by people who aren't me.

I could call a car to Oliver's, but I stroll leisurely along the river, letting the last of the day's June sun warm my skin. The air tonight smells of croissants and lilac, and I think that I would be content staying in Paris forever if I wouldn't miss Haxahaven quite so much.

The pitched roofs of the Sorbonne are glowing gold with the day's dying light by the time I arrive. My veins thrum with anticipation as I cross the cobblestoned paths that lead to his room. I picture the look of surprise on his face when he opens the door to see me in my beautiful gown. His mouth will form a soft O of surprise, but his green eyes will be sharp as they take all of me in. I hope he hasn't combed his hair today. I like it best when the waves fall messy over his forehead. It's only been a few days, but I ache for his face, for his touch, already. I can't wait to make everything up to him; he deserves the world, and tonight I will begin the process of giving it to him piece by piece.

I'm only nineteen and I'm still learning what love is, but I know that I love him. I know, because it's easy. It doesn't feel like bruised ribs in a basement, or sharp knuckles brushing against mine on a boardwalk in Coney Island.

No one told me love would feel like coming home, but that's what Oliver has always been to me, a home.

But it feels like fear, too. It's a nerve-racking feeling, this constant game of *do you like me too? Do you feel it too? Please tell me it's not just me. Please say you haven't changed your mind.*

My heart is in my throat when I finally make it to his door. I take a breath and rap three times. Will I kiss him right away? Is that too forward?

He leaves me too much time to decide. It's strange he doesn't come immediately. He may be at dinner—this is, after all, a surprise—but I knock once more just to be sure.

I rap my knuckles against the door a little harder, and this time the door gives a little, like it's unlocked. I try the knob, which turns easily, cold in my palm.

Something icy crawls up the chambers of my heart.

With sickening ease, I push the door open.

"Hello?" I call, praying I find Oliver napping in bed, waking surprised and delighted to see me.

But I don't.

The room is dim, the sun is sinking lower by the minute. I would light the lamp, but it's smashed all over the floor.

The whole room is in disarray, like a tornado tore through it only seconds ago. The coatrack is tipped over, clothing strewn across the floor, one shirt with a muddy footprint planted directly on it. The red quilt Oliver's mother made him for his fifth birthday is rumpled in a corner, as if tossed. The mirror is shattered, shards of it everywhere. One piece reflects my stunned face back up at me from the floor.

It's a horrible moment of stillness, like the lights have been flicked on and the music stopped at a three a.m. party. All at once, with shattering clarity, every ounce of hope leaves my body. Like it was all an illusion to begin with. Nothing today was real, but this is.

Something terrible has happened.

Someone put up a fight.

But against who?

Why?

When?

And most importantly, where is Oliver?

CHAPTER TWENTY-TWO

I want to collapse to my knees in fear. The warmth I felt moments ago dies in my chest, leaving nothing but the prickling cold of pure terror.

I scan the room for clues but there is nothing distinctive to be made out of the chaos.

I don't have time to search. All I have is instinct and the awful feeling this can't be a coincidence.

I think of the dead boys, splayed out on the altars of churches across the city, of the veil, of Finn walking away from Maxine's flat this evening.

I turn for the door, and I run.

If anything happens to Oliver, I'll kill Finn with my bare hands. I don't know how I'll go on. Maybe I'll fling myself into the veil to join him.

I sprint through the campus and down the sidewalk. I'm not far. I'm on the right side of the river, it's a straight shot up Boulevard Saint-Germain. But my legs feel like sandbags after climbing the Eiffel Tower today. Every slap of my boot against the pavement is accompanied by a horrible image: Oliver dead, his green eyes unseeing, his body laid out on an altar.

I think of the day they dragged my brother's body from the river, how something permanent in me died, how I thought I'd never go on. If Oliver leaves me too, I really don't think I'll survive it this time. I wouldn't want to.

I run until my lungs are screaming and my bones are aching and my muscles won't go anymore.

I run until I reach the doors of the Abbey of Saint-Germain-des-Prés. This late, the doors are locked, but I remember how my magic worked once I was close to the veil. I'm likely standing right on top of it now. It flickers below the sidewalk, six stories down, like the flames of hell.

This close to the catacombs, I can feel my magic spark awake again. "*Briseadh,*" I whisper the unlocking spell. Agonizingly slow, the lock in the door turns, and the door opens with a low thud.

The church is dark, shadows dance in every corner, and my frantic steps echo all the way up to the pitched roof.

The chapel is quiet and still. Perhaps that is good news, perhaps it is not. The heavy silence is holy or it is cursed, I will soon find out which.

The storage room leading to the staircase is even more terrifying at night. I bang my shin on an abandoned pew, cursing as pain radiates up to my knee, but I press on. I don't know how much time

I have. I don't even know if my hunch is correct, but I feel in my bones it must be.

"*Briseadh,*" I whisper to the locked door on the far end of the room. The magic comes quicker this time, as if sensing I'm closer to the source.

Down and down I climb, as if into the belly of the earth itself. The spiral staircase creaks under my frantic steps, but I do not slow. Each beat of my heart sounds like Oliver's name. What if I'm too late? I can't be too late.

My entire body is shaking with exhaustion by the time I feel the sharp buzzing. Like earlier, it stings, like a paring knife through the juncture of my jaw, tracing along the fissures of my skull.

Then, from out of the darkness, there comes the low rumble of voices—male and angry.

They're fighting.

With careful steps, I traverse the hallway of bones, illuminated in flickering red by my prayer candle.

I tuck my body behind a corner and peek a single eye down the hall I know leads to the veil.

It's still there, flickering like a silver pool of water up the far wall. It's who's in front of it that makes my heart stop.

There is Finn, one of the angry voices was his, but I already knew that. I recognized his accent and the chest-deep rumble of his syllables from a mile off. The collar of his fine white shirt is ripped and his lip is bleeding, like he's been in a fight. He's arguing with three boys who look to be about our age, his hands balled into fists at his side. The boys are solidly built, with mean faces and tree-trunk-thick arms. They too look a little worse for the wear. The sneers on their mouths are slicked with recently dried blood.

One, I do recognize. I haven't seen him since the Louvre. *Pascal.* It's the first time I've seen him with a frown on his face, so different from the jolly boy who once stole us a bottle of wine to drink on the steps of the Sacre Cœur. Was this their plan all along?

But I cannot dwell. I have no time.

Because directly in front of the veil is Oliver.

He's tied up, with ropes crisscrossing the front of his chest. His hands are bound behind his back, and stuffed in his mouth is a gag. But he is alive.

Next to him is another boy, flopped over and completely unconscious, tied up as well.

"I didn't say *him*," Finn yells at the boys.

"I thought you hated him. I thought you'd be happy," Pascal says.

"I *do* hate him. But he's still my friend. I don't want him dead."

"Well, he's here now, let's just kill him and move on with our lives," the blond, stockier one replies.

Before I can process what is going on, one of the boys pulls a dagger from his breast pocket and asks the other, "You know the spell?"

"Got it, boss."

"Let's just do it then, we're already here."

"No—" Finn starts to say, but his protests are abbreviated by the flash of a dagger flying through the air, aimed directly for Oliver's neck. A quick stab to the artery would have him bleeding out in seconds, it would be so quick.

My heart nearly stops beating in my chest. I'm running for him before I know what my feet are doing.

Finn flings himself in front of the knife right before it lands in Oliver's pale throat.

The knife thuds dull and sickening as it hits flesh, imbedding itself in the front of his shoulder, right by the joint.

"Fuck!" Finn screams. Swiftly he pulls the knife out. Blood spills from the wound, staining his white shirt red.

"I was just recovering from a gunshot wound, you absolute asshole," Finn spits at Pascal.

The two boys cry out in French and then in English as they see me round the corner. "You didn't tell us you brought someone with you!"

I ignore them, kneeling behind Oliver to undo the ties that bind his bruised hands. One of the boys lays a hand on my shoulder, but with one quick flick of my magic, I have him stumbling backward. Rage has always made casting easier and it's coming off me in waves right now.

"Frances!" Finn exclaims, then, strangely, kneels to help me with Oliver's ropes. "You have to believe me, I didn't ask for this."

Finn pulls the rag from Oliver's mouth. He stutters a breath. "Didn't stop your friends from jumping me in my dorm and dragging me here."

I reach out and slap Finn square across the face. He pulls back, eyes watering and face stunned.

"I'd give you worse if you weren't already bleeding." *If you didn't just nearly sacrifice your own life for Oliver's.* I pull the key from my pocket, it glints against the dark ripple of the veil. "We're ending this now." I still don't know what to do with the key, but I have to try something.

"No—no, not yet, I still have to . . . ," he sputters, and looks between the three boys and Oliver and me.

The one I flung against the wall is still catching his breath, and the other looks like he's debating whether or not a go at me is worth it. Pascal looks conflicted.

He pulls another knife from his breast pocket. It glints, terrible and sharp in the flickering torchlight.

In a flash, he magicks it toward me, aimed directly at my heart. With my own power, I force it to the ground, where it lands with a clatter.

I levitate the knife up off the dirt floor and send it careening in the direction of Pascal's knee. I don't want to kill him, but one good wound to the leg should slow him down enough for us to overpower him and end this.

But my aim is off and he sidesteps my attack.

"Stop her!" the taller one shouts at Finn. "Let's just kill them both, two birds, one stone, eh?"

"We're not killing either of them," Finn spits. "That's not the plan."

At that moment, a clatter of footsteps from behind startles me. I turn my head to see the source of the noise, but immediately pay for my lapse in judgment. One of the bones from the wall, an arm bone if I had to guess, comes flying at me, smacking me square in the chest. I fall backward, landing flat on the dirt floor, all the air pushed from my lungs.

A hand reaches through the darkness, sure and steady, and rights me on my feet. I look up through the dim torchlight to find Maxine. She's panting, her blond hair plastered to her forehead with sweat, Lena right beside her looking equally winded.

"How did you know where to find me?" I gasp.

She darts her eyes between Finn, the boys, and me. "A messenger came with this."

She flashes me a note that's been fisted in her sweaty hand. Scrawled in frantic handwriting are instructions on how to enter the catacombs and where to find us.

"From who?" I ask.

She shakes her head. "We don't know."

Before I can ask more questions, one of the boys sends another knife careening at Lena. She dodges it and picks it up from where it clatters to the ground.

"What the hell is going on?" she asks.

"That's what I'm trying to figure out."

"Jesus, more of them?" the shorter boy sighs.

"Let's kill them all, eh," the taller one replies.

I reach out with my power and take hold of the taller one, freezing him in place. His eyes go wide with panic, but he spits, full of bravado, "You don't scare me, witch."

I point my dagger at him. "Explain, now."

He sighs and rolls his eyes. "Just here doing exactly what your beau wanted of us. We're here for you, too."

"But why help Finn?" I know how he operates, he doesn't deal in violence or threats. He deals in hope, in offering people exactly what they've always wanted. "What has he promised you?" I won't get the truth from Finn himself. He'd manage to spin it into some half thing to make himself look better. I need these boys covered in his blood to tell me.

The blond I don't recognize spits blood on the floor and replies, "Because he promised he'd make us immortal."

The unconscious boy tied up on the ground stirs. He blinks open his watery eyes and stares up at us arguing.

"Sir," he moans, looking up at Finn with pleading eyes. In accented English, he begs, "I am Benny. You know me. I am a member of Les Selectionnes. Please, help me."

I turn to Finn in horror, the pieces slotting together. Finn never told the magicians at the lake his name. I found that odd.

How'd this boy get from an hour outside of Paris to the tunnels of the catacombs?

How convenient it was that every body found was an unidentified young transient, a runaway.

"You were supplying the sacrifices," I say to Finn. It isn't an accusation. It's a fact.

Finn shakes his head, but I can see in his face that it's the truth. "Frances . . ."

"Did you create the whole community for this? You gave them hope! Was it nothing more than a body farm?"

He takes a step toward me, but I stop him in his tracks with my magic. "I did it for us."

The words of his letter echo in my head. *What I'm building, I'm building for us.*

I take a step away from him and shake my head. "What did you do, Finn?"

"I needed a way in with the Brothers of Morte d'Arthur. I heard they could make a man immortal, it only required the life of another. So I provided them with the necessary bodies. People no one would miss. I didn't want to do it, but I needed to."

"You *needed* to murder people who trusted you?"

Finn runs a hand through his curls, frustrated, like I don't understand at all. We'll never understand each other. "I just needed the Brothers to trust me enough to show me how to do the ritual. So I could perform it for *us*, Frances. Then we'll close the veil and never let anyone use it to do harm again."

It's all so horrifying I don't know where to begin untangling it. Finn sold out his own followers and led them to slaughter. He agreed to help us and stole the key with the sole intention of performing the ritual for the two of us.

Forever with Finn? The concept has me shaking, sick to my stomach.

I turn to Finn with disgust. "You really are mad, Finn." My voice cracks on his name. "You thought I'd ever want an eternity with you? You thought I'd let you take Oliver's life the way you took William's? You'll never learn, will you? You'll never understand me, you'll never understand friendship or love."

"No, no, not Oliver. They weren't supposed to take Oliver," he protests.

"But if it wasn't Oliver, it would have been some other poor boy."

Finn meets my eye, steely in his resolve. "I need to atone for what I've done. I need more time, Frances. It'll take more than a lifetime. I'll do good with it, *I promise*. We could make a world that's better than this one, just like we always talked about."

There is nothing Finn can do to remedy the harm he's done, no steps, no perfect words or actions that will bring my brother back to me. He cannot undo the pain it has caused. They say all is healed with time, but that's not true at all, is it?

"You can't fix it, don't you understand?" I cry. "Not by more killing. And even if you could, do you really think it would make me love you again?"

He looks so wounded, standing in the flickering torchlight, covered in blood and bruises. "I—" he begins, at a loss for words. "Maybe I need more time to prove to you that I've changed, but everything I've done has been for you. You don't see it now, but you will."

In my distraction, I've let my hold on the taller boy slip. He lunges at Finn, a knife in his hand. The shorter boy goes at Oliver.

On the ground, Benny struggles against his ropes.

All at once, we unleash a torrent of magic. Maxine flings the knife out of the taller boy's hand. Lena magicks the ropes up off the floor and whips the shorter boy in the face. Pascal sends a shower of dirt our way, momentarily blinding me. It's all so ugly and quick. The catacombs already smell of death, but now they are filled with the deep, guttural sounds of eight people trying to overpower one another.

A skull comes careening off the wall, directly into the soft spot under my ribs. Something snaps as the breath is knocked from me. Another bone comes flying, sending me stumbling to my knees. I'm immediately hit in the back of the head by another blow.

They're trying to kill us. Pascal, the other boys, they're fanatics. They'd kill for this, the chance of eternal life. They don't see that Finn would just as easily sacrifice their lives too.

I'm gasping for a breath I can't catch against broken ribs, trying to push myself up off my bloody knees, when another set of footsteps comes running down the passageway.

I clench my eyes shut. *This is it, then*. More Brothers of Morte d'Arthur are here as reinforcements and my breaths are certainly numbered. They'll tie me up in front of the veil and drive a dagger through my heart. I only wish I hadn't gotten my friends so tangled up in this mess.

I open my eyes to see two bodies round the corner.

It's so dark I can't quite make out their faces. It's a man and a woman, I think. The man raises both his arms and, in a torrent of magic, sends three bodies slamming against the side wall. The woman clasps her hands in front of her chest and produces a light spell so bright, I have to blink away the tears from my eyes.

All at once, the fighting goes still. Pascal and the two others are collapsed on the ground. Oliver, Finn, Lena, Maxine, and I are all a little worse for the wear, but panting and alive.

And illuminated in golden light, standing perfectly still, her brown eyes full of fear, is *my mother.*

Next to her stands my father. He's trying to catch his breath, beads of sweat pooling on his brow. "Been a minute since I've done that," he says. "Come now, let's tie up your friends."

"They aren't our friends," Maxine corrects.

"Maxine, Lena, good to see you again," my father greets them, bending to gather ropes up off the ground.

My mother stands next to him, frozen in place, her eyes unblinking as if seeing to some far-off place.

"Mom." The sound of my voice seems to rouse her. Her eyes meet mine, and it is then that I realize they're full of tears.

She lets the light in her hands snuff out as she stumbles toward me to pull me in her arms. I've long been taller than her, but she manages to make me feel small as she burrows her damp face in the crook of my shoulder. She's shaking.

"Shh, Mom, it's all right." I comfort her in the quiet voice I always use with her. "What are you doing here?" I ask.

She pulls back and looks at me. "You're still here."

I'm confused. "Of course I'm still here."

From behind me, I hear the moaning of the three boys as my father and the others tie them up. I glance over my shoulder and see the same frozen fear in their eyes as they had when I took control of their bodies. My father is controlling them too. He makes them empty their pockets and wait patiently with their wrists behind their backs, their faces contorted with frustration.

I turn back to my mother. "Mom, please explain, I beg of you."

"I saw—" She heaves in a breath as if to keep herself from crying. "I saw—"

My father interrupts. "Lena, Maxine, I've met. You boys are?"

"Oliver Callahan, sir. Nice to see you again, Mrs. Hallowell," he calls to my mother.

I see the moment my father's eyes land on Finn. He lunges at him, landing a blow square in his gut. Finn sputters, gasping for breath.

My father punches again and again until I scream, "Stop!"

Finn heaves and stumbles back from my father, who looks at him with such ire, I'm afraid he might actually kill him.

"Tie him up," I command. "But please, no more."

My father nods silently, unhappily, and binds Finn's wrists behind his back. To my surprise, Finn lets him do it, making unyielding eye contact with me all the while.

I turn back to my mother, who is shaking and clutching herself around the middle. We need to close the veil and get her out of the catacombs as quickly as we're able. I take off my overcoat and wrap it around her thin shoulders.

I turn to the others. "We have the key, we're in front of the veil, let's close this and be done with it."

"But—" Finn protests.

"But you want to be immortal?" I snap. "You're out of luck."

Oliver strides over to Finn and reaches into the breast pocket of his coat to pull out the golden key. It looks smaller in the shadows of the catacombs.

He passes it to my father, who rolls it around in his palm a few times, then holds it up to the flickering torch on the wall to get a better look. "We will be deathless?" he translates the words on the key.

"Is it the spell?" It must be.

I walk over to my father, who hands me the key, and then take two more strides to where the veil ripples silver and unnatural on the back wall. This is the closest I've come to it. It makes me feel as if there are a million insects buzzing under the surface of my skin. It takes all the strength I have not to put my hands on my knees and wretch up the contents of my stomach.

"Do you feel it?" I ask weakly.

"Feel what?" Lena asks at the same moment as Finn whispers an emphatic "*Yes.*"

Despite the sickening feeling, it pulls me closer. It feels familiar somehow, as if we are made of the same stuff.

Suddenly Finn appears at my side. I extend a hand, fingers nearly brushing the quicksilver surface before he swats my arm down with an elbow.

"Curious," he breathes.

"I know," I whisper in return.

From behind us, I hear faint voices. But the buzzing in my ears is growing louder by the second, a swarm of locusts descending on my mind.

"*Frances.*" The name is faint; I can't tell who is calling me.

"FRANCES!" A hand fists the neck of my dress and yanks me back. I stumble and catch my breath, coming back to myself.

Maxine pulls Finn back too. I imagine the glassy look in his eyes is the same as in mine. The rest of them look at us confused and concerned.

My mother's mouth is moving quickly, her words too faint to hear.

"Do we just say the spell then?" I ask.

"It seems as good an idea as any."

I search the hallway for any visible keyhole, but there is just dirt and bones and the rippling wall.

My father nods. "Go ahead."

"I say go for it," Maxine speaks up, sensing my hesitation.

My mother's breathing is ragged and wet. I need to finish this quickly and get her to safety. I take a deep breath, filling my bruised lungs to the apex. I close my eyes and attempt to feel the words with my soul as the boy to my left once taught me to do in a forest far away from here.

I place the key in the center of my palm and say the spell, "We will be deathless."

The veil ripples, indifferent and unchanged.

I glance back to my father, who looks just as confused as I am.

I place the key on the ground on the edge of the veil next, like I laid out the items that allowed me to speak to my brother in the basement of the Commodore Club. "*Si sin morte,*" I try this time.

Still nothing.

It seems reckless to toss the key, but I don't know what else to do with it. "*Si sin morte!*" I shout so loud it reverberates off the walls.

Noiselessly the key is swallowed. It becomes nothing. And the veil just keeps on shimmering, rippling like nothing has changed at all.

"Did it work?" I ask, but I already know the answer.

Finn hesitates, then shakes his head. "I still feel it." I do too.

My mother is crying now, full body-racking sobs. "It's not going to work," she says, finally audible. "It's not going to work."

I walk over to her and place my hands on her shoulders. "What are you talking about? Why are you here?" I turn to my father. "Why is she here?"

My father looks nearly as lost as I feel. "She arrived in my office an hour ago in a similar state to what she's currently in. Said only that we needed to get to the catacombs and showed me the way here. She said you were in trouble. I sent your friends here a message by courier to meet us. Your mother said there was no time to explain. Vera, please, will you explain now?"

"How did you get to Paris?" I ask.

Light sparks in my mother's eyes and she looks almost like herself once more. "I took a ship, silly," she says weakly.

"And why did you take a ship, Mom? Why are you here?"

Tears fall down her hollow cheeks and she sits down on the dirt floor, collapsing in on herself. “Because I cannot lose another child.”

It is as if the air is sucked from all of our lungs simultaneously. “What do you mean?” I ask, my heart hammering so loudly I can scarcely hear myself over the blood rushing in my ears.

“I had a vision,” she says. My mother and I haven’t spoken at length about her magic since her release from the asylum, but we have discussed it a time or two. She’s a clairvoyant, like Lena. And from the little I’ve gathered, an awfully good one, when she isn’t trying to suffocate her power. It’s part of why Mrs. Vykotsky was so disappointed when she left Haxahaven.

“A vision?” I prod.

She nods. “Of you, of us, here.”

“And?” I ask.

She swallows, “And you die.”

Pascal, the two Brothers of Morte d’Arthur, and Benny are safely tied up a ways down the hall. There is no more looming threat. I don’t know what she means. The danger is gone. “Maybe you were mistaken.”

“No . . . no.” She cries softly.

“How do you know for certain?” Lena asks gently. “Sometimes, I misunderstand my visions.”

My mother shakes her head sadly. “I know for certain, because I know the story. I know how to close the veil.”

Her words settle like dust.

“What?” I gasp.

She takes a shaky breath. “That key was nothing. But you already know that, don’t you?”

I grab her by her narrow shoulders and duck to look up into her eyes. "How do you know? I thought only Mrs. Vykotsky and Boss Olan knew."

My mother sniffs but the tears keep falling. She makes no move to scrub them away. My father reachers out with a handkerchief and gently pats the skin under her eyes. "Ana Vykotsky wasn't supposed to tell me." She doesn't look at any of us as she recounts the memory. "She was sworn to secrecy by virtue of her position, but she thought I needed to hear it, so she told me anyway. Ana only cared for rules she herself created. It was about a witch much like myself, one in love with a Son, one about to leave Haxahaven to be with him, which Ana regarded as being the biggest mistake of my life."

"Mom, I know." I interrupt her. "Dad told me this story already."

My mom shakes her head. "But your father doesn't know the ending."

Next to her, my father places a comforting hand on her shoulder.

"Ingrid was a gifted witch, she knew magic demanded balance." My mother explains, "She felt the veil calling for her. So she—" My mother hiccups a sob and forces the last part out. "So she flung herself into the veil, dead and gone, and magic was restored. Mrs. Vykotsky wanted to dissuade me from falling in love with a Son. 'Look at where it leads,' she told me. 'Nowhere good.'"

The truth feels like a slap to the face. Right in front of me, something I should have seen coming, but it stings all the same. The key was nothing. A diversion created by the Sons. This is the real price. The veil demands life, *my* life.

We stand in stunned silence as the weight of her story settles. I watch the shadows from the torchlight dance along the wall, unable to let her words sink in.

I think of my mother and father, both cursed by the veil in such different ways. My mother was told to stay away and picked my dad anyway. She paid in a life of loneliness. My father in his attempt to avoid ruin left a pile of wreckage in his wake anyway. His price is guilt.

My heart is broken in so many places.

But I know without a doubt, this needs to end tonight before another innocent boy like Benny ends up with a sword in his heart.

"We'll find another way," Lena speaks up. "This can't be the only way."

My mother nods rapidly. "I cannot lose another child. Please. I came here to stop you. I saw what happened to William but I couldn't stop it. I can still stop this. Let me stop this."

But I feel the way the veil is calling for me, and I know she is wrong. This is the answer we've been so desperately searching for.

"So we leave it open," Finn says decisively.

"No," I say. "As long as the veil is open, the murders will continue. If not here in Paris, then at other places around the world. Dad, you said yourself Paris isn't the only weak spot. We can't guard every rip. We can't control it. We can only end it."

I look in my friends' panicked faces. My father looks as though he may vomit. My mother is scrunching her eyes shut to stop more tears from falling.

And Oliver—

Oliver is looking at me.

"Frances," he breathes as my eye meets his. "You can't really be considering this."

I step to him and bury my face in the warmth of his chest. I savor the sound of his beating heart against my ear. I can't believe I ever took a single second for granted with him. I make these last ones stretch on as long as I am able. I pull back, leaving his shirt wet with my tears.

"I hope you know how thoroughly and completely I am yours. What an honor it is to have been loved by you, Oliver Callahan."

"No!" he shouts, face contorted in anger. "You don't get to say goodbye like you're considering this. It's ridiculous, you can't."

There are so many versions of myself I have yet to meet, so many people I haven't yet gotten the chance to love.

But I should have known better than to have assumed I was guaranteed time. None of us are. It's better this way, at least I can go knowing I saved the ones I loved rather than in a random act of chaos, or drowning in the East River.

The most horrible part of me wonders if I deserve this, after all the death and destruction I've caused.

The terrifying truth is maybe it would feel nice to forget about the things I can't forgive myself for.

Oliver, Lena, and Maxine tell me it's all in the past, but is it in the past if I'm still living it over and over in my head every moment of every day?

Perhaps I deserve oblivion. Maybe I'll get lucky and it'll feel like peace.

I turn to face Lena and Maxine, whose faces are tear-streaked and full of rage. How do I say goodbye to them? How do I make them understand how fully I love them?

Before I can open my mouth, Oliver speaks up. "Absolutely not. It has to be Finn. This is absurd. I'll shove him myself."

The idea settles in the silence of the group.

My dad agrees immediately. "Yes, it should be the boy."

"It should be Finn," Maxine concurs.

"Wow, thanks, Maxine," Finn says under his breath, like there is any humor to be found here.

"I was the one who insisted he do the spell with me. The whole thing was my idea," I say.

"You only had to do the spell because he killed William," Lena reasons.

Finn looks down at his shoes. Is he ashamed? Is he thinking of a clever trick to get out of all this?

But what I'm wondering most of all is why I don't want him to die. I should, I should want it with every beat of my broken heart, but I don't.

Finn and I belonged to each other the moment he told me he'd seen me in his dreams his whole life, and we still belong to each other now. But when the warmth and affection and something that might have been love died, all we were left possessing of each other were the crimes. We still hold them now, the awful, ugliest parts of each other, fisted in our sinful hands. We're tied together forever, bound by blood and pain and mistakes. But we are still each other's.

"I killed Mrs. Vykotsky. I deserve this," I say. "Please, let me do this. Please, just let me go."

I take a step toward the veil and they all shout, "No!" or "Stop!" at the same time.

Finn raises his face from his boots, something determined in the set of his eyes. "Nah," he says casually. "Let me do it." He quirks a half smile.

"No," I say quick and decisive. It strikes me with a blow straight to my chest just how fiercely I don't want him gone.

He takes three careful steps and closes the distance between us. His eye is still bruised, a trickle of blood is half dried across his cheekbone. And here's that look. The one that's just for me. The one where he looks like he loves me with a ferocity so intense, neither of us can bear it. I wrap my arms around his waist, almost an embrace, and with a tug, undo the ropes around his wrists.

He reaches up and for once, I don't recoil from his touch. With shaking hands, he tucks one strand of hair behind my ear. I lean my cheek into the callused palm of his hand and close my eyes.

"I wish you'd have let me give you forever."

"No." The tears stream down my face, silent and unstoppable.

"I have to," he says so gentle, just for me.

"But I don't want you to go." I can't make sense of it, my ugly heart, the way it's shattering. "It should be me," I protest.

He shakes his head. "You know that isn't true. You're . . . good, Frances." *Good.* What a strange word. I don't feel good now, I haven't felt good in a long time. And Finn may have blood on his hands, but mine are irrevocably stained too.

"Mr. Hues, the commissioner, Mrs. Vykotsky . . ." I name my crimes between gasping tears.

"Oh, love." He shakes his head and runs a bruised hand through his curls. "There's something I should have told you a long time ago. I killed the old witch. I walked into the foyer of the Commodore Club and was so filled with anger with how she treated you. I snapped her neck before I could think twice. Our magic was already bound. It couldn't've been you. I shouldn't've let you believe it was."

"But I—" It wasn't me? The guilt doesn't dissipate. It still sits heavy as a rock in my throat. She came to the Commodore Club that day for me. "But I still don't want you to die," I say, voice somewhere small and far away, thick with tears.

He smiles, revealing the dimple right under his left cheekbone. "Ah, I'm none too crazy about the prospect myself."

"But you're going to do it anyway?" I ask.

He nods and takes two large strides toward the veil. I want to cry out. I want to stop him. I want it to swallow him whole. I want to take back everything I've ever done that led me to this moment.

Right before he reaches the shimmering surface, he pauses and looks back. His curls in a riot around his head, his full bottom lip split down the middle, his jaw sharp and determined.

He's looking at me like he wants to crawl inside of me, unspooling, unnerving, and punishing.

"Why?" I sob, broken.

He takes a breath, then smiles, softly, like we are seventeen and in Forest Park again. "Because I love you."

There are some truths you just can't swallow.

Finn steps into the veil and disappears.

CHAPTER TWENTY-THREE

And here it is, the terrible truth of my life: there isn't anyone who has loved me and gone unpunished for it.

"No!" I cry, falling to my knees in my dirt. "No, no, no—" I sob over and over again, crying for a boy who deserves no tears from me.

Maxine and Lena haul me up off the ground, and I collapse backward into their chests.

"Shh, it's all right," Lena soothes me. "It'll be all right now."

"Look, Frances." Maxine extends a finger and points at the veil. "It's already working."

I open my swollen eyes to see the veil flickering. It's as if it's collapsing in on itself like a dying star. The unreality of it all is hard to take in.

The silver surface ripples and glints, growing smaller and dimmer by the second.

Then—with a mighty gust of air, the torches are extinguished, leaving us in total darkness.

The veil flashes brilliant white, leaving spots in my eyes, then winks out completely.

There is a boom so loud it makes my ears hurt, and then there is nothing.

For a minute, there is silence. Then there is the noise of my tears once more, dripping on the dirt floors of the catacombs, leaving little spots where they fall like confetti at the end of a terrible party.

It's over. He is gone.

The veil is no longer the veil, it's just a wall.

I fall back to my knees and sob but no sound comes out, it's all stuck in my throat and I'm choking on it. *He's gone, he's gone, he's gone.* Lena and Maxine appear on either side of me and haul me to my feet. "C'mon, Frances," Lena encourages gently. "We need to go."

We round the corner where the Brothers of Morte d'Arthur and Benny sit tied up. Oliver undoes Benny's ropes and helps him to his feet. "Thank you, thank you." Blubbers.

"What about them?" Oliver whispers to my father, and gestures to Pascal and the others who still lie unconscious.

"They'll be all right," my father says. "The next guard watch will be here at midnight. They'll untie them."

Oliver turns to Benny. "Tell the others," he says. "Tell Les Selectionnes who Finn really was, that he's dead."

I swallow the new sob that bubbles up in my throat. Oliver's eyes are full of pity, but I know he doesn't understand my tears for Finn. I don't know if I'll ever have the words to explain them.

"And what will they do now that the veil is shut?" Oliver asks my father.

My father replies, "They'll do what they have always done. They will stand watch in holy places and pray it opens once again."

"And what about the men who used the spell to make themselves immortal?" Lena asks.

My father makes his way for the exit, and we follow him as he explains. I trip over my own feet, my eyes still too swollen to see clearly. Maxine takes her arm around my waist and steadies me. "Who knows if the spell is worth anything. We'll have fifty more years before we can know for certain. And if there is a small group of men who have cursed themselves to walk this earth forever, living until she dissolves into flames, well . . . that is their own problem to solve, isn't it?"

But some part of me remembers the strange duke and believes it to be true.

We navigate the serpentine halls by the light of my mother's spell and climb the rickety staircase up out of the depths of the earth. Maxine all but carries me out, my hiccupping sobs echoing off the walls of the catacombs no matter how hard I try to quiet them.

We enter the hall of the church just as eight p.m. Mass is beginning. We walk through the crowds of people, looking so nice in their church clothes, the five of us covered in dirt and blood and bone shards. Sister Evangeline stands near the pulpit watching with silent, understanding pity.

We stumble out of the church onto the street and heave in deep breaths, letting the fresh air soothe our aching lungs.

I look up into the sky, seeing the stars for the first time in a world without him. *Gone.*

"What now?" Lena asks.

"We go home, I guess," Maxine answers.

Together we walk down the block, turning down a much quieter side street, freckles of starlight glinting in shop windows as the sun sinks below the horizon.

I tilt my head up at the sky and try to calm my racing heartbeat. It's over. But I can't help but feel some part of me is dead too.

I may not have killed Mrs. Vykotsky with my own spell, but her death is still my fault. But I don't believe I am irredeemable. I am not even fully myself yet. I am still finding me, tucked away in people and places. In Lena and Maxine and Oliver. In the kitchens of Haxahaven and the steps of the Sacre Cœur and in an apartment on Hester Street. I wonder where the other parts of me lie? I look forward to finding them in all the people I have yet to meet and places I have yet to see.

There is comfort in that. I don't like myself very much right now, but this version of me is not a forever, stagnant thing. There will be a new Frances eventually, and maybe she won't hurt this badly.

If I'm going to become a version of myself that I like, I have to stop hating the person I've been.

Because life is long. If you're lucky, it is long.

And I might be lost, but there is so much of me left to be found.

Was Finn truly irredeemable? I'll never know now.

My father turns to me and reaches a hand up to wipe the tears from my swollen face. I recoil from his touch.

"I am sorry," he says. "But if it wasn't that, the Sons would have had him killed soon enough."

I remember back to the gunshot the night of the Louvre.

"Was it you who tried to kill him last week?" There's no real accusation there, just resignation.

"He killed my son . . . Boss Olan, my friends. It's for the best he's gone. You'll see that in time."

I can't yet picture a future version of me that feels better. But I pray she exists.

CHAPTER TWENTY-FOUR

My father and mother return to Saint Bosco's for the night while Lena, Maxine, and I go to Maxine's flat together.

I run a steaming-hot bath and throw my bloodstained dress in the garbage.

As I lie in the bath, I bang the back of my head softly against the hard porcelain, and magick the cold tap back and forth with a simple flick of my fingers. The power is back in full force, like it was never gone at all. But I'll never forget what it cost.

Staring up at the ceiling, I memorize his face, knowing it'll fade with time, just like my brother's.

I don't even have a picture of him, just a letter and a pair of hand-knit gloves shoved in the back of a drawer back home.

I want to picture him like he was in the woods of Forest Park with his grin and his curls and the coat that hung too large off his frame. I press my thumbs into my closed eyelids until I see spots, as if I could make the image stick forever. All I see now is the silhouette of his shoulders as he turned to face his death.

After, when my bruised skin has been scrubbed raw, I walk to Maxine's room. Lena is already there, sprawled on her blue silk duvet.

"How are you?" they ask as I enter.

"Alive?" I joke weakly.

"That won't be funny for at least ten more years," Lena scolds. "I can't believe you tried to die today."

"The audacity, truly," Maxine concurs.

"Ten years, all right. I'll mark my calendar." I settle into Maxine's bed and stare up at her canopy. The ship back to New York is leaving in just a few days. We won't be together like this for much longer.

"Ten years seems so far off," I say. "I can't imagine who I'll be at twenty-nine."

"Do you ever see us?" Maxine asks Lena with a jab. She never speaks much about her visions of the future, and it's always seemed invasive to ask.

Lena purses her lips, thinking. "Sometimes. Just flashes."

"Flashes of what?" Maxine prods.

She laughs like it's a private joke. "You and Frances are going to cut your hair."

This, I wasn't expecting. "Oh?"

Lena nods. "Maxine will spend a lot of time talking you into it. You shouldn't let her. You look terrible."

"I'm fragile, and yet you mock me." My laugh is still watery from all my sobbing, but it's nice to picture a future version of myself.

"I'm saving you. It looks like a long way off. We look older. But we're together. We look happy . . . happy-ish. My hair is long. I don't let Maxine talk me into it."

"How does Maxine look?"

"Oh, she looks magnificent. You look like a newspaper boy."

"Where are we?" I ask.

Lena closes her eyes and rubs the space between them. "New York, I think. It's brighter in the future. More lights. Oliver is there too. He loves you despite your terrible hair, it appears."

That's a comforting thought, Oliver and I together so many years from now. He's always felt like a constant thing, but it is nice to have it confirmed, as much as the future can ever be confirmed.

All at once I can see it, a life with him, a brownstone with hydrangeas out front and a bench in a bay window to read in. Years of dinners and waltzes and his fingers playing with mine while we take the subway uptown. I long for a life made up of quiet moments with him. I picture opening a door after a long day of teaching and having his face be the one that greets me with a smile. I want it. I want it so badly I could cry.

"So, what do we do now?" I ask.

Next to me, they sigh. "Whatever we want, I think."

It's a nice thought.

"My painting teacher here is putting me in touch with a gallery in New York. They're interested in my work," Lena says. "I meant to tell you yesterday. It could mean a lot of money. I'm going to be a real artist."

"You already were," Maxine says.

"Yes, but now I'll be one with works in salons and a house all my own, bought with my own money."

I feel so hollowed out, but happiness soars in me, picturing Lena in a gallery standing in front of her paintings. "Well deserved. I never doubted you for a minute."

"What about you, Maxine?" Lena asks.

She flops down on her pillow and announces, "I'm staying."

"Staying?" Lena and I both ask in unison.

Maxine pops back up and looks us both in the eyes. "Well, not staying exactly. Anais invited me on a European tour and I said yes."

"*Anais?*" I'm shocked.

Maxine nods, her cheeks a little pink. "She's really nothing like her family. She lives most of the time in a flat with her aunts."

"And?" I prompt. I've been a little distracted, but I'm trying to figure out exactly how we landed from Anais cornering us in a basement to taking Maxine on a European holiday.

"And we got to talking the night at the Louvre, and then at the ballet the night you were at the opera, and then on a stroll around Père Lachaise while Lena was painting and you were off with Finn."

"My, my, Maxine, you are full of secrets," Lena chides.

Maxine laughs, embarrassed, and ducks her face into the bed, hiding the way her cheeks flush. "No, just one, and now it's out in the open. She's just . . . she's lovely."

"She'd better think you're lovely too," I say.

Quiet, her voice muffled by the quilt, she replies, "She told me I was magic itself."

Lena pokes her between the shoulder blades. "What was that?" she teases.

"I'm not saying it again!" Maxine protests.

"You really do like her," I say.

Maxine smiles something private, just for her. "I do."

I barely trust Anais, but if Maxine does, it has to be good enough for me, and I really am thrilled. Finally, an adventure when she's been craving one so desperately.

I take her in my arms and squeeze. Lena joins us, and for a moment we just hold one another. This is a forever kind of love.

"I'll miss you terribly."

Maxine brushes an errant tear from my face. "I'll be home in October. I'll bring you the greatest souvenirs you've ever seen, and Frances, seems you've got your whole life ahead of you, despite the stunt you pulled today. What will you do with it?"

What will I do with it? When my brother died, I was worried I would never have a family again. How wrong I was.

Then I was worried I would spend my life living in fear. I don't feel that way anymore either. Now I'm mostly just curious.

"I'm not sure," I say. "I'll keep teaching, I think." I don't know yet how to make the world a better place, but helping others figure out how to use what already exists within them feels like a good place to start. I don't have to have the rest figured out yet, but I know who will be beside me as I do.

There is still so much I haven't seen, so much I don't know, so many people left to love. I clutch the thought to my chest, and let it warm me from the inside out.

Lena and I board the ship bound for New York four days later. We spend our last days in Paris eating croissants, sprawled out on jade-green lawns, the sun warming our faces.

At night I practice magic, having missed it for the months it abandoned me. I ripen and wither berries on top of a tart, I float a balloon across a courtyard and into Nina's hands, I send a rosebush into a riot of blooms even though it's too hot for the blossoms to survive the day. The next morning the sidewalk is littered with petals that get stuck to the soles of our shoes. Maxine and Lena treat me with kid gloves, making sure I eat and sleep, always asking me how I'm feeling.

I reply with a polite "Fine." How do I admit I'm grieving the person I hate the most?

Sometimes at night I cry. Sometimes I don't. My sleep is dreamless and dark. I crawl into bed with Maxine or Lena to stop it from feeling so lonely.

In the evenings I meet Oliver at his dorm and place my lips on each of his bruises. He watches with equal parts patience and awe and I relearn how to use magic. He's uncomplaining as I spark flame after flame, lighting and extinguishing the lamp beside his bed. He lets me manipulate his fingers until I have enough finesse to drum them smoothly along his desk. I want to wrap him in blankets and swear to never allow harm to come to him again, but I don't. I'm still learning what it means to love someone like I love him, but I think it means letting go of the big promises. Instead, I make him small ones. I will wake up each day and try to be a little better than the day before. I will tell him the truth, even when it is hard. I will trust him to make decisions for himself. I will give him the space to grow into the person he is becoming, and we will love each other through all the parts that still ache.

On our final night together in Paris he slips a small emerald band around my ring finger and whispers, "Eventually. Only if you want to."

"*I want to.*"

It isn't quite a proposal, but he smiles like wedding bells, and I want to be the kind of girl who deserves a forever with him.

My parents, Finn, even Mrs. Vykotsky made love sound like a curse, something to be defeated or ruined by. But with Oliver it's so much simpler. Love is a relief.

Oliver, who reacts to any situation first with kindness and understanding, who is curious and humble. He sets down his book every time I speak and looks me in the eyes like he always cares what I have to say, even if he's studying something important and I'm just informing him I've accidentally let my tea go cold. He's the kind of person who brings me a cake with pink icing on my birthday because he remembered me liking a similar-looking cake five years before. He is careful and soft around the edges in all the places I still feel too reckless and sharp. But here's how I know it's him, it'll be him forever; he has never once made me feel as if I am a difficult person to love.

And so I say yes. I will love him tomorrow and I will love him the day after that. He's an easy boy to make promises to.

I trust we'll figure out the rest in time.

He'll join me in New York in August, but one month isn't so long in the grand scheme of a lifetime together.

Maxine takes us to the docks, and waves goodbye, her hat swinging in her hand, as the ship pulls away from the port.

I miss her immediately.

In the stateroom across from Lena and me are my parents. Whether it was my guilt trip or my mother who convinced him, my father is going to give New York and being a husband another try. I still sometimes have the urge to push him overboard, but my mother is smiling brighter than she has in years and that is enough for me. When we return to the city, she's going to stay with him in Manhattan for a bit as they get to know each other again.

Lena paints the entire journey. I lounge next to her, letting the sun warm my face and my injuries heal as I watch her create something from nothing.

She paints flowers for me and landscapes for herself. She really is an extraordinary talent.

It is still difficult when Lena and I go our separate ways upon docking in New York City. She doesn't hug me too tight, my ribs are still broken from the fight in the catacombs, but she holds me close enough for me to get my tears all over her dress.

"Don't cry, silly," she says. "I'll be in the city all the time. You'll be bored of me soon enough."

"Impossible."

I return to Haxahaven alone. More alone than perhaps I've ever been. Even on my first day here, I had Maxine by my side. But I don't feel lonely. I feel the tethers of their love stretching across states and oceans, a promise to be together again that can't be broken.

I push open the double doors to the school and am greeted by shrieks of joy, and a dozen small bodies colliding with mine.

I've entered just as the girls are walking to lunch. "Miss Hallowell!" little Bernice screams. "We missed you so much! How was France? So much has happened while you were away! Thomasina broke her arm, and Kitty set the curtains in the dining room on fire and I aced my practical applications test and there's a new girl here named April who can find people just like Maxine! It's amazing! You have to meet her!"

A dozen other little voices shout their updates, clinging to my skirts, and I drag them to the dining hall with me. How could I have ever been afraid of being alone, here, where I'm never given more than an inch of space?

In her office I find Florence. She takes my report of all that happened in France with a grim sense of humor. "Dear Miss Hallowell, please promise this is the last adventure you'll have."

I want to say yes, but I've long learned not to make promises I can't keep. "You know I can't do that," I reply with a smile.

And so, I return to the life I left behind. It's waiting for me like I never left at all. There's an empty glass I left on my bedside table the day I left, the stack of letters from Oliver tied with ribbon in the drawer, my same midnight-blue quilt, rumpled a little because Mabel did let the little girls sleep in my bed while I was away. I find one of their dolls shoved under the covers and deliver it back to Mabel with an eye roll. She gives it to little Flossie Maynard, who clutches it to her chest and mutters, "Sorry, Miss Hallowell," like she's not sorry at all.

It is good to be home. Even if I still feel a little hollow.

Nothing has changed except for me.

For the first few days I'm back, I walk through my life at Haxahaven like a ghost, haunting the halls of the school late at night when I can't sleep. I wanted him gone, I got what I wished for, but every part of me aches like a broken bone that wasn't set right. It's healing, but in the wrong places.

I thought what happened in the catacombs was an ending. As

it turns out, it was a beginning. This is my task now; I have to learn to live with it.

My brain runs in circles as I complete my daily routines. As I weed the garden, I think of magic and death and wonder if Finn flinging himself into the veil felt like drowning.

While I wander the dark halls on night patrol, I think of his love for me too, and try to untangle it from what he did, forever picking at the knots in my brain like a skein of yarn that won't come undone.

My heart isn't a traitor. It doesn't love him, but it remembers loving him, and really, what's the difference in the middle of the night? They say time heals all things, but waiting and healing have never been my strengths.

Three weeks later, Oliver comes home. I meet him at the docks with a sandwich from his favorite Lower East Side deli in my bag and a smile on my face so big it hurts.

He picks me up and spins me around as we collide on the docks. Then he pulls back to take in my face.

"How is it possible you've gotten prettier?" He grins.

I swat his shoulder, but he captures my wrist in his hand and extends it, admiring the way the small emerald ring he gave me glints in the sun.

"You haven't changed your mind?"

"Nope," I say, looping my arm through his. "You're stuck with me."

Life isn't all darkness. I may have broken magic, but I fixed it too. And now I live a life where Mabel studies with me in the library and my students make me little handwritten cards for every holiday.

In September, as the leaves start to turn, I enroll in an art history class at Barnard just to see if I can do it. If my transcripts are the result of magical forgery, so be it.

Lena is often in the city now that every art collector in New York seems to want one of her pieces. When I see her, we sit on the Great Lawn in Central Park and we paint. She says I'm getting better, and it's kind of her to lie to me.

Maxine comes home in October sporting trousers she purchased in Constantinople and bearing a stack of black-and-white photos of her and Anais. She'll be back in Paris for Christmas, but Haxahaven is still her home. If Anais's constant letters are any indication, she misses Maxine exactly as much as Maxine deserves to be missed.

On the weekends, Oliver comes to Forest Hills and lounges by the fire as we both study, or I meet him in Manhattan and he continues my waltzing lessons. His mother wants us to get married at the Plaza. We're holding her off for now. I think we'll probably sneak off somewhere upstate, have Lena and Maxine by our sides at the first courthouse we run into on the road. I still can't quite wrap my head around it, a *wedding*. I wanted a home, I wanted to be loved. I have that now, white flowers in a ballroom won't change anything. We're in no hurry. At night, when his dorm room is dark and quiet, his hands wander up my spine and he whispers, "Forever?" His breath is hot against my collarbone. He doesn't need to ask, but I'm always happy to affirm. "Forever."

There are so many things left to do and be and learn in the world. And now I have the time to explore all the people I could become.

I live enough for two people, collecting experiences and sights for my brother, too, wherever he is.

It's a life I've earned, a good one.

Except for the dreams.

CHAPTER TWENTY-FIVE

Three months after returning from France, after a grueling day of preparing the garden for fall, I sink into bed and let the waves of sleep pull me under like a shipwreck.

I'm used to the silence now. I don't fear sleep like I used to, nothing waits for me anymore.

But then—for the first time in months, something ripples in the dark, silvery gray like the light I once saw in the tunnels of the catacombs.

The dream is hazy at first, like the sky on the first day of September. The landscape comes into focus slowly. A sprawling green field, greener than anything I've ever seen in New York. The grass is soft, waving in the light breeze. A ways off, sheep graze high on a hill, calm and quiet.

First, there is just the low whistle of the wind. Then, there is a voice.

"Hi, love."

I clutch my chest over my dress, gasping as I turn around.

I'd know his voice anywhere, even in death. Standing in the field, wearing a hand-knit cream-colored sweater, his curls blowing in the breeze, is Finn.

"No." I turn away from him and clench my eyes shut, willing myself to wake from this dream. It's too cruel, this imaginary version of him the deepest recesses of my brain have dredged up.

"No," I say again. This time it sounds more like a sob than a word.

"Are you that unhappy to see me?" he asks.

"You aren't real," I say. *You're dead. It's my fault.*

The dream-Finn extends a hand out to touch me on the shoulder, but I recoil before he makes contact. I shut my eyes as tight as I can. *Wakeupwakeupwakeup.*

I come to, drenched in sweat, alone in my room. Mabel must still be up patrolling. At least I don't have to explain why I'm crying.

After that, I fight sleep, like it's a battle I can win. I stay up reading novels and texts on forgery magic until my eyes grow so heavy, I wake with the book still open on my chest and the kerosene lamp on the bedside flickering as it burns through the last drops of oil.

Weeks pass and the dream doesn't come back. It waits just long enough that I am lulled into submission.

But then, in the dark, in the same green field, he is waiting.

He looks so calm, the personification of all my stinging, awful, ugly hurt.

"I missed you," he greets me.

I can't help it, I march up to him and I hit his chest, solid and real under my fists. I punch and punch and punch against his breastbone until I am sobbing, and he catches me just before my knees hit the wet earth.

"You're dead," I cry.

He pulls back and looks at me with those sharp hazel eyes. "I am."

"Then how are you here?"

He shrugs casually but there is fear in his eyes. "I don't know."

He once told me I'd been haunting him his whole life. Am I to suffer the same fate? Are we truly that tied together?

I refuse to accept it. "No."

"It doesn't seem either of us have a choice, love."

I turn to walk away. My bare feet sink into the damp grass, but no matter how many steps I take, the landscape remains the same. The clouds don't move gently across the sky, the hills on the horizon don't come any closer.

"Don't you see?" he asks. I turn and he's right behind me.

I don't. I don't understand it at all.

When I wake, Oliver is breathing gently beside me. I stare at the dark ceiling and I try not to panic.

Oliver doesn't mention the dark circles under my eyes until a few weeks later at dinner. "Have you been sleeping?" he asks kindly, passing me the bread.

I shrug, noncommittal.

"You did the right thing. Even he knew that."

He.

That's who he is between us. Finn's name is never spoken aloud.

It's only when I've convinced myself I've imagined the whole thing that I find Finn waiting for me again. He smiles like the sunrise as I appear in front of him, but it's a little broken at the edges.

"This is happening, then," I greet him.

"It appears so."

And so, the dreams continue. He's not there every night. Not even every week, but he never goes away. My own personal ghost.

"What do you do when I'm not here?" I ask one night. We're lounging against the grass, and Finn has magicked cups of steaming tea into our hands. Sometimes we play cards. Sometimes we talk. Sometimes we don't talk at all.

He shrugs. "I wait for you."

"That sounds horrible." If Finn is my personal ghost, he's trapped in his personal purgatory.

He sets his teacup down in the grass and turns to face me. "You want to know something? I was twelve years old the first time I saw you in my head, and I knew then my life's purpose was to find you. I would've gone to the ends of the earth. And if you weren't there, then I would have kept walking. Everything was for you. It was always about you."

I shake my head with pity. "And look at you now, stuck here at the ends of the earth forever."

"You're missing the point."

"What's the point?"

"I'm with you, aren't I?"

If Oliver is a warm hearth, Finn is a house on fire. In my dreams, it's easy to imagine the flames feel like home. Love and pain are so intertwined, sometimes I can't tell the difference when I look at him.

In my waking hours, life marches on. I finish my first semester of classes at Barnard. I get a new class of students. The carrots growing in the patch outside the kitchen are picked and the earth is turned over. The dirt is cold in my hands, sharp as it gets stuck under my fingernails.

I tell Oliver everything. Every detail of my day, every secret I hear in the Haxahaven faculty lounge, every scrap of gossip from Anais's letters.

I tell him everything except one thing.

What is a secret, if not an act of love?

There's nothing he can do to fix it.

"Does he know?" Finn asks one night. That's who he is between us. Finn never speaks Oliver's name out loud.

"No." I won't give Finn the satisfaction of his jealousy. I won't give Oliver the pain of Finn's continued existence, even in this terrible half state. He isn't a person anymore, he's a cold spot in an empty room, a horrible promise to love me forever fulfilled. He's a hand on the back of my neck and it's squeezing and I don't know when the last time I took a full breath was.

"Is it because you'd know he'd be jealous?"

"You think Oliver is the kind of man who'd be jealous of you? You're barely even real."

"You're afraid of how he'd react," Finn volleys.

I shake my head. "I'm not."

"He's weak."

I resist the urge to hit him. "You're dead."

Finn smiles, sure and smug, but I know he must be lonely trapped here all alone. "He'll never make you happy."

I gesture to myself. "And yet look at me. Happy. Engaged, too." It's petty and venomous to tell him, but the fire in my chest flares as I say it. In my dream, the emerald band is not on my finger. I am forever dressed as Finn last saw me in the catacombs, in Maxine's borrowed baby-blue silk gown.

I get the reaction I want from him immediately. Finn furrows his brow, something terrible flickering in his eyes.

"That's not a funny joke."

I smile at his anger. "I've never been good at telling jokes, you know that."

He shoves his hands in his pockets and tilts his chin up, defiant. It only has the effect of making him look younger. "You're already married to me."

I laugh. "That wasn't a marriage, that was a trick."

"We said vows."

"I hate you."

He takes a step toward me. "I love you."

I look him square in the eye. "One day, I will die happy and loved, at the end of a full life, and be at peace forever, and you'll be left alone to go mad in an empty dream."

I expect him to respond, but instead, Finn just *looks*.

And I look back. At his freckles and curls and sharp eyes and arms that tossed my brother's body in a river.

The wind rustles through his hair, mine too. It blows across my face, but I don't brush it away. We're standing too far to touch, but we don't need to. There are already so many ways we are entangled. His fingerprints are all over my soul. I've been so thoroughly marked up.

There is fog on the false horizon. It rolls in, slow and gray, like it knows it has all the time in the world.

I wake, leaving him alone.

Oliver is next to me. The ring is on my finger.

But I know I'll be back to break my own heart, again and again.

This is how it goes, he's always in the dark. That is how I have him, now.

And in daylight, Oliver glows golden and I tilt my face toward the sun and I build something worth having. I take full breaths, filling my lungs to the very top.

But Finn is waiting in the shadows, just like the very first time I saw him in the woods.

I keep my promise to William, I live my life enough for the both of us. I live for Oliver and Maxine and Lena, too.

But my dreams, I keep to myself, knowing Finn will be trapped under the floorboards of my heart, listening to Oliver and me slow dance over his body forever.

ACKNOWLEDGMENTS

I was warned that second books are harder than first books, and this book was no exception. At times, writing this story felt more like a great excavation attempt than anything else. I spent many nights digging through this story, through myself, for what felt true. But stronger than the anxiety and the exhaustion was the immense gratitude I felt. I'm so lucky to have gotten to write this book. I don't think that sense of awe will ever really go away. Writing is a solitary act, but I've never once felt as if I was in this alone.

My first and biggest thank-you goes to you, the readers of this story. To pick up a sequel is no small thing; to care enough about a group of characters to commit to an entirely new novel about them is an act of real love. It is because of you that I get to keep writing, and I'll never have the right words for what a profound gift that is. Thank you for saying hi in bookstores, emails, letters, and DMs. Your enthusiasm and love for this story and these characters have made writing this book the most fulfilling, terrifying, and joyous thing I've ever done.

Thank you to Hillary Jacobson, the agent of my dreams. Cheers to more stories, more lunches, more midnight "I think the planets are being weird this week?" texts. I'll forever be so grateful you saw the potential I didn't see in myself all those years ago.

To my editor, Nicole Ellul, a true word witch. Thank you for pushing me and for understanding the heart of what this book needed to be even before I did.

To the Simon & Schuster team, whose commitment to storytelling continually blows me away: Nicole Valdez, Cassie Malmo, Alyza Liu, Emily Ritter, Justin Chanda, Kendra Levin, Katrina Groover, Chrissy Noh, Lisa Moraleda, Anna Jarzab, Victor Iannone, Christina Pecorale, Emily Hutton, and Lauren Castner.

To Faceout Studio and Sarah Creech for designing this absolute banger of a cover.

To the bookstores and libraries that showed *The Witch Haven* so much love, it is because of the effort of so many of you that this series found its way into the hands of readers. A particular thank-you to my local independent bookstore, One More Page in Arlington, Virginia.

I spent a lot of lonely days at a seventh-grade lunch table wishing for friends, so I can't believe how many incredible people I have to list here. Friends who bought me coffees and read drafts and responded to all my "Hey, is this any good?" texts. To Diya Mishra, Susan Lee, Alexa Lach, Sabrina McClain, Jenna Voris, and Kristin Lambert, who cheered me on through every page.

To Shelby Mahurin, Jordan Gray, Rebecca Ross, Adrienne Young, and Isabel Ibanez for being the best Airbnb roommates a gal could ask for.

To Kristin Dwyer, who I believe really would fight someone behind a dumpster for me.

To The Beans: Hannah Carter, Mary Dombrowski, Emily Sonneland, and Leah Smith for more than I can list here, but mostly for listening to all my Taylor Swift opinions.

To Kristopher Kam for asking, "How can I help?" and always meaning it.

To my best friend, Casey McQuiston, who made me a charcuterie board, sat on the floor of a haunted farmhouse with me, and asked, "What if Oliver studied abroad?" I love you so much, it's honestly a little embarrassing. There's no one I'd rather sit next to on a roller coaster (both literally and metaphorically).

To Emilie Sowers, who offered to give me the only shower with good water pressure in a dorm bathroom over a decade ago. I knew in that moment we'd be friends forever. I don't know what I'd do without you.

To my husband, Charles, who cooks every meal, who keeps our house running, who celebrates even the smallest victories as if they're big ones. I'm the luckiest. Truly.

To my family, whose love has given me everything.

To Frances Hallowell, who isn't me but is parts of me. Really, she is the parts of me that scare me the most, shoved into a book about grief and fear and love in all its forms. In so many ways, I grew up right alongside Frances. I began this series at twenty-two, alone, sitting in my childhood bedroom, terrified of what my life was going to be. I finished this series at thirty, married, settled into a life filled with so much love, it sometimes feels like I might burst. I like to imagine Frances found herself a similar kind of life, that she learned to live with the ghosts in her head too.

A final thank-you and hug across space and time to everyone who saw themselves in Frances. If I could leave you with one final message, it is this: you've never been difficult to love, not for one minute. I happen to love you a lot.